HUNTIN' JUSTICE

CHARLES LEMAR BROWN

Broken L Press

To Coach Sanders & Coach Taylor

CHAPTER 1

Tonight, Sheriff Billie Hilton would die. A goodbye present from the Panther to the good folks of Love County. A prelude to what one day would set the record straight. Grandmother Mosley would be proud of him. She would know. She would understand. She alone would see that Coahoma had begun the reckoning, for she alone called him Coahoma.

He remembered well the night she had told him his Choctaw name. He sat on the front porch of the only home he had ever known, an old frame three-room shotgun house flaked with weather worn white paint. His mother turned and waved as she climbed into the cab of an old Chevy stepside pickup. It was faded black with several primer-gray areas and no rear bumper. She wore a yellow tube top, a denim miniskirt, and no shoes. As the newest boyfriend pulled away, she took a final draw from her joint and flicked the end into the dirt. If he closed his eyes, he could still smell the dust that the old truck kicked up as it spun out and headed up the road. It was the year of Coahoma's tenth birthday.

"I think we will not see her again." Grandmother Mosley's brow crinkled as she spoke. Coahoma sat silently staring down the road.

"It is time you knew," her brow relaxed, "you are still young, so I will tell you a little now and more as you grow older."

"Okay, Grandmother." His palms felt sweaty. He could hear his heart beating, feel it in his chest. He and Grandmother often sat out on the porch and had visits, but this was different somehow.

"First, it is time you knew your Choctaw name."

"I didn't know I had one." He looked up into her dark eyes, and she smiled.

"Yes, your grandfather gave it to you before he passed over to the other side," she paused, "it is Coahoma. In the Choctaw tongue, it means—the panther."

"Coahoma," he repeated, "the panther."

"It is not a name for the ears of others," she warned, "it is for you and me only. One day you will understand why, but for now, we will keep this to ourselves."

"Okay, Grandmother."

"Your mother was not always like she is now," Grandmother began, paused, and then continued, "once she was very pretty and very sweet. Then some men changed all that."

Now the Panther sat motionless across from Billie Hilton's house. He sat as he had sat many nights, well back from the road, cross-legged, leaning against a giant old hackberry. The distant full moon shining through the light bar on the top of the Sheriff's squad car beckoned like a neon bar sign to an old drunk cowboy. But the Panther was neither drunk nor a cowboy. He was part Choctaw and part unknown, and all purpose, thanks to Grandmother Mosley. The smell of the dirt and new leaves, the sounds of the night, the feel of humidity in the air, each in its own way told him all was well. Like all wild creatures, his every sense was attuned to the world around him.

The squeak of rusty hinges followed by the slam of the old wood and wire storm door on the Sheriff's weathered cedar-sided house told him it was time to move. With no wasted motion, he crossed the road, slid along the edge of the house, rounded the corner, and stood silently listening through the screen. Many nights he had stood just so, listening to the house, knowing that the right time would come, and tonight, it had. Five minutes passed slowly. The Panther waited patiently.

Inside, Johnny Carson's laugh rolled from the television and Billie chuckled. The Panther smiled, opened the screen, and slipped inside.

"Damn cat," Billie snapped. "Peckerhead, I ain't lettin' you back in." He sneered over his shoulder toward the screen door.

With the silent ease of much practice, the Panther passed through the kitchen and picked up a knife from the counter. It was one-piece stainless steel. Stepping through the dining room, he smiled and nodded at the cat sitting in the middle of an old wooden table. Rounding the corner into the living area, he stopped behind the sheriff. Billie sat in an overstuffed chair, old and worn like all the furniture in the room. His socked feet were propped on a scarred, cheap wooden table. In his right hand, he held a jelly glass with a little Wild Turkey and a couple of melting ice cubes.

The television cut to a commercial. Music started to play as a DJ put on a record: "Here are some cool sounds coming at you on a sizzling summer day." Two bikini-clad girls carrying Cokes walked away from the viewer across a beach toward the water. "Have a Coke and a smile…"

Billie smiled as Coahoma grabbed a handful of hair and wrenched his head back. With his other hand, he cut the sheriff's throat from ear to ear. Blood sprayed, covering the front of Billie's shirt and splattering the jelly glass as it slipped from his hand and shattered on the hardwood floor. The smile faded. His mouth opened and shut, but the only sound was a strange gurgle.

As the light faded from his eyes, the commercial ended. Coahoma wiped the blood from the knife on the sleeve of Billie's uniform shirt, ripped the badge from his chest, and left through the screen door. Peckerhead followed him out and watched him until he disappeared into the woods across the street.

Love County Under-Sheriff, Ed Hughes stared down at his boss as a shiver ran up his spine. He was smart enough to know he was in over his head, but not intelligent enough to figure out what to do about it. His rise to second-in-command of the Love County Sheriff's Department had been fast and easy. Three deputies with more seniority had found better paying jobs elsewhere, and a fourth, who had pissed off the judge's wife, was asked to resign.

Now, barring any resistance, he would step into the role of interim sheriff, and with any luck come election time, well… the possibilities were endless.

CHAPTER 2
22 Years Later

"What in the hell were you thinking, Wyatt?" Assistant Chief of Police Brad McClain asked.

"I ain't Wyatt; I'm Virgil, man, get it straight." Virgil sat on the curb beside his brother.

McClain hitched his gun belt higher on his pudgy midsection, stretched his five-foot-six-inch frame to its max, gave Wyatt a go-to-hell look, then turned and wobbled back to his squad car. Through the gap in his front teeth, Wyatt shot a stream of Copenhagen at the retreating officer.

"Webbles wobble, but they don't fall down." Virgil giggled and shouldered Wyatt.

"Virgil, you're a dumbass," Wyatt stated flatly.

Wyatt stared past his brother at the old model blue Chevy Silverado and shook his head. Even from a block away, he could see the front bumper wrapped around the light pole at the corner of East Main and Second Street. The jackknifed sixteen-foot John Deere flatbed, somehow still attached to the back, was only partly visible through the cloud of angry bees. Marietta might be the county seat, but it was still a small town, and like most small Oklahoma towns, everyone knew everyone's business, and business like this drew a crowd. Wyatt figured all two thousand seven hundred and fifty-nine citizens of the wonderful city of Marietta had made it out for the fiasco, and perhaps half of Thackerville, but then it wasn't every day you saw a swarm of pissed-off honeybees take over two blocks of a town.

Virgil and Wyatt Muncy were identical twins. So identical that even their mom had trouble telling them apart, at least until they started talking. Not to say Wyatt was an Einstein, but with Virgil as comparison the words "rocket scientist" might get tossed around. Both were six feet four inches tall in their bare feet, and both weighed in at a buck seventy-five. What they lacked in bulk, they made up for in pure, unadulterated mean. When they had hair, it was flaming red. On this day, both had shiny, shaved heads. Each of their scalps was adorned with a series of red welts. Wyatt ran his hand over his head and muttered a curse under his breath.

"What's your problem, man?" Virgil glared. "I was the one drivin'."

"Yeah, well that don't matter," he jerked his chin towards a white Chevy Tahoe, "Here comes Deputy Dawg, and you and me both know he'll find a reason to put our asses back in a cell."

Deputy Dan Sanderson was a foreigner, at least in the Muncy boys' eyes. But then anyone who came from farther north than the Arbuckle Mountains was a foreigner. Sanderson was from Stillwater, a Cowpoke through and through. He met his wife on the Oklahoma State University campus, and when she finished her teaching degree, he followed her back to her hometown. She taught third grade at Turner Elementary; he chased bad guys, and he considered the Muncy brothers bad guys.

"Wyatt…" he began.

"It wasn't Wyatt, it was me. I was driving." Virgil cut him off.

"Shut it," Wyatt hissed.

Sanderson chuckled, "Virgil, stand up, turn around, and put your hands behind your back."

"Kiss my ass." Virgil rose to his feet and turned.

"Save the pillow talk for the boys down at county." Sanderson smiled as he put the cuffs on. "I'm sure they've been missin' you."

"You think you're some kinda badass," Virgil sneered. "You ain't nothin' but a low-down dirty Yankee prick."

"Once again, Virgil, I was born and raised in Pawnee, Oklahoma, just north of Stillwater."

"Yankee prick," Virgil repeated. "Like you said, from up north."

Wyatt shook his head and sat quietly, watching as the deputy delivered his brother to Officer McClain. He rubbed at a bee sting and wondered why some fellows had balls and some didn't. Were some guys just born with big cojones, or had some event or events in their lives caused them to grow so large? By his figuring, if jobs were handed out by testicle size, Sanderson should be Sheriff, and McClain should be chasing stray cats down back alleys. Anyway, wasn't this a city problem? It was within the city limits, so McClain should have made the arrest.

Sanderson strolled back over and stood with his right hand resting on his .45 Smith & Wesson. Dressed in faded blue Wrangler jeans, a khaki uniform shirt, a straw Stetson, and black ostrich boots, Sanderson stood beside Wyatt and glared down the street at the wrecked truck. Cars circled the four-block area that had been barricaded off for everyone's safety. Some of them were just detouring around the chaos, but not all. Wyatt could already see lines of cars parked up the side streets and people meandering toward the scene.

Wyatt stretched his long legs out into the street and crossed one ankle over the other. His bibbed overalls were greasy and sweat-stained, and his steel-toed work boots had seen better days. He could hear his brother ranting through the cracked window of the police vehicle.

"So, what happened here?" Sanderson asked, still staring up the street.

"If I tell you, are you gonna haul my ass in?"

"Maybe," Sanderson shrugged. "Maybe not."

"Man, I didn't break no laws."

"Got insurance on that truck?" Sanderson asked.

"I wasn't drivin', Virgil was." Wyatt looked up. "You got a cigarette?"

"Don't smoke," Sanderson answered as he watched a city police officer hauling ass away from the trailer, trying to get away from several bees that had decided he was the problem.

"Can I get one from McClain then?" he asked and nodded towards the chubby officer.

"Maybe, maybe not," Sanderson looked down at him. "What happened here?"

"Well, you see…" Wyatt began, then paused, watching a fully clad bee wrangler shuffle past, then continued, "Virgil had a dentist appointment day afore yesterday."

"What does that have to do with anything?" Sanderson looked down at him.

"Well, that's how all of this started," Wyatt explained. "The dentist has a house over there in that new addition. The one at the edge of town where they been clearin' out all those trees on the other side of the railroad tracks. You know, that big two-story that sets back off the road a bit?"

"Yeah, I know which one you're talkin' about," Sanderson nodded.

"Anyway, he had 'em leave a big old hackberry in the back, so when his kids get bigger, they could build a tree house up in it. Only then, the other week when that storm came through, it knocked down the biggest limb from the top of the tree, and he noticed a bunch of bees comin' in and out of a hole in the limb. That's where me and Virgil came in."

He paused to watch the bee fellow step up onto the back of the flatbed trailer with a funny-looking contraption that had smoke coming out of it. Then continued, "Virgil had to go in cause his tooth was hurtin' him, and the dentist was talkin' to another patient in the next room about needin' someone to move a limb that had bees in it. Virgil tells me we should do it, so we get with the dentist, and he says he will give us a hundred dollars if we haul it off."

"He pay you in advance?" Sanderson wondered aloud.

"Sure enough," Wyatt answered. "Matter a fact, he paid one fifty, cause when we got over there, that limb was still hangin' up in the tree. I told him it would cost more cause we'd have to get a ladder and a chainsaw to get it down."

The sound of a ratchet strap drifting from the direction of the trailer drew their attention. The bee man was reattaching the straps that had secured the limb in place on the trailer prior to the collision with the lamppost. Bees swarmed around him in a cloud.

"You see how big that damn limb is?" Wyatt asked, looking off toward the trailer, then continued before Sanderson could answer, "We eased a ladder up against the trunk of that hackberry, and then, real careful-like, I climbed up and, usin' that blue tarp you see down there, I duct-taped it in place over the hole."

Sanderson shook his head. From this vantage point, he could tell the limb in question was close to twelve feet long and at least three feet around. The whole length of it must be hollow, considering the number of bees plaguing the area around the trailer.

"Then we pulled the trailer up under the limb, and I cut it so's it fell right down on the trailer." He paused, sighed, looked down at the scuffed toe of his boot, then continued, "That sure pissed them bees off good. I was up on the ladder with the chainsaw when it let loose. Virgil was down by the trailer. When it hit, a piece of that duct tape let loose, and them bees just started pilin' out. Man, was they ever pissed. Virgil got stung 'bout twenty times 'fore he got that tarp duct-taped back in place, and me, I got hit a few times myself."

"How, in blue blazes, did these boys ever live past puberty?" Sanderson muttered under his breath.

"What'd you say?" Wyatt asked as they managed to get the limb strapped securely to the trailer once again.

Sanderson ignored his question and asked, "So, what was the plan once you got the limb loaded?"

Wyatt watched as the beekeeper tried to unhitch the trailer from the wrecked truck. The way it had jackknifed was making it difficult. Sanderson cleared his throat and said, "The plan?"

Wyatt shrugged, "Well, I got a buddy out on D Ranch Road. He's got a big ol' brush pile. He said we could bring it out there and maybe find a way to get the honey out."

"Let me get this straight," Sanderson cocked his head to the side, crinkled his forehead, and looked down at the seated man. "You loaded this limb at the dentist's new house, which is on the far east edge of town, planned to take it to D Ranch Road, which is even farther east of town, and ended up crashing on Main Street. I may not be the brightest crayon in the box, but that's kind of like goin' from here to Dallas through Nebraska."

"Yep," Wyatt agreed, shaking his head in disgust. "Good ol' Virgil."

"So, once again, we return to good ol' Virgil, huh?" Sanderson shook his head.

"Yeah, Virgil. He's got this hard-on for that Gwen chick down at the Sonic. He wanted her to see his big honey-filled limb, plus it was Happy Hour, and he figured we needed us a cold drink," Wyatt explained.

"So, you loaded up a branch full of angry bees and drove through downtown Marietta so Virgil could impress a chick? Hell, when she hears about this, I bet she falls down, throws both legs up in the air, and just waits for him to come a runnin'," Sanderson could not suppress a smile.

"That's real funny, asshole," Wyatt hissed. "It was Happy Hour."

Sanderson continued to smile as he pushed his hat back on his head and said, "So now you're at Sonic. Then what happened?"

Wyatt shrugged again. "Well, Gwen brung our drinks out and says that there's some bees flyin' around and we better get goin' before someone got stung. So, we lit out. We was passin' by the Family Dollar when Virgil started lightin' up a cigarette..."

Sanderson interrupted him. "You mean a joint?"

"Whatever," Wyatt rolled his eyes. "About that time, I looked back and noticed the wind had blown a corner of the tarp loose and bees were pourin' out of that hole again."

As Sanderson watched, a second bee wrangler approached the trailer. Between the two of them, they got the flatbed unhooked and swung the tongue out into the street. A white extended cab Chevy Silverado with a County Sheriff's decal on the side backed into place, the trailer was hitched to the truck, and started slowly away, followed by a swarm of bees.

"I told Virgil we better get the hell out of town, and he put a foot in it, but then we caught that first red light and had to stop. A bunch of kids on bikes were waitin' to cross the street when we stopped, and those bees just went crazy and attacked them. They was hollerin' and screamin' and runnin'. One of them left his bike right out in the middle of the road. When that light turned green, Virgil took off like the devil was after us, only he must have been lookin' in the rearview, cause he sure wasn't watching where he was going. Then, on top of that, his cigarette," Wyatt used his fingers to emphasize, "fell in his lap, and it was still lit."

"So, he swerved to miss the car stopped at the second light and smacked into the lamp post," Sanderson finished the story for him.

"Yep," Wyatt replied, then asked, "So am I free to go?"

"It ain't my call. Ask Officer McClain." Sanderson looked down at Wyatt as he settled his hat back in place.

"McClain's a pussy," Wyatt snarled.

Sanderson, already walking away, smiled.

Sanderson stepped from his vehicle and walked cautiously toward the flatbed trailer. The bees had been subdued. A few still crawled along the top edge of the limb. Several hundred lay dead on the wooden planks beneath the hackberry branch.

The bee wranglers stood to one side, both still in their white bee suits, holding their white hooded hats. Sanderson's boss, Love County Sheriff Ed Hughes, looked across the trailer as he approached. He was a large man with a massive head covered with curly brown hair that always looked in need of a comb. A mustache and goatee of matching color hid thin lips beneath small blue-grey eyes. He towered four inches above Sanderson's six foot one and weighed nearly three hundred, which dwarfed Sanderson's one ninety.

"Dan, these boys say they think there's somethin' besides honey up in that hole." Hughes jerked his head toward the tree branch.

"Okay."

"Crawl up there and give'er a look," he ordered, thus explaining why he had called Dan out in the first place.

Sanderson's eyes narrowed, his brow furrowed, and his mouth set, but he crawled up on the trailer and eased up to the opening. At the bottom of the knothole, honey had begun to pool. Squatting down, he could smell the honey and see part of the comb up in the hollowed-out limb. What looked like the edge of a leather pouch was visible. Sticking his hand up inside, he grasped the leather and pulled. The aged leather broke into sticky pieces in his hand, and something fell into the pooled honey.

"What is it?" Ed wanted to know.

"I don't know yet. It's something. Everything is sticky and a mess. Give me a second."

Sanderson reached down through the pooled honey and ran his hand along until it struck something hard. Grasping it, he lifted it out through the hole. In his hand was a honey-covered badge. A Love County Sheriff's badge.

CHAPTER 3

"You ain't foolin' nobody, asshole." She stretched onto her tiptoes to apply eyeliner in the bathroom mirror. The navy-blue silk robe hung open in the front and rode halfway up her ass as she leaned forward. "You're awake. I know. I can feel your eyes on me."

"Yeah, well if that robe rides any higher, you're gonna feel more than my eyes," Noble shot back.

"Vacation's over. I've gotta get to the office, and you gotta go chase bad guys." She finished her makeup, dropped the robe, and began to dress.

Noble propped himself on a pillow and watched. Jacqueline had always amazed him. At thirty-seven, she was three years younger than he was and moved with the graceful ease of a deer. Her driver's license said she was five foot eight and weighed one hundred and twenty. He figured it was off by about ten pounds.

"You enjoyin' this?" she asked, wiggling into a black bra that matched the lace panties she wore and fastening the clasp between her breasts.

"As always," Noble smiled and winked. She cupped a breast in each hand and wiggled the bra into a more comfortable position.

He reached for her as she passed the bed. She side-stepped, turned, wiggled her eyebrows up and down twice, and mocked, "Nice try."

Noble tossed the covers back and exposed the full length of his six-foot frame. Jacqueline threw her hands over her mouth, gasped loudly, and feigned shock. Then she twirled, bent at the waist, paused long enough for him to get a good look, and picked up a pair of shoes in each hand.

"Which pair do you think I should wear today?" she asked as she turned back to face him.

"Depends on what else you're plannin' on wearin' I suppose." He grinned.

"Maybe I wasn't plannin' on wearin' anything else." She grinned.

"Then, I'd say those black strappy things with the heels." He nodded.

"You're such a smart ass." She reached back into the closet, pulled out a little black dress, and shimmied into it.

"Smart whatever," he replied with a chuckle.

She looked down at his naked body, ran her tongue over her lips playfully, and asked, "Are you gonna just lay there, or are you gonna get dressed?"

"Why? Is it gettin' to you?" A half smile turned up one corner of his mouth.

"You wish…" she snorted, then questioned, "You want a goodbye kiss?"

"Yep," came the answer.

"Okay, but no funny business. I don't have time to shower again." She leaned over, kissed him on the cheek, and hurried from the room.

He sat quietly and listened as she grabbed a Dr. Pepper from the fridge, her purse from the table, and left. Then he swung his feet to the floor and stepped into the bathroom. The scale registered one hundred ninety-seven. Either the week's vacation or the big four-oh had added the seven. Time would tell.

He showered quickly, shaved carefully, and stood staring into the mirror. Hazel eyes stared back. Silver streaks along the temples of his short black hair reminded him he was not getting any younger. He ran his thumb over the scar that ran along the left side of his square jaw and thought it would sure be nice if all of life scars could be seen from the outside.

Half an hour later, he backed his black extended cab GMC Sierra from its parking spot at the side of his apartment, circled the building, and sat idly watching as the security gate rolled open. He turned left onto Lyrewood Lane followed it for a quarter of a mile, then waited at a long red light. Another left, found him on Northwest Sixty-Third Street headed east. Fifteen minutes later, he swung into the parking lot of the Oklahoma Bureau of Investigation at 6600 North Harvey, found an empty space, and pulled in.

The rumble of a Harley Davidson made him smile as he stepped out of his truck. He shut the door and leaned back against it as the motorcycle swung around the rear-end of his vehicle. The driver stopped, kicked down the stand, stepped off the bike with a smile, and thrust a hand out. Kent Davenport might manage five foot eight if he tiptoed. Built like a college fullback, many folks along the way had let his short stature fool them. There was no one Noble would rather have in a fight than Kent. The office buzz had him with one foot over the insanity line due to his multiple tours in Afghanistan, but no one seemed to be able to pin down any specifics, and Kent was not the talkative type.

"How's it hangin'?" Noble grinned as he shook the offered hand.

"Slightly to the left," Kent grinned back, then added, drawing deeply on the remnants of his New Jersey accent, "to the left of my right knee."

"I see you're still full of shit," Noble stated.

"What… who… me?" Kent laughed. "You only been gone a week. You really expect things around here to change that much?"

"Reckon not," came the reply.

The two started up the walk. Noble stared up at the four-story glass and rock building with a sigh of appreciation. Home away from home. In the early years, he had spent more time in this building than he ever did in his apartment. The last four years, with Jacqueline, had changed that somewhat, but he still loved this old building. And he loved his job. Well, most days anyway."

"Man, I'm glad you're back," Davenport chuckled, holding the door open for Noble.

"Miss me that much, did ya?" Noble queried.

"Hell no," he answered, then added, "but the old man got a case from that hillbilly shithole you call home, and I was afraid he was gonna send my sexy white ass down there. Man, I'm sure as hell glad you're back."

"Marietta ain't a hillbilly shithole," Noble glared as he pushed the up button for the elevator.

"Says you," Davenport replied as the doors slid open.

Noble stepped into the elevator, held the door for Davenport, then pushed the number two button to the left of the doors. Leaning against the back wall, he waited for Davenport to elaborate. Davenport did not.

The bell dinged, the doors slid open, and the two men stepped into the second-floor hallway. Noble ran the gauntlet of 'welcome backs' and 'how was the vacation' on his way to his desk, followed by Davenport, who just smiled and nodded. Still grinning, Davenport pulled the chair out from his own desk, which faced Noble's, and eased into it.

"You're such a dick," Noble shook his head, removed the straw Stetson hat he wore, and tossed it on his desk.

"Get in here, Noble," Tom Jack hollered from his office at the end of the room.

Tom Jack Laughlin was the old man. Tough as nails, he showed no favoritism. Respected by all, he was fond of quoting W.C. Fields and would often state, "I hate everyone equally," with such finesse that, somehow, one got the feeling maybe W.C. Fields had actually borrowed the quote from Tom Jack.

"How was your vacation?" Tom Jack asked as Noble seated himself in a short-backed leather chair across the desk from his boss.

"Good, really good, but too short," Noble answered.

"Okay, well, time to get to work." Necessary pleasantries out of the way, Tom Jack slid a drawer out, plucked a plastic evidence bag from inside, and tossed it to Noble.

"Got a case down your way," he said, as Noble caught the bag. "That there badge belonged to a sheriff who was killed sometime back—'bout twenty years ago or so. Anyway, it's a cold case, and the locals want some help. Maybe you remember it?"

Marietta, Oklahoma, is the county seat of Love County. A rural town of just over two thousand seven hundred God-fearing, down-to-earth country folk. An hour and forty-five-minute drive straight south of Oklahoma City on Interstate 35, and an hour and a half straight north of Dallas, it is the gateway to Lake Country. At least, that is what the sign at the edge of town used to claim.

Noble's first memory of Marietta was that damn sign. Fifteen years old, seated on the passenger side of an old two tone blue and white Chevy farm truck, he saw it and wondered how far it was to the lake. Granny swung into the feed store, backed up to the loading dock, jumped out, and shuffled inside to order and pay for the cattle feed they had come to town to purchase.

Noble stepped out of the truck, strolled to the back, and dropped the tailgate. A slim young man about his age with a sideways grin stepped out of an open doorway and walked to the edge of the dock.

"New 'round here." It was more like a statement than a question.

"Yes, just moved in with my grandmother," Noble replied.

"Got a name?" the young man asked.

"Noble," he answered.

"So are you?" the young man grinned.

"Am I what?" Noble's eyebrows furrowed as he looked up.

"Hey, easy there, I was just funnin'," the young man's grin never wavered. "My name's Lincoln, you know, like the seventeenth president." He jumped down from the platform and stuck out his hand.

"Lincoln was the sixteenth president," Noble stated as he took the hand.

Lincoln laughed, "Yeah, I know, just testin' you. You pass."

Noble had chuckled himself. It had felt unnatural. Too soon to be happy. Too soon to enjoy life. He had looked at Lincoln and wondered if he would ever feel like life was right again.

Now, twenty-five years later, he angled his truck into an empty spot in front of the glass doors of the Chickasaw Trading Post at the Davis exit for a pit stop and a fresh Dr. Pepper. A little over halfway between Oklahoma City and Marietta, it had become his favorite stopping place on his infrequent trips to see Granny.

"Hey sexy, you come to rescue me and take me away from this God-forsaken place?" The body behind the voice was not one that would go unnoticed in any setting.

"Maria," Noble tipped his hat and smiled, "Now, what would your husband say if he heard you talkin' like that?"

"Well, cowboy, I won't tell if you don't," Maria shot back.

"I just bet you wouldn't at that." Noble escaped to the restroom in the back corner.

Damn, that woman was sure tempting. If he was not with Jacqueline and if she was not married… Well, as old Uncle Eli used to a say, "If ifs and buts, were candy and nuts, we'd all have a Merry Christmas." Or a Merry Whatever. He finished at the urinal, washed his hands, and wondered if he did not stop here just for a little flirting.

"Haven't been by in a while," Maria stated slyly as she rang up a Dr. Pepper and a pack of beef jerky.

"Been missin' me," Noble flirted back.

"You know it, darlin'," Maria leaned forward over the counter, giving a full view of her cleavage, "Who is she? Is it serious?"

"Same one. Little over four years now. How much do I owe ya?

"Six thirteen," she stretched her hand out, then added, "Been with my current fifteen long years, but you just say the word, Honey, and…" she winked and smiled.

Noble slipped a ten-dollar bill into her outstretched palm and winked back. "Keep the change," he smiled, "I better get on down the road."

"Okay, then, but when you're ready, you know where to find me, Sweetheart."

Forty minutes later, still wondering what a romp in the hay with Maria would be like and kicking himself for not being able to get it out of his head, he rolled past the Love County Courthouse, turned south on Fourth Street, and found a parking spot. Two blocks further east on Main Street sat the Post Office. The first post office in Marietta had opened its doors on December 20, 1887, making Marietta a town twenty years before Oklahoma became a state. The courthouse itself was completed in 1910 and was listed on the National Registry of Historical Places in 1984, three years before Noble arrived in Marietta.

Two stories, with a raised basement that made it look like a three-story building, the courthouse had all the charm of the old western territory. Brick and stone, with large white columns, and a beautiful clock tower, the historical marker out front stated, "The building houses all county offices and is a point of pride and focus of community activities."

Noble watched as a line of orange-clad county convicts marched along the sidewalk to the courthouse and struggled up the steps into the side door. He gave them a couple of minutes to clear, then stepped out of his truck and followed the walkway around the well-manicured lawn himself. Once inside, he took a set of steps up to the second floor and slipped onto a bench in the back of the courtroom.

Deputy Sanderson rustled the convicts into the jurors' box and stood waiting for the judge to enter via the door behind his bench. His secretary and the court reporter were already set. Two attorneys and several civilians sat scattered around the courtroom. Movement outside the window caught Noble's attention, and he turned. Old Glory flapped gently in the breeze, just above the state flag of Oklahoma.

Judge Hall entered. Deputy Sanderson announced him, and everyone stood.

"Be seated," he said as he settled into his chair and addressed the convicts. As he droned on about their rights, Noble shifted on the wooden bench and wondered how long this was going to take.

Sanderson's attention, drawn by movement, shifted from the judge to where Noble sat on the backrow. As their eyes met, Noble smiled and winked at him. Sanderson's eyes quickly swung back to the judge, and he shook his head in disgust. He and Noble had struck a friendship up the first year he was on the force in Love County. That had been several years ago, and he still was not used to Noble's crazy antics.

It was two hours later before the judge retired to his chambers, and Sanderson marched the convicts back out to their transport. When the last of the prisoners were loaded, he turned to find Noble leaning against his truck.

"You're an asshole," he sneered at Noble.

"What?" Noble feigned innocence. "Does this mean you didn't miss me?"

"Don't you take anything serious?" Sanderson asked.

"Only my job," Noble replied.

"Yeah, well, I do too," Sanderson shot back. "Do you have any idea what would happen if one of those convicts saw you wink at me?"

"Oh, so that's what's got your panties all wadded up." Noble laughed.

"Keep laughin', asshole," Sanderson swore. "But if I hear so much as one 'Broke Back Mountain' joke this week, I'll hunt you down and kick your ass."

"Okay, okay." Noble raised his hands to signal truce, stepped away from the vehicle, and stuck his hand out, then added, "So, I guess next time I shouldn't blow you a kiss."

"You do, and I'll shoot you dead right in the courtroom, you shithead."

They both laughed as Sanderson shook Noble's hand.

"So, where's the bee tree now?" Noble asked.

"Out east of town at the wrecker yard," Sanderson answered.

"Reckon that's the best place to start." Noble nodded, then pointed at Sanderson's vehicle. "You drivin' or am I?"

CHAPTER 4

Death drove a white Ford F150 slowly down Main Street. Black eyes stared through the bug splattered windshield. A stalled train backed traffic up through the red light on Second Street and brought him to a stop in front of the town's only antique store. Well, some things had not changed. He put the truck in park and laughed. The sound was odd, almost foreign.

Almost as foreign as the memory that unexpectedly surfaced—a young man walking north, along this same set of tracks, over twenty years ago. It seemed like much longer, and he had changed more than he would have ever imagined. He had walked through the night to get to the bus station in Ardmore, stopping only once at a small creek to wash the blood from his hands—the sheriff's blood. He smiled at the thought. The trip had given him time to think about what he had done and the possible repercussions if anyone ever figured out it was his doing. It had taken several years before the fears of being identified as "the Dog's killer" had begun to disappear.

If he closed his eyes, he could still smell the scent of creosote and feel the railroad ties under his feet as he left the only life he had ever known for the new one his Marine recruiter had promised him. He recalled the sound of night insects and the vibrations of the rails when a train grew closer. Twice he had slipped into the woods, and once, when no trees were near, he had stretched out in a patch of tall Johnson grass until the tracks were once again clear. Leaving Marietta was the best choice he had ever made.

Twenty years with the Corps had changed him in many ways. His years as a sniper had toughened him in ways that most could never understand. He had left conflicted with two names—the one on his birth certificate and his Choctaw name, Coahoma, the Panther. He had left unsure of who he was or who he would become. He had returned knowing exactly who he had become and who he was… he was Death.

Twenty minutes later, the train started to move, jolting him back to the present. He waited patiently as the tracks cleared. Four blocks east of the tracks, he nearly missed the turn. What once had been East Fifth Street was now South Elmwood. A small green sign indicated the cemetery was somewhere to the south. He turned south and soon found himself leaving town. The cemetery was not far outside town limits. It had two entryways, each with a metal archway that read "LAKEVIEW CEMETERY." It sat on a hill overlooking the town.

"You bury me in that white man's cemetery, and I'll dig my way back outta the ground and haunt you forever." Death remembered Grandmother Mosley's words as he drove past the second archway. Half a mile further along the same road, he slowed to a stop. He stared up at the American flag waving gently in the breeze above the single metal archway that read "PRAIRIEVIEW CEMETERY."

"Grandmother?" he whispered aloud.

An old red truck eased past, with one set of wheels pressing down the tall green grass that grew along each side of the narrow road. Death turned west under the archway and drove along the gravel road through pastureland for another half mile. Nestled on the backside of nowhere at the edge of the train tracks, he found the other cemetery. Here, those who were not white found their final resting place. He knew this was where Grandmother Mosley wanted to be buried and that he should be happy. He would try.

The cemetery was small, with few graves. It took him less than five minutes to reach it and park. Grandmother Mosley's headstone sat in the far back corner, closest to the train tracks. Somehow, this seemed appropriate. He and Grandmother had always lived close to and on the wrong side of the tracks. Now, she would rest there forever.

A patchwork of greens and browns topped the grave, giving it a strange appearance. He knew, eventually, the mound of dirt would settle and grass would reclaim the whole area. He knelt beside her headstone and picked a sprig of grass from the freshly dug dirt along the front of it. In the distance, a train whistle blew. He listened as it approached. As the train rumbled along, passing on the tracks just across the fence and behind the tree line, he found himself back on the porch of their old frame house, listening to Grandmother Mosley once again.

"The *ofi* is a bad man. He hurt your mother. You should kill him first, but he is not the worst of them. *Impa Shilup* is the worst. He must be killed last. He is the one that met with *biskinik* and *sinti* and *nashoba,* and they made *fvla* lie. I will not feel sorry for *fvla* when he dies. He did not have to lie."

The last car rumbled past, and the train faded off into the distance. Death plucked the last few pieces of grass, stood, and looked off down the tracks. Like the tracks, he was empty. He knew himself well enough to know that inside there was nothing. Whatever there might have been died with Grandmother Mosley. Perhaps he had always been empty. Perhaps *Impa Shilup*, the soul-eater, had taken his as a small boy, and when he killed him, he would get it back. Maybe then he would not feel so empty. Maybe.

It had taken him years to piece together what, at the time, had seemed like the ramblings of an old woman. As a young boy, he had heard stories of *Impa Shilup*. He had known that *ofi* was a dog, *sinti* a snake, *nashoba* a wolf. Later he learned that *biskinik* was a bird, more accurately a 'sapsucker' or a yellow-bellied wood-pecker. And even later still, that *fvla* was a crow. Grandmother had a way of leaving a lot of gray areas in her stories. In the end, it was a letter—or, more accurately, a list of names included in a very short note—that he had received just days after her death that answered some of his questions.

Sheriff Billie Hilton had been the dog, the *ofi*. It was he who had ruined the life of the Death's mother. Had his mother been a white girl when she met Billie Hilton, things would have been different, but she was not. She was a young half-breed Indian girl with a baby at home and no husband. She lived with her grandmother on the wrong side of the tracks and walked to and from work.

Just weeks after Death's first birthday, the sheriff had picked up his mother on the way home from work, driven her out to an abandoned house, raped her, and left her to find her way back. By the time she walked home, Billie Hilton was having coffee at a café on the other end of town.

Now, Death knew who each of the others were, but not what they had done to be included in the story. The Woodpecker, the Snake, the Crow, and the Wolf had all done something for which they deserved to die. And when they were all dead, then he would kill the Shadow. The Shadow last, just as Grandmother wished. Yes, all deserved death. And he was Death.

"Grandmother, the *ofi* is dead." He spoke aloud, "Now I will kill *biskinik*."

Emptiness closed in around him as his truck rolled through the archway, and he turned south onto the narrow blacktop. Dodging potholes along the way, he reached a stop sign and turned west. He kept to back roads as he made his way to Interstate 35 and headed south toward Texas.

A copy of Marietta's weekly newspaper lay neatly folded in the passenger seat. Death did not believe in signs, but he could see the irony in the front-page story. Two rednecks had found the badge of the *ofi* in the tree. He wondered what had happened to the knife.

The *ofi*, Sheriff Hilton—he remembered the first time he counted coup on the sheriff and the hell Grandmother Mosley had given him for doing it. By the time he had cut the sheriff's throat, he had counted coup on him twice more. Grandmother Mosley never knew about either of those times.

The muddy water of the Red River looked a little low as he crossed the bridge from Oklahoma into Texas. A hundred or so years ago, by crossing the river, he would have left Indian Territory. He wondered if, perhaps, he had been born a century and a half too late. He was a warrior. This he knew. He had seen battle. He had killed without remorse. He would do so again, but this was different. This was not war. It was not revenge; it was something else, but what? It would come to him in time.

Gainesville fell behind him and he drove on. The smaller towns of Valley View and Sanger drifted past, and soon he found himself in Denton. Not so long ago, one would pass through Denton and, sometime later, enter Dallas. Now, progress had connected Denton to the rest of the metropolis that was the Dallas/Fort Worth area.

This was the perfect place to lose himself. Staying in Marietta was not an option. It was too small. Within a week, someone would begin to wonder about him and ask questions. Gainesville would have worked but was still too close to Marietta for comfort. Denton was perfect. Forty-five minutes from Marietta and big enough so no one would notice him.

He pulled off the interstate at Exit 469, turned east at the stoplight, then back north on Mesa Drive. Easing past the Waffle House and several chain motels, he worked his way to the rent-by-the-week suites in the back corner of this small section of town.

Candy was bored. It had been a long day. She flipped idly through an old issue of *Tattoo*. Her own tattoo was hidden beneath the pale green uniform shirt she wore. "Stay Strong" in cursive with a feather along her left clavicle, a proud reminder of her senior spring break trip to Panama City Beach, Florida. She was twenty-eight now, that trip was ten years behind her.

Sometimes, it felt like it had been just yesterday. Other times, it felt like it had been an eternity ago, in another lifetime. She thought maybe she would like another tat. Maybe one on her back. One between her shoulder blades or perhaps a dream catcher with some feathers just below the top of the bikini line on her lower back.

The sound of the chime that signaled the front door was opening interrupted her thoughts. Pushing the magazine aside, she put on her sweetest smile. "Welcome to Denton Suites, how can we help you this evening?" she asked as she looked up into the blackest eyes she had ever seen.

"I need a room," the man behind the eyes answered.

"How… how long?" she stammered. His voice was smooth, sweet with a soft southern drawl, not a voice that matched those eyes.

"A week, maybe two," he spoke. "Let's start with one week."

"I'll need a picture ID and a credit card." Candy regained her composure and began maneuvering a mouse on the desk in front of her as her eyes moved from his to the computer screen.

"I'll pay with cash, if that's okay." His voice was like warm honey, and she felt herself shiver.

He passed her a Georgia driver's license and a military ID. "Do you have a military discount?" he asked.

"Yes," then, without thinking, the reply she had been trained to give escaped her lips, "And thank you for your service."

She took the license and the military ID and turned to a combination scanner/printer. As she scanned both, she felt his eyes on her body and realized that she liked it, even enjoyed it. A quick check of the information on his identification surprised her. Only five foot nine inches tall, somehow, he seemed much taller. Perhaps it was the lean one hundred and seventy pounds. Even more surprising was the date of birth.

He did not bother to hide the attention he was giving to her figure as she turned back toward the counter. Candy watched his gaze move up her body to her eyes and blushed. "That will be five hundred seventy-eight dollars and sixty-nine cents with tax."

He handed her six one hundred-dollar bills and watched as she made change from a drawer beneath the counter. He found himself appreciating the way her body moved beneath the tight black slacks and the loose blouse. His experience with women was limited. He knew the effect he had on them. Why they were attracted to him, he was not sure. He had been with a few, but somehow, it never felt right. In his mind, there was an unwavering belief that he should love, or be in love with, a person before he had sex with them. He also knew that love was not something that he had ever felt, and after many years, he was pretty sure it was not an emotion he would ever feel. Just another of the many contradictions that caused turmoil in his mind and left a cold hard stone where he knew his heart should be.

"Twenty-one dollars and thirty-one cents," she said as she handed him change and then a key attached to a pale green plastic keychain with the number eight embossed in black on both sides. "That's a lucky number in China," she added with a flirtatious smile.

"Maybe I'll get lucky," he winked and smiled back, then turned and disappeared through the front door.

She watched him go, admiring the fluid motion. The muscles danced beneath the black shirt stretched across his shoulders each time his polished combat boots struck the ground. And those tight Levi's jeans. *Goodness, girl, he's nearly fifteen years older than you*, she thought to herself. Then, *so what? Give me a chance, and I'm gonna ride that...* she giggled to herself and picked up her magazine.

A trip across the interstate to Walmart for food, toiletries, and a few other necessary items, and the Panther made his way back to his new home. A fair-size living room, with an open kitchen/dining room, and a bedroom with a bathroom attached completed the layout. The kitchen had a small refrigerator, a midsize microwave, and a two-burner stovetop, but no oven. The windows faced north, and across the street, he could see a school. Beyond the school building, there was open grassland as far as he could see.

In the bedroom, he removed the pictures from the walls and carefully placed them in the closet. He put his laptop on the bed, pulled a pair of scissors from one of the plastic bags he had carried in, and began to cut articles from the newspapers.

The first two articles, one from the local paper and one from the larger town just to the north, were both about the two redneck brothers who found the badge. The third article was a write-up about the Shadow. It told about his many years of service to the community, of how he was to retire soon, and how blessed the town was to have had such a wonderful leader for so many years. There was a picture included with the article of the Shadow shaking hands with Woodpecker.

Death pinned each article to the wall at the foot of the bed. Then, he opened his suitcase and carefully pulled out a large dream catcher. He hung it on the wall above the headboard. Perhaps it would keep the evil away—perhaps not.

After a long shower, he lay on his back, naked, staring at the articles pinned to the wall. Tomorrow, he would do research on his computer and rest. The next day, he would drive back to Marietta and do some reconnaissance. Within a week, the Woodpecker would die.

CHAPTER 5

"This should be good." Sanderson grinned as he opened the door of his Tahoe and stepped out.

A short, fat fellow covered with tattoos and a shaved head was yelling at a tall, thin elderly man with a long, grey beard that matched the thinning hair on his head. *Duck Dynasty* meets *Justified*, Noble thought to himself as he and Sanderson approached the two along a patch of gravel that passed as a drive.

"That's my trailer!!!" Tattoo Boy yelled up at the older man.

"I don't care if it is your trailer. There's evidence on it, and you can't take it." Grey Beard spoke evenly and calmly.

"Fuck that!!" Tattoo shook a pudgy finger at the old gentleman.

"I don't like that word." Came the stern warning as Sanderson and Noble reached the two.

"What's goin' on here, Mr. Greeley?" Sanderson's voice surprised Tattoo, and he turned.

"What's goin' on? What's goin' on? I'll tell you what's goin' on, Deputy Dawg." Tattoo's naturally high-pitched voice reached new heights with each word, and he shifted his head from side to side as if to emphasize his point, "This old faggot says there's evidence on my trailer, and he won't release it to me."

"Well, that is key-wrecked, Brucey." Sanderson raised the pitch of his own voice a notch.

Brucey sneered at Sanderson and turned back to Mr. Greeley, "Fuck that and fuck…

A sound, like that of a high-powered rifle shot, interrupted his sentence. Mr. Greeley's fist connected perfectly with the left side of Brucey's jaw, and he dropped like a heart-shot hog. Mr. Greeley looked sheepishly at the two law enforcement officers and then down at the shaved head of Brucey lying in the tall grass.

"I warned him about that word," he said dryly, "you both heard me tell him."

"Sure did." Sanderson shrugged and chuckled. Turning to Noble, he pointed to the unconscious man, "Let me introduce you to Bruce Bobby Brennan. He likes to refer to himself as the Cube."

"What brings y'all out this way?" Mr. Greeley asked, interrupting Sanderson's introduction.

"Noble wanted to look at the tree," Sanderson answered.

"Noble? Noble Harris?" Mr. Greeley cocked his head sideways and looked down at Noble.

"Yes, sir." Came the reply.

"Ain't seen you in a while. Wouldn't have recognized ya." He straightened.

"It has been a while," Noble agreed, "You've lost some weight and grown a beard since I saw you last."

"Yep," Mr. Greeley snorted a reply, then hoisted the straps of his overalls, "'bout two hundred fifty pounds lighter these days."

The three left Brucey lying where he had fallen and ambled over to the trailer. The tree was still strapped securely in place. Mr. Greeley and Sanderson watched as Noble climbed onto the trailer and began to examine the evidence.

"That big hole is full of honey," Sanderson explained as Noble squatted down near the center of the trailer, "That's where I found the badge."

"Did you check all the way up into the hollow?" Noble asked.

"What?" Sanderson asked with a look of confusion.

"Up...", Noble pointed up into the hole in the tree, "You know, up."

"Oh, up...", Sanderson said, "Well, now. No, I didn't think anything else would be up there."

"Guess we better check anyway," Noble suggested.

Brucey began to stir on the ground behind them. With a groan, he rolled himself into a seated position and looked around bewildered. A pudgy hand raised to his jaw, and he flinched at the touch, "You hit me?" he half asked as he pointed at Mr. Greeley.

"I told you I didn't like that word," Mr. Greeley explained, then turned his attention back to the trailer.

"He hit me!" Brucey wailed as he pushed himself up off the ground.

Noble finished rolling his shirt sleeve up and reached up into the hollow tree, trying hard to avoid the worst of the honey. Mr. Greeley and Sanderson watched patiently. Brucey waddled toward the trio.

"Hey, he hit me!" he whined loudly. "I wanna press charges!"

Mr. Greeley ignored him. Sanderson turned slowly away from the trailer. When Brucey was ten feet away, he raised a hand palm out. Brucey stopped and looked at the hand.

"I want to press charges," he stated again, still staring at the hand.

"So, the big bad-ass gangster wannabe Bruce Bobby Brennan wants everyone in Love County to know that old Mr. Greeley knocked his ass out cold?" Sanderson asked, then over his shoulder, "No offense, Mr. Greeley."

"None taken," Mr. Greeley chuckled.

"That's Cube to you, Deputy Dawg," Brucey sneered. "And that old faggot hit me."

"Yeah, that's right, Brucey," Noble chimed in. "He whooped your fat ass with one tap on that chubby little chin of yours."

"I want his ass thrown in jail," Brucey insisted.

"Sanderson, cuff him," Noble ordered. "Then call Mr. Nelson and tell him to get someone from the paper out here. Tell him to make sure they bring a camera."

"What's the camera for?" Brucey began to look nervous as reality of the suggestion filtered through his pride and into his brain.

"Okay," Sanderson pulled out his cuffs turned to Mr. Greeley. "Sorry, Mr. Greeley."

"Wait, wait, wait just a minute," Brucey raised a hand. "What's the camera for?" he repeated.

Sanderson paused, looked at Noble, and then back at Brucey. Slowly, the picture cleared in Brucey's mind. Mr. Greeley, in handcuffs, on the front page of next week's newspaper. The headline would read, "Elderly Man Knocks The Cube Out With One Punch." Brucey shook his head, trying to clear the picture from his addled mind.

"I change my mind. I ain't gonna press charges," he snapped.

"There's something else in here," Noble said.

Sanderson replaced his handcuffs as he turned back to the trailer. Brucey turned and waddled to his red Chrysler 300. He crawled behind the wheel, started the engine, and threw gravel as he sped through the gate and then fishtailed violently as he hit the blacktop.

"It's feels like the handle of a knife," Noble gave a tug.

"Can you get it out?" Mr. Greeley asked.

"I think so," Noble tugged again, and the knife came free.

He held it up. Honey dripped down the length of it and covered his hand. Sanderson turned and walked back to his vehicle.

"You think that there's the knife that killed old Billie Hilton?" Mr. Greeley voiced the question aloud that was on all their minds.

"Could be," Noble whispered, more to himself than the others.

"What's next?" Sanderson asked, returning with a large plastic evidence bag.

"There's someone I need to see," Noble answered. "Maybe she can help."

Sanderson swung into the parking lot of the Sheriff's office and dropped Noble at his truck. Ten minutes later, Noble took exit 21 off Interstate 35 and headed west on Oswalt Road. A mile past the Abner Church, he turned north once again, this time up a gravel lane that twisted through mountain cedars, scrub oaks, bois d'arcs heavy with horse apples, and an occasional mesquite tree.

Rounding a final bend, he crossed a cattle guard into a twelve-acre clearing. He recalled his first summer on the ranch and smiled. Granny had given him the job of making sure the place was mowed. He had never driven a tractor, never even sat on one, truth be told. By the end of that summer, he damn well knew his way around a tractor and a brush hog. Pulling to a stop in front of the sprawling white frame house that sat at the far north edge of the clearing, he stepped out and started up the stairs to the front porch.

"I'm 'round back," Granny shouted.

Noble followed the wrap-around porch to the backyard, only to find Granny perched atop an eight-foot step ladder with a pair of pruning shears. She dropped a freshly cut pear limb to the ground as he stopped, shaded his eyes from the sun with a hand, and stared up at her.

"What are you doing up there?" he asked as she clipped another limb and let it fall.

"What's it look like I'm doin'?" she returned. "I'm pruning the pear tree."

"Granny Harris," he chided, "I think, maybe, you should get someone else to do that."

"Really? And just who should I get? That no-account grandson of mine, who only stops by once in a blue moon?" she shot back.

"Yes," he raised a hand. "Just come on down, and I'll do it."

"Too late," she grinned, clipped another limb, watched it fall, and said, "It's done. I'm finished."

Noble held the ladder steady as she climbed down. Once on the ground, she set the clippers on the porch and gave him a big hug. She stepped back, pulled her leather work gloves off, and looked him up and down.

"You've put on some weight since you were here last," she stated. "It looks good on you."

"Thanks, I guess," Noble grinned. "You haven't changed a bit."

"At my age, there ain't gonna be a lot of change, I reckon." She started up the steps.

"You know, at your age, you really shouldn't be climbing around on ladders when no one's around," he scolded.

"You may be right, but it needed doing," she said over her shoulder as she opened the back door.

"Granny, you're gonna be eighty next month," Noble followed her in. "I think it's about time you slowed down a little."

Granny dropped her gloves on the kitchen table, turned on dime, and stuck a finger in his chest. "Now, you listen here. I've been running things around here since before you were even a thought. I'm just as fit as I've ever been and just as capable of taking care of this place, and if you don't want me climbing ladders and pruning trees, then maybe you should find the time to come around a little more often. And as for what you think, when I want to know what you think, I'll ask."

Noble raised both hands in submission, laughed, and said, "Yes, Ma'am. Yes, Ma'am. You're right. I give up."

"Alright, then," Granny took her finger from his chest. "You want something to drink?"

"Whatcha got?" Noble asked.

"Water and sweet tea," she answered, as she walked to the kitchen sink, turned the water on, and began to wash her hands. "Oh, and there's beer in the back of the fridge from the last time you were here if you'd prefer that."

"Just sweet tea," Noble said. "I'm on duty."

Granny shut the water off, picked up a hand towel, and turned to her grandson. "And here I thought you'd driven all this way just to see me. So, I guess, you ain't gonna wanna have a sip of Jack with me either?" She raised one eyebrow in question.

Noble shrugged. Granny finished drying her hands, took a mason jar from down from the cabinet shelf, handed it to him, and said, "Tea's in the fridge. I reckon you can get it yourself while you're tellin' me what business has brought you back to Love County."

"You remember when the Sheriff was found with his throat cut some years back?" he asked as he made his way across the kitchen.

"Sheriff Billie Hilton, I do," Granny said over her shoulder as she placed a jelly glass on the countertop and poured three fingers of Gentleman Jack into it.

"And?" Noble prodded as he pulled a chair away from the kitchen table and eased himself into it.

Granny took the chair opposite him, took a sip from her glass, and said, "And what? That was years ago."

"I know that, Granny," Noble shook his head. "And I also know not much goes on around this county that you don't know about."

"Now you listen here," Granny's eyes narrowed, causing the skin above her nose to wrinkle. "You can't just waltz in here and call me a busybody. I'll have you know…"

"Wow, easy now, Granny!" Noble interrupted with a chuckle. "No one is callin' you a busybody. I was just acknowledging that you are well-informed."

Chin a bit stiff, Granny lifted the glass to her lips once more, then as she set it on the table, she pursed her lips, shot him a sideways look, and said, "Well-informed, huh? Now that just might be true, but don't you think for one minute that I go a-pryin' about tryin' to stir the proverbial shit pot, cause I don't. I just have lots of friends, who like to talk, and who am I not to oblige when they need someone to spill their guts to?"

"That's all I meant," Noble agreed. "So, what can you tell me about Sheriff Billie Hilton's murder?"

"I'd say what I can't tell you is more important than what I can tell you." Granny fiddled with her glass of whiskey for few seconds. "I can't tell you who killed him. I can't tell you one single person who seemed all that broken-hearted about his death. And I can't tell you why there wasn't more of an investigation at the time he got his throat cut."

"So, it was common knowledge that his throat was cut and his badge was missing?" Noble swirled his tea, causing the cubes of ice to clink against the inside of the glass.

"Seems, as best I can recall, we knew within days that his throat had been cut," Granny said, "but I don't recall anything about the missing badge until those two yoo-hoos crashed with that limb full of bees down on Main. Then it was all over the papers."

"Interesting," Noble said and then sat quietly, mulling it around in his mind.

After several minutes of silence, Granny tossed back the last of the Jack, got up, and headed for the sink. Over her shoulder, she asked, "You stayin' the night?"

"Think I'll mosey back north," Noble answered and finished off his tea. "Jacqueline will be waitin' for me. I didn't tell her I was gonna be outta town."

"Jacqueline, humph," Granny rinsed her glass, put it on the drainboard, and turned. "When are you gonna marry that girl and make an honest woman out of her?"

"Now Granny…" Noble began but she waved him off.

"Don't need to hear any more of your lame-ass excuses. You just remember how often I've warned you when you wake up one mornin' all alone and can't figure out why."

"Yes, ma'am." Noble had long since given up on getting anywhere with this discussion.

"At least promise me you'll bring her to see me soon." Granny shot him a scowl.

Another, "Yes, ma'am," as he rose and took his glass to the sink.

"Soon," she reiterated with a finger on his chest as he reached out to hug her.

"Yes, ma'am."

As Noble pulled onto Oswalt Road, his phone rang. The name on the screen displayed as Sanderson.

Noble hit the accept button and said, "I was just fixin' to call you."

"Really? Guess I beat you to it," Sanderson said. "Listen, something is hinky about Sheriff Hilton's cold case. I can't put a finger on it, but every time I'm around Hughes, I feel like the new girl at the dance that none of the other girls want there."

"Sanderson, if this is your way of tellin' me you're comin' out of the closet," Noble chuckled, "I'd say it's about time."

"Dammit Harris, I'm serious," Sanderson barked. "I've got a bad feelin' about this one."

"I hear ya, buddy," Noble grew serious. "I hear ya."

CHAPTER 6

Death pulled a small flashlight from the side pocket of his black BDU pants and laid it on the ground, pointing back the way he had come when he crossed the floor into the Woodpecker's nest. He smiled. Just as he had figured, there were so many overlapping shoe prints in the dust and grime that covered the floor that his own prints just faded into those already there.

Blending in was something he had always excelled at, and tonight he was at the top of his game. His white truck was parked across the tracks less than half a block away. Backed up to a pile of railroad ties, just as he remembered seeing the BNSF railroad company trucks do so when he had walked home from school years ago. The tag would only be visible if someone was willing to get out on foot and check it. He seriously doubted anyone employed in small-town Oklahoma was going to put forth that much effort.

It had taken him less than thirty seconds to cross the tracks, pick the lock on the side door of the newspaper office, and let himself in. Now, with his back to the far wall, he pressed the button on the flashlight, and everything went dark, completely dark. This was his element. Slowly, his eyes grew accustomed to the darkness, and he could make out shapes. A sliver of light blinked briefly beneath the underside of the door he had entered as a late-night driver passed on the road outside.

With care, he crossed to the door he figured led into the main office of the establishment. After a thorough search for any sign of an alarm, he turned the doorknob. It was locked from the other side. With a smile, he slipped the tools from his pocket and began to count silently. On the count of seven there was a click. He turned the knob, eased the door open slightly, and returned the tools to their place in his left front pocket.

Light from the opened door cast eerie shadows through the room behind him, but he did not notice. His attention was on the front window some twenty feet away. Through the cracked door, he watched as a car slowed for the traffic light at the far end of the block. When he could no longer see the glowing reflection of its brake lights on the glass, he slipped quickly into the room and pulled the door closed.

Keeping a wary eye out, he worked his way through the building, keeping to the deepest shadows. He knew the Woodpecker would be the first one to arrive. Two days of careful observation was all it had taken for him to learn the little news bird's routine.

The desk closest to the front door, he figured, must be for the receptionist. Two additional areas had been partitioned off, possibly for reporters since both had small desks with computers on them. In the far back of the building, he found what he was looking for—the Woodpecker's office. Centered in the room was a large antique mahogany desk. Behind it, built into and spanning the entire wall, were shelves made of the same wood that reached nearly to the top of the ten-foot ceiling.

The door to the office had been standing open when he had entered. He swung it back and forth, testing the hinges for squeaks. There were none. *Silent as a grave.* A smile played at the corner of his mouth as he checked the time. The Woodpecker had less than an hour to live. He stepped behind the door, bent, and pulled a knife from the inside of his boot.

Noble stared at the ceiling and wondered if there was something wrong with him. That he had feelings for the beautiful woman curled up against him was beyond doubt, but was it love? Was it something that could, if given the chance, last forever? He just didn't know.

As was his custom when he wanted to avoid such questions, he turned his attention to the case. Billie Hilton had been brutally murdered, but why? And why take his badge?

He hated cold cases, and this one was not just a little chilly; it was North Pole Arctic cold. Over twenty years, and the only new evidence was a badge and the murder weapon. The idea that a fingerprint could be lifted from either of the objects after being submerged in honey seemed absolutely ludicrous. The optimistic side of his brain reminded him of advancements in technology. The pessimistic side told him to piss off and get ready for endless hours of going over dusty folders of long-forgotten reports and faded crime scene photographs taken with cameras that actually required film.

Jacqueline muttered incoherently and pressed closer. He slowly reached down and pulled the comforter up over her shoulder. No sense getting all worked up about it. Most likely it would be a matter of two or three wasted weeks ending in a dead end. And he knew that was what was really bothering him—two things he absolutely hated: wasting time and not being able to wrap a case up in a pretty little package and call it done.

Sanderson was just stepping out of the shower when his phone vibrated on the countertop. He dried his hands quickly and swiped to accept the call as he wrapped the towel around his waist.

"Sanderson, you meet me at the newspaper office as soon as you can," Ed Hughes spoke fast and sharp, then the line went dead, leaving the still dripping deputy staring blankly at the screen.

"Who was that?" his wife, Crystal, asked through the half-open bathroom door.

"Ed," Sanderson answered, pushing the door fully open.

"Everything alright?" she asked, looking up from where she was seated on the edge of the bed, buckling the strap on a pair of leather sandals.

"Don't know for sure," he shrugged. "Ed said get there ASAP and then hung up."

"Well, I'm headed for school," she stood up, stepped around the edge of the bed, and leaned in for a goodbye kiss. "I'll see you tonight. Be safe. Love ya."

"Love ya, too," he returned as she vanished down the hallway.

By the time she had gathered up her satchel, lunch, and car keys, Sanderson had managed to get himself dried and into his pants. Five minutes after her car pulled out of their driveway, he stepped into his police unit and started for town. Unsure about the level of emergency, he decided to forego lights and sirens but still made the fifteen-minute trip in just under ten.

Half a block from the news office, a young city officer stood beside his police unit directing traffic north and south. He motioned for Sanderson to continue on. At the far end of the block, Sanderson could see where sawhorses and yellow tape had been stretched across the road. It looked like every police and emergency vehicle in the county was on site. Easing into an empty space across the street from the news office, he stepped out of his vehicle to see Sheriff Hughes motioning him to come on.

"What's goin' on?" he asked as he reached Hughes' side.

"Frank Nelson's been murdered," he answered.

"How?" Sanderson could feel the hair rise on the back of his neck as he asked.

"Someone slit his throat from ear to ear," Hughes raised an eyebrow. "That's why I called you in. Looks like there might be a connection between this and Sheriff Hilton's cold case."

"Does seem a little odd," Sanderson said.

"I guess 'odd' is as good a word as any," Hughes agreed. "Reckon you better see it all. Chief Fields is waiting inside for us," he added as he opened the door and stepped inside.

Sanderson followed him in and quickly scanned the room. Nothing seemed to be out of place, as far as he could tell. On a normal day, the receptionist would have been seated behind the chair to his left, but today was not a normal day. Her chair sat empty, as did the two further into the room along the wall to his left. Marietta Police Chief Duncan Fields leaned against the far desk with a cellphone pressed against his ear.

"Yes, sir," he spoke to whoever was on the other end of the conversation.

"Frank's in his office," Hughes pointed past the Chief at the open door.

Sanderson's eyes scanned the floor between where he stood and the entrance to the office and wondered how many people had already traipsed through the crime scene. The low-pile commercial carpet, with its pattern of neutral brown and tan stripes, reminded him of a hotel room. He noticed it was worn and covered with stains.

"Gonna have to call you back," Fields said, looking up at Hughes.

Through the open door, Sanderson could see Mr. Nelson's body sprawled on the floor in front of his desk. Even from twenty feet away, he could see the blood splattered across the desk and the shelves behind it.

"Y'all come on back," Fields said, as he pressed the screen of his phone, ending the call, and offered his hand to Sanderson. "Ed says there's a chance this may tie in with something you're working on.

Sanderson shook his hand and asked, "Because of the way the throat was slit, or is there something more?"

Fields stepped to the edge of the office door, pointed to the desktop, and answered, "Something more." Then, as he stepped around the body of Frank Nelson, he added, "Watch your step. There's a lot of blood splatter, and forensics hasn't been in yet."

Hughes stepped back as Sanderson followed Fields into the office. The coppery scent of blood was more powerful inside the room. The telltale smell that reminded Sanderson of a nursing home indicated that decomposition had already begun, and that, if the body wasn't removed soon, it would not be long before it became nearly unbearable to remain in the room.

Directing Sanderson's attention, once again, to the top of the desk, Fields asked, "What do you make of that?"

That turned out to be the murder weapon, a ten-inch tactical military knife. The killer had stabbed it into the mahogany wood hard enough that Sanderson could tell it would take a bit of effort to remove it.

"Anything taken?" Sanderson asked as he turned his attention from the knife to the body lying on the floor.

"Not that I can tell," Fields answered, "but then, we haven't moved the body yet."

"So, this is exactly the way everything was when you got here?" Sanderson squatted and began a visual examination of the body.

"Yes," Fields answered, then added, "I figure the killer waited behind the door; then, when Mr. Nelson stepped into the office, he grabbed him from behind and slit his throat."

Sanderson studied the position of the body and the blood splatters. "And what makes you think it's the same person who killed Billie Hilton?" he asked. When Fields did not answer, he looked up and added, "That's why I'm here right?"

Fields nodded and pointed again at the knife. "The knife and the fact that the throat was cut like Billie's. Factor in that just last week the badge was found, and it seemed likely there may be a connection."

Sanderson listened, then spoke as he stood up. "I suppose it's possible, but the killin's are over twenty years apart. Why now?"

Fields shrugged.

"I reckon we better get Noble back down here," he looked to Hughes for confirmation.

Hughes nodded, and Sanderson said, "I'll make the call."

"You think it's okay to let forensics in and start gettin' the body ready to move?" Fields asked.

"Give me a minute," Sanderson answered, reaching for his phone.

CHAPTER 7

Noble was headed south on Interstate 35 when his cellphone rang, and Sanderson's name appeared at the top of the screen. He tapped to accept and then hit the speaker button. "What's up?" he asked.

"I hope you're headed this way already," Sanderson said.

"Just passin' the Wynnewood turnoff," Noble could hear tension in Sanderson's voice. "Something goin' on?"

"Frank Nelson's been murdered," Sanderson explained. "Someone cut his throat. Might be connected to the Billie Hilton case. Thought you might want to have a look before we bring forensics in."

"Yes, I would," Noble agreed. "Any chance of keepin' a lid on it?"

"Well, considering they've already barricaded off a whole city block, I'd say the lid's already off."

"Damn," Noble said. "Well, try to keep it as clear and under wraps as possible. I'll be there in half an hour."

"Will do," Sanderson said before breaking the connection.

Noble waited for the beep that indicated the call was finished and then said, "Siri, call Tom Jack on speaker," and waited.

Tom Jack answered on the third ring. "Whatcha got?" came his usual response.

"The newspaper editor in Marietta was murdered this mornin'. Looks like someone cut his throat. The locals think it may be connected to our cold case," Noble filled him in. "I'm twenty minutes away. Just wanted to let you know ahead of time."

"Alright," Tom Jack acknowledged. "Offer them our help, and if they need forensics, call it in. Keep me posted."

"Will do," Noble said as he sped past the first Davis exit. No flirting with Maria today.

Sanderson was standing outside the entrance to the news office with Sheriff Hughes and Chief Fields when Noble pulled his truck to a stop at the curb. As he stepped out and looked around at what had become quite a circus, he swore softly under his breath. He hoped what he found inside was less chaotic.

Gathering himself, he took a deep breath, nodded at Sanderson, and slowly scanned the faces of the people who had gathered just beyond the yellow crime scene tape stretched across the east end of the block. At the moment, no one person stood out. He had done this enough to know that, most of the time, no one did, but his ability to remember faces and the places he had seen them had served him well on more than one occasion.

When his eyes reached the last face in the crowd, he turned his attention back to the west. A deputy sheriff's SUV and a Marietta police cruiser combined to block traffic coming from that direction. The drivers of the vehicles leaned against the squad car chatting, while a third officer directed oncoming traffic left and right onto Second Street. Inside the restricted area, he counted seven vehicles—five police units, including his, and two civilian cars.

"Glad you made it," Sanderson said as he stepped off the sidewalk, "how do you want to do this?"

"I'm here to help," Noble answered. "I called my boss after our call, and he said to let y'all know whatever you need."

"Kinda figured you'd say that," Sanderson nodded. "I've been talking with Chief Fields, and he'd like all the help you can give him."

"Okay then, let's start by havin' a look inside." Noble stepped up onto the walkway, and Sanderson followed.

A quick handshake and brief conversation with both the

sheriff and chief, and Noble followed Sanderson into the building. It had been years since he had been inside this business, but little had changed. The same outdated wood paneling covered the walls and the front of the counter. He recalled the first time he had stepped into the building with Granny. She had needed to place an ad, but for the life of him, he could not remember why the ad had been necessary.

"I've been through the building and can't find any signs of forced entry," Sanderson's voice brought him back to the present.

"Well, walk me through it," Noble said. "Maybe a fresh set of eyes will pick up somethin'."

Nothing appeared out of the ordinary in the front room as they passed through. As they stepped into the editor's office, Sanderson voiced what Noble's nose detected, "Probably best if we move the body soon before the smell permeates everything in here."

Noble nodded in agreement and said, "As soon as we're done, better get someone here to take pictures. Lots of pictures."

After Noble had studied the room for a minute, Sanderson asked, "Any thoughts?"

"Whoever did this is physically strong," Noble answered, pointing down at Mr. Nelson. "Death from that cut isn't usually instantaneous like you see in the movies. It looks as if Mr. Nelson never got a chance to turn around, so he was very likely held upright while he bled out. Look at the blood splatter and the way his body is positioned. Both hands are up under him, and he looks like someone slowly eased him to the floor. I'm betting when we move him, the pattern of the blood will confirm it."

"Anything else?" Sanderson asked.

"With this much blood, the killer had to have gotten some on him," Noble looked silently around, then said, "There's too much of Mr. Nelson's blood in this room to figure much out without forensics. Did you see any in the rest of the building?"

"I checked the front room pretty thoroughly, but only did a quick pass through the room used for storage and supplies," Sanderson answered.

"I've seen enough in here until they remove the body," Noble said. "Let's go see the storage room."

Following Sanderson back through the building, he did a more thorough scan of the path he suspected the killer had taken, but to no avail. Sanderson opened the door to the back room and stepped back to allow Noble to pass.

Noticing that the door could be locked, Noble asked, "When you went through this door earlier, was it locked or unlocked?"

"Unlocked," Sanderson answered. "Why?"

Noble shrugged. "Just wondering. Could be nothin', but it's worth lookin' into. Who found the body?"

"Mrs. Samples did. She's the receptionist," Sanderson answered.

"Where is she now?" Noble asked.

"At the Sheriff's office. She was pretty shaken up. Hughes had one of the deputies take her over and put her in a room. As far as I know, she's still there."

"I'll need to talk to her later and confirm it," Noble said as he stepped through the door. "But for now, let's assume this door was usually locked."

"Okay." Sanderson followed him in and reached to turn on the light switch.

"Leave it off and shut the door." Noble stopped him as he pulled a penlight from his pocket.

As Sanderson pulled the door shut, Noble clicked on the light. Turning in a slow circle, he studied the room through the slim cone of light the flashlight generated. Like most spaces used for storage, this one was dusty. Everything the light shone on had at least a thin layer on it, and small particles were visible in air as the beam made its arc across the room.

Turning back to the door, Noble first checked the lock. It was old and worn, with years of scratches and scars, but along the left side of the keyhole, there was a fresh scrape that shone brightly. Moving the light up to the right side of the door facing, he followed it up to the header, then back down.

Motioning for Sanderson to take a closer look, he pointed out the scrape, and then as he moved the light back up the door facing, he said, "This is no run-of-the-mill killer. Look here along the edge of the door."

Sanderson stepped closer as Noble continued, "See the lack of dust along the crack like someone ran their finger up the facing and across the top?"

"Yes," Sanderson answered.

"I suspect they were checkin' for an alarm," Noble said. "Most folks who haven't done somethin' like this don't check interior doors for alarms."

"So, he came through this door?" Sanderson said.

"Maybe," Noble answered. "At least that's a working theory, but it's one I'm leanin' toward."

"Okay to turn the lights on now?" Sanderson asked.

"Not just yet," Noble answered as he turned and using his flashlight walked into the room. Bending down, he laid the flashlight on the floor and moved it in a slow back-and-forth motion. "I think we may have somethin'," he said, stopping the light and standing up. "Go ahead and turn on the lights," he said over his shoulder, not taking his eyes off the floor.

When his eyes had adjusted to the light, he walked slowly toward the spot he had located. With each step, he checked the floor carefully before placing his foot down. Once across the floor, he motioned for Sanderson to do the same. When Sanderson was standing beside him, he pointed to a small reddish colored spot on the floor not much bigger than the eraser end of a number two pencil.

"If I'm not mistaken, that is blood," he said. "There are so many footprints on the floor, it's unlikely forensics can do anything with them, but if that turns out to be blood, it could give us a better picture of how the killer got in and out. Still not much to go on, but at least it's a start."

"Do you think this is the same guy?" Sanderson asked. "I mean in your gut, do you think it's the same guy?"

"I don't know," Noble answered. "I'm a little scared to listen to my gut right now."

"Why?" Sanderson asked.

Noble sighed. "Because, on the one hand, if it is the same guy, it'll be easier than working a cold case, but on the other hand, if it is the same guy, he's already gotten away with one murder and disappeared for over twenty years. If forensics doesn't come up with anything, and he waits another twenty years to kill again, well, you can see where I'm goin'."

"Yes, I can," Sanderson said. "So, if this is our guy, our best chance to catch him is for him to kill again."

"That is the dilemma," Noble shook his head and repeated, "That is the dilemma."

CHAPTER 8

The long shrill whistle of a southbound train cut through the gentle morning breeze. The smell of freshly cut grass and an approaching rainstorm filled the air. Death squatted at the foot of Grandmother Mosley's grave, staring at but not really seeing the headstone ten feet away. In his mind, he worked through the stories Grandmother had told him looking for clues to who he should kill next.

"Do you know the Choctaw word for snake?" Grandmother asked.

"No, Grandmother," he had answered.

"It is *sinti*," she said, "and there is one who slithers around this town. One who thinks I do not know his part in your mother's story. In others' eyes, he is a big man, an important man, but to me, he is just a *sinti*."

"Why is he a *sinti*?" the Panther had asked.

"Why is not important," Grandmother's eyes narrowed, the way they did any time her opinion was questioned, "that he is a snake is enough. And what do we do with a snake?"

Death had smiled then because he knew the answer to this question: "We cut its head off."

The clickety-clack of the train drawing near brought him back to the present. A smile played at one corner of his mouth, as the thought of how that first talk about the snake had fueled his fantasies of using a knife. The smile disappeared as the old realization that while other teenage boys were dreaming about having sex with this girl or that one, his thoughts had been about death and those whom Grandmother said needed it.

The problem had been for years, and still was, that except for *Impa Shilup*, Grandmother had not given him an order in which to carry out their deaths, so he was left to figure it out himself. The dog, Sheriff Hilton, had been an easy place to start, but where to go from there was a more difficult decision.

He had come to the cemetery today to tell Grandmother *biskinik* was dead, and had hoped that there would be a sign telling who would be next, but so far, none had appeared. A dark gray spot appeared on Grandmother's headstone and then another as the edge of the rainstorm arrived. Death rose and stared out across the land at the gray clouds pushing the last of the sun from the sky. A lightning strike flashed toward the ground not far off, and as the thunder rolled across the space between him and it, he looked down once again at the weathered granite marker at the head of Grandmother's grave. His vision, distorted by the flash, momentarily caused a weird zigzag pattern on the rock.

"Okay, Grandmother, the *sinti* it is," he said aloud, then turned and started for his truck.

Noble stared at the folders strewn across his desk in frustration. The faded yellow pages of the statements taken over twenty years ago created a sharp contrast to the white forensics report he had just tossed into the center of the pile. He glanced at the cardboard box on the floor beside his chair to confirm that it was empty. With a sigh, he looked up and noticed Kent Davenport staring at him from his desk on the other side of the room.

"What are you starin' at?" he snapped.

"Not sure," Davenport grinned, "but I think maybe a cranky old bastard who's having trouble with his case."

"Kiss my ass." Noble shot back.

"You ain't my type," Davenport spoke in his best Southern accent, then changed to his own Jersey brogue, "but if you need someone to run that case by, I'm here."

Noble glanced once again at the paperwork cluttering his desk, then shrugged and said, "I guess it couldn't hurt, but don't you have cases of your own you're workin' on?"

"Nothing big at the moment," Davenport assured him, "just a string of break-ins at a few gentlemen's clubs and some missing drugs over at the Veterans Hospital. Nothing as pressing as two murders, even if they did happen down in Hicksville, America."

"Not even gonna dignify that one with a response, Capone," Noble shook his head.

"So, what about the case has you all tangled up?" Davenport asked.

Instead of giving a verbal response, Noble reached down and retrieved the cardboard box from the floor and removed its lid. From the desk, he took all the folders filled with faded documents and placed them in the box. Standing, he crossed the room and placed it on Davenport's desk.

"A county sheriff gets murdered. Not just murdered, but someone comes into his house and slits his throat from ear to ear. Inside that box is a handful of folders, a few statements from neighbors, all of whom saw or heard nothing, and fourteen pictures of the crime scene, which were taken with an old Polaroid camera and have faded badly over the years. And the last date I can find on anything in that box tells me that in less than three months, the investigation ended." Noble tilted the box towards Davenport and then asked, "What does that say to you?"

Davenport leaned forward and peered over the edge of the box, then sat back and said, "They ran out of leads, and/or nobody really cared."

Noble recalled what Granny Harris had said about there not being one single person who was brokenhearted about the sheriff's death. "I think maybe it was the latter," he said, "I don't think anyone cared, and that doesn't make sense."

"Why?" Davenport asked.

"Well, think about it," Noble answered as he picked the box up and shook it. "If you or I or any other law enforcement officer we know had been murdered in such a manner, the paperwork from the investigation sure wouldn't fit in one box, and this one doesn't even fill up a third of one."

"I agree," Davenport rocked further back in his chair and placed both of his hands behind his head. "Anything else about the case eating at you?"

"Yes," Noble answered. "I'm not sure if the new murder is connected to this one."

"So, you're not sure if you're working one case or two, then?" Davenport pushed his elbows forward as he spoke.

"It's all a bit frustrating at this point," Noble admitted as he returned to his desk.

"Want a suggestion?" Davenport asked.

"Sure," Noble answered.

"Work them as two separate cases until you're sure they're not connected," he proposed.

"Either way, it's not lookin' good at the moment," Noble said. "A honey covered badge and murder weapon don't really give me any new leads from the old case, and unless forensics comes through with something, there's nothing in these reports Sanderson sent up here to give me a direction to work on with the new one."

"Hate to say it, but another murder, well…" Davenport left the sentence unfinished.

"I know what you mean," Noble said, "but I don't know if Hicksville can handle another one."

By the time Death pulled his truck onto Interstate 35 just north of the Winstar Casino, rain was falling in sheets so hard that other drivers were moving to the side of the road to wait out the storm. He pressed on, keeping his speed reasonable while constantly searching for any sign of other vehicles on the road. A slow mile passed and then another before faint flashing red lights ahead caught his attention. As he closed the distance, the alternating red and blue lights on top of an emergency vehicle further down the road came into view.

As he pulled to a stop well behind an older model sedan, he engaged his emergency flashers and hoped whoever was behind him on the road saw them in time to stop. Keeping a wary eye on the rearview, he wondered if he should pull to the shoulder out of harm's way. The answer came in the form of the distant whine of a siren. Without hesitation, he eased off the road. Seconds later, a slow-moving fire engine followed by an ambulance passed in the far lane, and then for the next twenty minutes, he sat quietly while the rain faded to a drizzle and the traffic began to back up.

Just as he was beginning to think about moving back onto the highway, another fire engine and two additional ambulances passed. *Must be a bad one*, he thought to himself, and then his mind turned to *fvla*, the Crow.

He knew where to find the Snake, the Wolf, and the Shadow, but where the Crow was, he did not know. It had not been a pressing matter in his mind until just this moment. The possibility of fatalities in what he assumed must be a wreck ahead made him wonder if the Crow might already be dead. The muscles in his shoulders tightened and his jaw clenched. This could not be. He was Death, and he must deal with the Crow. He would not be cheated.

Inhaling deeply through his nose, he forced himself to relax. The Snake was next. He needed to focus on him, but it would not hurt to try to find the Crow again.

Toby Keith's I Love This Bar restaurant had always been Jacqueline's favorite, but tonight was even more special. Four years ago, they had met here. He had just finished a case and, as was his custom, he had decided to have a celebratory drink. His usual place was closed for renovations and Davenport had been talking about Toby's for days. He remembered thinking how odd it was that someone from New Jersey would have such adoration for a place that was owned by a country music singer and that played country music.

Jacqueline had been sitting at a table not far from the bar, waiting for her date to arrive. Noble had spotted her as soon as he walked in, and when she began to fidget with her watch, he knew she was growing uncomfortable sitting there by herself and that whoever she was waiting on had either stood her up or was running very late. Figuring it would not hurt to keep her company, he had ordered another drink, walked over to her table, and said, "Looks like they're runnin' late."

"Who?" Jacqueline had asked with a look of confusion.

"Whoever you're waitin' on," Noble answered. "I'm Noble, Noble Harris. Would you mind if I sit with you while you wait?"

"I would like that." She had smiled, and now four years later, she sat across from him at the same table where they had first met, picking at the last of her Caesar salad.

Noble finished chewing the last bit of his ribeye steak, pushed the plate away, and said, "That was wonderful, but I'm stuffed."

Jacqueline laughed. "You say the same thing every time we come here," she teased.

"Because every time we come here, I eat too much and end up stuffed," Noble wiggled his eyebrows. "Then I say what I always say, and you laugh. And you are absolutely beautiful."

"Only when I laugh?" she asked, eyes narrowing.

"No," Noble said with a smile. "You're always beautiful, but when you laugh, there is an extra little twinkle in your eye that I absolutely love."

"Oh, now you're just tryin' to get lucky tonight," she said pushing her plate away and reaching for her glass of chardonnay.

"Did you not just hear me say that I'm stuffed?" Noble feigned shock.

Opening her eyes wide, Jacqueline lowered her head, looked

across the table at him, and said, "Mister, this is our anniversary, and I, for one, am plannin' on getting' very lucky tonight."

Noble laughed aloud. "Maybe we should take a stroll down the Riverwalk to work some of it off before we head back to the car," he suggested.

"I'd like that," she said, swirling the last of the wine left in her glass.

CHAPTER 9

Death watched the Snake step out of an older model green step-side Ford truck, walk across the parking lot, and enter Carl's Jr. It had been six days since he had cut the throat of the Woodpecker. Both local television stations had run segments on it the same evening it happened, and at least two newspapers had printed articles the following day. Cutout copies of both were pinned to the bedroom wall back in the motel.

For two days, he had stayed away and kept an eye on the television for any further developments. On the third day, he had chanced a visit to Grandmother's grave. That night, the six o'clock news aired a short piece asking for any information on the murder. When it ended and the phone number flashed across the bottom of the screen, he smiled knowing law enforcement did not have a clue.

This was his third day of surveillance, and the problem he was finding was that the Snake was living up to his name. Except for his morning stop for coffee at Carl's Jr., his schedule was erratic and unpredictable. Most people had a fairly set routine. At least, that had been his experience. The lack of structure in the Snake's was slowing things down, and he found that irritating.

Just as irritating was his search for the Crow. A web search showed him practicing medicine in Ardmore, Oklahoma, but when he had used a burner phone to call and ask for him, the receptionist had informed him that the Crow was no longer with that office. When he asked where he had moved to, she asked him for his name. He hung up immediately. Not willing to take any chances, he wiped the phone clean of prints and tossed it.

Forty-five minutes of frustration passed before the Snake

exited the restaurant. From his vantage point at the convenience store across the road, Death watched as he stood visiting for another ten minutes with a group of elderly men. Not much of a talker himself, he pinched the bridge of his nose and wondered how some people could just chat away about nothing for hours.

Finally, he thought, as the Snake broke away from the group and got into his truck. The growing glow of light from the east told him it was nearly seven o'clock. He checked his watch anyway just to confirm it. For the next four hours, he shadowed his target while jotting times and notes in a small spiral notebook. Like the previous two days, no discernible patterns seemed to emerge. The man was all over town—the water department, City Hall, a haircut at the barbershop, a stop at one bank, and then across town to the other. Not one single place he stopped had he visited before today, according to Death's log.

Five minutes before eleven o'clock, the Snake swung by his residence, left his truck running, and went inside. Ten minutes later, he stepped back outside, got in his truck, and was off again. A quick check of his notes, and Death smiled for the first time in three days. The Snake drove away, not realizing he had just signed his own death warrant.

Death made a slow turn around the block and then pulled into the alley. Clipboard in hand, he marched straight to the gas meter and squatted in front of it. After a slow count of twenty, he tapped the gauges and pretended to scribble notes. Then, he stood up and surveyed the yard between the meter and the house. The neighbors to the south had a six-foot privacy fence. The one to the north had a chain-link fence bordered by a hedge they had let get out of control.

Tomorrow then, Death smiled. *Tomorrow, the Snake dies.*

Noble held the forensics report up as he flipped through its pages. Nothing. No prints besides those they expected to find. The blood in the storage room had been analyzed. It was Frank

Nelson's blood, but that was what Noble had suspected. He laid the report on his desk and picked up his cellphone.

When Sanderson picked up after the second ring, Noble said, "Thought you'd wanna know I got the forensics report back."

"Anything in it?" Sanderson asked.

"Not really," Noble answered. "No prints, but the blood in that back room was Nelson's."

"Well, that's something, not much but something," Sanderson said.

"How do you figure?" Noble asked, unsure of how that information helped.

"I've been doing a little legwork down here," Sanderson explained, "and it lines up with a notion I have."

"Like a notion that might be a lead?" Noble leaned forward in his chair.

"Possibly, but more like a gut feeling at this point." Sanderson paused, then added, "The officer on patrol the night of the murder remembered seeing a white truck parked alongside the track in the morning hours before he got off his shift. He didn't think much of it because the railroad sometimes leaves a truck there overnight. The thing is, I checked with BNSF, and they don't have any record of any work being done around here for the last couple of months."

"I don't suppose our officer got a tag number," Noble said.

"No, it was backed up to a pile of railroad ties," Sanderson said, "but if I'm right, our killer parked it, crossed the tracks without being seen, and came in through the side door."

"Okay," Noble interjected. "Still doesn't seem like much."

"Maybe not," Sanderson agreed, "but we have the murder weapon—two if the cases are connected—and we know that he possibly drives a white truck."

"Still doesn't narrow it down very far," Noble stated, the obvious.

Unwavering, Sanderson added, "I'm thinkin' that if whoever killed Frank parked the truck where the railroad parks theirs, there's a good chance he's local."

"I'm thinkin' that still leaves a shitload of suspects, partner," Noble responded.

"Bits and pieces, bits and pieces," Sanderson said. "That's what you've told me every time you've helped me with a case."

"Yes," Noble agreed, "but none of the cases I've helped you with in the past have included corpses and murder weapons."

"Good point," Sanderson said. "You comin' back down this way any time soon?"

"Maybe in a couple of days," Noble answered. "I'll give you a call when I start your way."

A police radio squealed in the background, and Noble listened as the dispatcher called for assistance with a wreck. When the call finished, Sanderson said, "Alright, gotta go. See you in a couple."

Noble placed the phone back on his desk. *What had Sanderson said? More of a gut feeling? Well, I see your gut feeling and raise you one*, he thought. *If we don't catch a break soon, someone else is going to die.*

Death parked his truck in the driveway of a house four blocks away from the home of the Snake. The place was for sale and, according to his research, had been for over a year. He could see why. The windows were all boarded up, probably due to vandals. Isolated at the end of a block that butted up to pastures on two sides, it would have been a very private residence in its day, a location that he, himself, might have chosen had he ever considered building in this town. The thought caused a mental chuckle as he stepped out onto the cracked driveway.

When the sun came up, the stolen license plate would be easily spotted by anyone who passed by, as would the tools and buckets in the truck bed that suggested someone was going to be working around the place. Standing in the dark, he breathed in the night. The smell of cut grass and a plowed field registered. The sound of a cricket far off floated through the air.

There was no need to hurry. He had given himself plenty of time to reach his destination before dawn. Leaving the side of the truck, he stepped around the corner of the house and walked its length to the backyard. There, he stood momentarily allowing his eyes to adjust to the lighting. The grass in the overgrown lawn was bent over with the weight of last night's dew. Someone's porch light from the adjacent block created a silhouette effect on the houses closest to him.

A dog barked somewhere off to his left, then another chimed in, and seconds later still yet another. He stepped away from the building and made his way across the yard to the alley, which was really just two furrows with grass growing between them. The switch from dumpsters to poly-carts had seriously reduced the amount of traffic along the city's alleyways. New technology, allowing water and gas meters to be checked remotely, had nearly finished it off. If not for the need for an occasional repair to one of the meters, the ruts would have long since disappeared. Choosing the first bare rut, he turned north. Slow, steady strides took him to the first of three paved streets he would have to cross before reaching his destination.

He paused briefly and checked both ways for any lights. None. Halfway down the next alley, he froze at the sound of an approaching engine. When the sound continued to increase in volume, he moved quickly to the trunk of a large tree and waited. As the rumble drew closer, light appeared in the street ahead of him, illuminating the faded pavement. A large dark-colored truck passed, leaving the odor of diesel in the air. When the sound of its motor had faded into the distance, he stepped away from the tree and started out once again.

He made it across the next two streets without incident and was working his way along the back of a privacy fence when he heard feet swiftly rushing from the other side of the wooden planks. Instantly, he dropped into a crouching position just as a dog began to growl its threats through the crack between two panels. Motionless, he waited. The low gruntled snarl stopped momentarily while the dog sniffed, trying to identify his scent. Unable to do so, it began to bark wildly, moving back and forth along a section of the fence.

A back porch light came to life, illuminating a large portion of the yard and filtering through the cracks in the fence. Death did not move. He did not breathe. He did not blink.

"Kimo, knock it off," a male voice, still heavy with sleep, shouted.

Kimo ignored him.

"Dammit, Kimo," the man shouted louder, "if that skunk sprays you again, I swear to God, I'm gonna take you to the pound."

Undeterred by the threat, Kimo continued to snarl and growl while Death waited. *If I have to leave and come back another day*, he thought, *a skunk is going to be the least of your worries*.

"Kimo!!!" The closeness of the man's voice caused Death to flinch. His movement covered by the commotion of the dog, Kimo's owner had managed to walk across the yard, and now the only thing separating him from Death was eight feet and the gray, weathered planks of the fence.

Instinctively, Death pulled a knife from his right boot and waited.

The sound of Kimo being dragged back across the yard, still growling, followed by, "Kimo, you're such a dumbass," made Death relax and slide the knife back into its sheath. The door slammed shut, the light clicked off, and Death slowly stood upright.

The first slice of morning light crept over the eastern horizon as he strolled the last few yards to a spot he had chosen the day before. As he squatted on his heels and leaned back against a giant pecan tree, his thoughts turned to Grandmother.

"I have never liked *sinti*," she had told him. "He slithers around town hissing first into one person's ear and then into another's."

"Why does he do it?" the Panther had asked. What he really wanted to know, but was too afraid to ask, was why it bothered Grandmother.

"Because it is his nature," she had answered.

His nature. Realization takes many paths and sometimes many years before it reaches its destination. How Grandmother had come to name each of the men she despised so much had always been a mystery to him. Once he knew who they were, the animals Grandmother had chosen for each did not align with their physical stature or appearance. If names had been left up to him, the Snake would have been Bulldog because of his short, stocky physique. Relaxing, waiting for the Snake to leave his house, Death realized Grandmother had assigned names according to the nature she considered each of the men to possess.

Ofi, Sheriff Billie Hilton, had the nature of a dog, unable to control his urges. A lot of bark, but no real bite if he could not overpower a person or situation. Death wondered, briefly, what power Billie had possessed over the others. Over the years, he had often speculated on the subject. Whatever it was, it must have been very damning for them to let him get away with rape.

Biskinik, Frank Nelson, tall, lanky, and completely bald, even back when Death had been in school, did not look at all like a yellow-bellied woodpecker, but then, Grandmother had not been looking at his outward being, but at his personality. He had flown around the county gathering little bits of news, then flown back to his nest and packed them into his weekly paper.

Sinti, former Mayor Sam Wilson, had already proven Grandmother's name selection had been accurate. Unpredictable as a serpent, Death had watched him slither around town far longer than he had planned. Like any cold-blooded reptile, the mayor crept early from his hole and then moved with seemingly random purpose.

Caution. The word slipped through the web of Death's thoughts like a spider running across its web. He retraced the last few minutes of his mental path. A dog is no trouble if you know its nature. A woodpecker is harmless. But a snake. A snake has the ability to be deadly. Perhaps there was more to Grandmother's names. Perhaps the names held warnings. Once again, that single word surfaced—*Caution.*

CHAPTER 10

Damn, what a night. Noble finished shaving and wandered from the bathroom into the bedroom. The unmade bed caught his eye. A tangled mess of sheets peeked out from under the blue and gray comforter he had thrown back when he had finally forced himself to get up. The aroma of last night's activities hung heavy in the air. *Damn, what a night*, he thought again.

For a brief moment, as he began to dress, he found himself wishing that Jacqueline's schedule had not required her to leave so early. Then, as if his self-conscious were chiding him, the chorus from Toby Keith's song "As Good As I Once Was" began to play in his head. He decided he was not going to give in and go quietly into this process people referred to as aging.

Picking up his phone from its spot on the nightstand, he unplugged it from its charger and wrote a short text letting Sanderson know he would be in Marietta later that afternoon. The message complete, he paused, not really in the mood to make the trip, but knowing it was overdue. In the end, he tapped send and finished dressing.

Death stood inside the door of the Snake's house. His stop against the pecan tree had been short—less than five minutes. The Snake's truck had started, its engine roaring to life and its lights casting strange shadows over the back wall of the open carport. Minutes later, a door had slammed shut, the Snake had crossed in front of the vehicle, gotten into it, backed out, and driven off.

When Death could no longer hear the sound of the motor, he had stood and walked quickly to the back door.

Now, he waited. The internet had told him that the Snake had been a widower for nearly ten years. His routine, and the absence of any additional automobiles on the premises, suggested a lack of any female companionship, but Death knew better than to assume too much. The sun rose slowly over the horizon, allowing enough light to filter through the curtain windows to make out the shape of the furniture in the room. To his immediate right sat an antique television, with a flat screen mounted to the wall above it. Along the wall, to the left, was a set of floor-to-ceiling bookshelves filled with books and knickknacks. A couch, a recliner, two end tables, and matching coffee table, all relics of the nineteen-eighties, completed the layout. Behind the recliner, to the left of the couch, was an archway.

Silently, he crossed to it and stepped into a small dining room that was separated from an even smaller kitchen by a breakfast bar, complete with glass cabinets above it. On the far side of the kitchen was the only indication that he had not been transported back in time to his high school years—a stainless-steel side-by-side refrigerator with an ice and water dispenser in the door.

In the opposite direction, a hallway led away from the dining room. Knife in hand, he eased along it until he could make out a door. Gently, he turned the knob, swung it open, and stared into darkness. Jaws clenched, muscles tensed, seconds passed. Unable to make out the interior of the room, he fished the penlight from his pocket and clicked it on. Washer. Dryer. Broom. Mop. He had found the utility room.

Careful to keep the light down and to a minimum, he continued checking doors along the short corridor. Two small bedrooms shared a bathroom and a much larger master with a bathroom of its own. All decorated to match the rest of the house.

Once assured that there was no danger to himself in any of the rooms, he closed each door and made his way back up the hall through the dining room and into the kitchen. A white plastic dish drain was perched to the left side of the sink, and across from it was an assortment of little brownish-orange prescription bottles carefully lined up across the back of the counter.

Caution. Something did not seem right. As he mentally processed the house's floor plans, it struck him. There was no good place from which to attack. The side door through which the Snake would enter opened against the refrigerator. He could not hide behind it. A check of the time told him it would be more than four hours before the Snake returned. He would figure something out.

Leaving Norman, Noble had told himself he was not going to stop at the Davis exit. Since he was in no rush, the reason had nothing to do with time. It was an attempt to turn over a new leaf as they say. He wanted to avoid the thoughts that plagued him every time he and Maria flirted.

Passing along the edge of Purcell, the notion that a little innocent playing around would not harm anything, as long as it did not become physical, entered his thinking, and the argument began. By Pauls Valley, he had once again decided a stop would not be necessary, and he managed to maintain the resolve through the Wynnewood exit. Nine miles of continuous debate later, he took Exit 55, turned right, and then right again into the parking lot of the Chickasaw Trading Post.

Old habit, one; new leaf, zero, he thought as he pulled to a stop and stepped out. *Maybe someday, but not today.* He opened the door and held it as an elderly couple exited. As he watched, the man helped the woman step down off the curb. He wondered if that would ever be him and Jacqueline, then turned and stepped inside. Maria smiled from behind the counter, and all his previous thoughts disappeared.

"Goodness gracious, looky here what the cat dragged in," she said as he winked and turned down the candy aisle toward the men's room.

Five minutes later, a twenty-ounce Dr. Pepper and share-size bag of M&Ms in hand, he stepped into line behind the only other customer in the store. When Maria handed him his change, the man hurried outside, leaving the two of them alone.

"I think this may be the shortest time between visits we've ever had?" Maria raised an eyebrow in question, as she reached for the items in his hands.

"Too soon?" he countered. "Should I stay away longer next time?"

"Depends," she said, running the candy under the scanner first and then the drink. "Did you stop by because you missed me?"

"You know it." Noble grinned.

"You ready to take me away from all this?" she asked, with a sweep of her hands.

"You still married to that husband?" he asked, as she passed him his items.

"You still hooked on that girlfriend?" she asked, instead of answering his question.

"Looks like we're gonna have to wait a bit longer," Noble smiled. "Besides, I don't think the boss would like it much if you just quit work and disappeared."

Maria giggled. "Maybe next time, then."

Minutes before eleven o'clock, the Snake's truck pulled into the carport. Death crouched against the cabinet door, knife held low and ready in his hand. The setup was not ideal, but it was the best he could do. He played the next ninety seconds out in his mind. The Snake would step through the door and close it behind himself. He would take a glass from the cabinet, possibly pick up his prescription bottle, move to the sink, and turn on the water. Death would stand, step up behind the Snake, and…

The door swung open, then closed as the Snake stepped around the refrigerator and reached for its handle. Death sprang from his position, thrusting the knife up toward the Snake's body.

The thrust missed as the Snake kicked out hard, catching Death coming up. Death staggered backward and then launched himself at the Snake, only to meet the refrigerator door as the Snake swung it open with all the force he could muster. Unable to avoid the collision, Death took the full force of the stainless steel to the right side of his head, and the knife left a groove just above the ice dispenser. Pain exploded inside his head, as if someone had detonated a small bomb. He sensed, more than saw, the Snake turn and start for the door. Reflex took over, and he launched himself across the short space, driving the knife up hard into the Snake's back. The Snake threw his hands out, bracing for the impact. They collided with the edge of the counter, and Death withdrew the knife in a swift practiced motion and cut the Snake's throat.

As blood sprayed the curtained window, backsplash, and sink, Death recalled Grandmother Mosley warning him about snakes. "A snake that is trapped, especially if wounded, is more dangerous than a snake that has a chance to escape. Its instincts tell it that it's a fight to the death and it will strike and bite until it can do so no longer."

Death leaned into the Snake's body, knife ready, keeping him pressed against the counter as the seconds turned to minutes. With one final convulsion, life slipped away, he went limp, folded at the waist, and fell forward against the counter. Death continued to wait until the last gurgle of air escaped from the severed windpipe, then stepped back, and let the body collapse onto the kitchen floor.

It was done. The Snake was dead. Teeth clenched, he drove the tip of the knife deep into the bloody countertop and scanned the kitchen. As he looked around, he realized he was in trouble. The blood on the refrigerator door was from his head wound. That, he could easily wipe away, but he had also bled on the floor and would certainly have transferred blood to the Snake's clothing while holding him against the counter. Wearing gloves kept fingerprints from being left, but a good forensic team would have little trouble finding his DNA in this mess.

He checked his watch, as if doing so would somehow set a

plan in motion. It did not. Cleanup would take too long, and the chance of leaving more DNA by doing so was not a good idea. His head was beginning to throb, and his thought process was not what it should be. He turned and made his way to the bathroom.

Once there, he took a quick survey of his head wound. A nasty inch-long gash, just below his hairline and to the right of his eye, where the edge of the door had hit him, was bleeding. The tissue around it was already beginning to swell, causing the cut to gape open. There was nothing he could do here, and every minute he stayed, the chances of discovery grew. He suppressed the urge to scream, took a beige hand towel from its hanger beside the bathroom sink, wet it, and pressed it against his head.

With the adrenaline already starting to wear off, he mentally struggled. Stop the bleeding. Make it to the truck. Try not to be seen. Get out of town. He pulled the towel away from his head and looked at the cut again. The bleeding seemed to be slowing.

Twirling the towel into a single long strip, he tied it around his head like a bandana and pulled the hood of his sweatshirt up. *No sense crying over spilled milk, or blood either, for that matter,* he thought as he stepped out of the bathroom and started for the back door. *It was time to disappear once more.*

Noble stood in the dining room, beside Dan Sanderson, and studied the new crime scene. The body of Sam Wilson, retired barber and business owner, lay crumpled on the kitchen floor of his home. If the murder of Frank Nelson had not completely convinced the two lawmen that the cases were connected, this one did.

"These are startin' to feel like revenge killings," Noble offered his opinion aloud.

"I don't know about revenge," Sanderson responded, "but someone is cleanin' house and I wouldn't want to be on their to-do list."

Noble nodded his agreement. "I'm beginnin' to think this one might go back a ways," he muttered more to himself than to anyone in particular.

Sanderson pointed to the blood on the refrigerator door and then to the gouge the knife had left. He said, "Bits and pieces."

"Looks like Mr. Wilson didn't go quietly," Noble spoke as he stepped into the kitchen, careful not to step on any evidence, and pointed at the bloody wound in the middle of the victim's back.

"If I were a bettin' man," Sanderson said, following him around the breakfast bar, "I'd give you two to one odds that blood on the fridge door is not Mr. Wilson's."

"I am a bettin' man," Noble stated. "You can keep your odds. I wouldn't touch that bet, but I sure hope you're right. A DNA match would be a really nice piece to stumble on right about now."

"How long before we know anything?" Sanderson asked.

Noble cocked his head and stared at the ceiling momentarily, then answered, "Forensics won't be done until tomorrow at the earliest. Then, if I can fast track it, maybe five days to a week."

"Do you think we have a week?" Sanderson asked.

"Maybe, maybe not." Noble ran his thumb along the scar on his jawline. "If we're lucky, the fight in Mr. Wilson will give the killer pause and slow him down. But if we look at the timetable between this one and Mr. Nelson, we have exactly one week."

"But, on the other hand," Sanderson shook his head as he spoke, "if he suspects we may have evidence that will lead us to him, he may feel the need to move more quickly."

"It would sure be nice to know how many more there might be," Noble said as he studied the tactical knife that had been thrust into the countertop. *Three murders. Three knives. But why leave the knives behind?* Noble wondered.

As Sanderson carefully backed out of the kitchen area, he said, "Maybe your first thought was right. Maybe this will slow him down and give us more time. Maybe we'll get lucky."

Noble looked slowly from the knife to the body on the floor and said, "I don't feel lucky."

CHAPTER 11

Granny Harris swirled the jelly jar in her hand, creating a miniature tornado in the amber liquid and causing the last pieces of ice to clink against the side of the glass. Noble could smell the bourbon and see the movement from the corner of his eye as he stared across the back pasture at the sun racing towards the top of the cedar trees. The wooden porch planks creaked as Granny placed her drink on the wrought iron table between them. Over the years, the two had shared many sunsets from these same two rocking chairs, but tonight, Noble was having trouble enjoying it.

He found himself reflecting on the rollercoaster people call life. Every once in a while, their cart manages to clank-clank-clank its way up, and for a moment in time, they are at the top of the world, staring out over creation. Then, in an instant, the bottom drops out, and before they can blink, they are back in the lowest valley, twisting and turning while life streaks past. The idea that anyone could ever remain at the top is, of course, ludicrous. Time would have to stop, and even if that were possible, it would not take long for an existence like that to become dull and boring. He knew it was life's valleys, with their hairpin curves and near-death drops, that made people appreciate those precious seconds at the top. He realized that it was the hanging on for dear life and the struggle to get back to the top that gave people strength, but damn, it would sure be nice if the moment at the top lasted a little bit longer.

If I designed a rollercoaster, he thought, after the climb to the top, there would be a long straight stretch that lasted…

"I never really liked Sam Wilson," Granny Harris said, and all thoughts of rollercoasters disappeared.

Noble mulled her statement over briefly, then asked, "Why was that?"

She continued to rock, and Noble knew she was thinking about her answer and weighing each word carefully. Finally, she said, "Sam was a busybody. He was always in everyone's business. I reckon it was because he was a barber by trade. They're pretty much the male equivalent of a hairdresser." She paused long enough to take a sip of her bourbon, then put it back on the table and continued, "Folks always figure most of the chatter in this town happens down at Claudia Mae's Hair and Nail Salon, but I'm telling you, those women can't hold a candle to the backstabbin' and gossipin' that goes on at the coffee shops and the barber shop."

Noble turned to look at her and said, "Seems like a lame reason to dislike a person."

Granny met his gaze, shrugged, and replied, "Well, he was also an asshole."

"Maybe you should have led with that," Noble suggested.

"I'll try to remember that bit of advice the next time I'm asked to evaluate my feelin's toward the deceased," Granny snapped as she reached for her glass.

Noble looked back to the horizon. The bottom edge of the sun had just reached the top of the trees. Streaks of reds and oranges spread out along each side of the gigantic sphere as if the treetops had somehow pierced it and the colors were spilling across the sky. Next came the yellows and pinks and pastels until the whole skyline was transformed into a picture so beautiful no canvas could ever do it justice.

As the last sliver of the sun disappeared and the golden hour began, Noble asked, "What about Mr. Nelson? How did you feel about him?"

Granny's response was immediate, "Oh, I liked him. Frank Nelson was a good man. A Christian man."

"Would you say most folks around here share your opinion of the two of them?" Noble asked the next question that came to mind.

Granny sat silent as if she were contemplating the question, then said, "Yes… Yes, I believe so. Most folks I know thought Sam was an ass. And like me, I think most folks liked Frank. Maybe not the ones who ended up in the paper looking foolish, but that's on them, not Frank."

"Can you think of anyone who might have a grudge against both men?" Noble continued to pick her brain.

Granny chuckled, "Nope. As a matter of fact, I'd say that would be an interesting find in and of itself."

"Why's that?" Noble asked.

"Because those two men hated each other," she answered.

Noble thought about that for a minute, then asked, "Do you know why?"

Seconds turned into minutes, and just as Noble was about to ask again, Granny stopped rocking and said, "Now that you ask, I seem to recall Frank helped Sam get elected mayor. As I recollect, Donnie Hartman had been mayor for years and stepped down. Sam was running against two other men and, for the life of me, I can't remember who they were, but you could probably find out at the courthouse. Anyway, I know Frank had a big hand in the election."

"Something must have happened for them to have that kind of fallin' out," Noble spoke his thoughts aloud.

"I reckon," Granny agreed.

The darkness of night pushed the last bit of sunlight over the edge of the world, and the first sounds of the night's symphony filled the air. Noble pondered his and Granny Harris's conversation. *Bits and pieces*, he thought.

"How long was Sam Wilson mayor?" he asked.

"Four years," Granny answered. "Just the one term, as I recall. Frank Nelson backed someone else in the next election. Let me see if I can recall who it was… was it, Jackson Hicks? Or the Williams man? I can't remember his first name. No, I think it was Hicks. Pretty sure." She finished her train of thought, picked up her drink, drained the glass in a single gulp, and said, "Let's move this inside before the mosquitoes get too bad."

Noble pushed himself from his chair and held the door open for his grandmother. Inside, she placed her glass upside down in the kitchen sink and then pulled her chair away from the table.

"Let's sit in here," she instructed as she sat down.

Noble settled into his usual seat before he spoke. "What kind of relationship did Frank Nelson and Sam Wilson have with Sheriff Billie Hilton?"

"Frank didn't like him much, if memory serves me right," she said, "but I just don't know about Sam. Why do you ask?"

"Just tryin' to put it all together," Noble answered. "I'm startin' to feel like there are a lot of movin' parts to this puzzle, and we're still missin' lots of pieces."

"Like tryin' to drive a herd when you can't find the cattle," Granny offered her version of the dilemma.

Noble shook his head and smiled.

"Oh, that reminds me," Granny perked up. "I was visitin' with Agnes down at the feed store yesterday, and I think I might have another piece of the puzzle. Mind you, it ain't much and may be nothin' at all, but she said she always thought it could have been one of the Muncy bunch that did old Billie in."

"You mean the Muncys from out Burneyville way?" Noble asked.

"Some live out in Burneyville," Granny nodded, "but there's some out towards Jimtown and Leon, maybe all the way to Rubottom. Seems like someone told me once that's where the first of them settled."

Noble rolled this new bit of news around and then asked, "Why would the Muncys want Billie Hilton dead?"

"Accordin' to Agnes, his people and the Muncys had some kind of feud goin' from way back when. I got the feelin' maybe over somethin' illegal," Granny said. "Anyway, once he got elected sheriff, I guess he made life hell for anyone named Muncy every chance he got."

"Someone would have surely checked all of that out, I'm thinkin'," Noble said.

"Maybe so," Granny tapped a finger on the table in front of her, "but it might be worth another look into. It's not like you've got other leads at the moment."

Noble nodded his agreement and said, "You're absolutely right, Granny. I'll call Sanderson first thing in the mornin', and we'll check it out."

Death lay on his back in the living area of his hotel room and watched a housefly work its way across the ceiling toward the outer wall. The cut above his eye throbbed, but the superglue and butterflies he had used to close the wound had stopped the bleeding. He knew tomorrow the area would be bruised, and he would have to do something with it so it would not draw attention. At the moment, however, this was the least of his worries. He had gotten sloppy. His ego had grown too big, and he had been careless.

Yes, the Snake was dead, but at what cost? There was no doubt in his mind that he had left evidence behind at the house. The trip from the house back to his truck had been uneventful, and, as far as he was aware, no one saw him. Of course, it only took one unseen, nosy neighbor for that to change. Mentally, he walked through his steps from the time he entered the house until he exited. There would be no fingerprints. He had worn gloves. DNA was another matter. They would no doubt find his on the refrigerator door and might be able to separate his from the Snake's on the counter and floor, or on the back of the Snake's shirt. He believed he had bled on it while holding him against the sink.

The military would have his DNA on record, but no one else, and, thankfully, it was not as easy to gain access to the military's databank, which would give him a little more time. But not as much as he would have had if he had only shown a little patience and not been caught off guard by the Snake. Now, he figured it would be less than a week before they knew his identity, and three kills in seven days made things a bit more complicated, especially since he still did not have a location for the *fvla*, the Crow.

With effort, he turned onto his stomach and pushed himself off the floor. His head wound pulsed with each step as he made his way to the bedroom and collapsed against the headboard. He pulled a burner phone from the nightstand drawer, looked up the phone number once more for the last known place the Crow had worked, and punched in the number.

"Health and Wellness Center, Linda speaking," a slightly nasal female voice announced, then asked, "How can I help you this afternoon?"

"Well, little darlin'," he answered in a deep southern accent, "if you could connect me with Doctor Hal Spencer, it would be very much appreciated."

"Oh," the single syllable that reached his ear was very close to a gasp, then after a brief pause, "I'm so sorry, Doctor Spencer doesn't work with us anymore."

"That's odd," Death said, "the last time we talked, he was so happy with his work there. I would never have guessed he would have moved. Can you tell me where I might find him?"

"I'm sorry," the receptionist said, "I'm not at liberty to say. Can I ask who is calling?"

"Sure thing, ma'am," Death answered, "I'm Charley Flinn. Hal and I worked together years ago when we were over at the Marietta Hospital. I'm passin' through town in a couple of days and thought I'd surprise him. I haven't heard from him in a while, and I can't seem to get him on the phone."

"Oh, dear," the voice broke.

"Ma'am," Death spoke, "are you okay?"

A sniffle and another pause, and she answered, "Yes, but I'm afraid I have bad news. I'm not really supposed to say." Another pause, "Mr. Flinn, was it? Or Doctor Flinn?"

"Either works," Death answered, "I wouldn't want to cause you any trouble…"

"Oh, no," she interrupted, "I think you ought to know. Doctor Spencer didn't have a lot of friends. Oh my, that came out wrong. What I meant was, except for those who worked with him, he didn't seem to have any. Since he's been sick, I heard not one single person, who wasn't a work acquaintance, has been to visit him. Not even any of his family."

"Goodness," Death feigned shock, "well just how sick is he?"

"Very sick," came the answer, "he's on end-of-life care."

"No," Death did not have to fake the emotion in his voice this time, "is he allowed visitors?"

"I believe so," she said, "you should call the hospital directory and ask them to connect you to the hospice building. They can tell you."

"Thank you so very much," Death said, "you have been more than helpful."

"I probably shouldn't have told you all of this," she sounded worried now that her emotions were in check, "please don't tell anyone I told you."

"I surely won't, young lady," Death assured her, "if anyone asks, I'll just say I learned it from a friend of Hal's, and if I'm guessin' right, I won't be lyin'?"

"No, sir, you would not," her words thick with the resolve that she had done the right thing.

"Well, then," Death said, "I'm sorry for your loss."

"And I for yours."

Burneyville was fifteen miles west of Marietta if Noble remembered right. He could not recall the last time he had traveled in that direction. Sanderson seemed lost in thought in the driver's seat as they passed the last of the residences at the edge of Marietta's city limits. The road stretched out ahead of them long and straight. The dips and rises of the terrain were the only things that kept him from being able to see all the way to Burneyville.

"I went to school with a Carla Muncy," Noble said, breaking the silence.

"Really?" Sanderson glanced over at him and raised an eyebrow.

"Yep," Noble said, as the road dipped and they crossed a bridge over a dry limestone creek. "What was that look about?"

"I guess I'd just forgotten you graduated from here and might know some of these folks," Sanderson explained.

"We didn't graduate together," Noble said. "She was a year ahead of me in school. I remember she was a looker - really stacked, if you know what I mean - but I don't think she ever had a steady boyfriend. But then, I kind of kept to myself except for sports. I wonder if she's still around."

"Can't say for sure," Sanderson said. "I've been out this way a couple of times, but mostly Ed takes care of things with the Muncy family himself."

"Really, now, that's interesting," Noble said.

"How so?" Sanderson asked.

"Well, from my observations, Ed Hughes doesn't do anything that he can pawn off on someone else," Noble explained, "so it makes me wonder why he shows such an interest in the Muncy family."

"Guess I never really thought much about it," Sanderson shrugged.

"Does our good sheriff know where we're going this mornin'?" Noble asked.

"Not unless you told him," Sanderson grinned. "It's been a while since Ed and I had much to do with each other. I'm not sure why or where it started, but I get the feelin' he keeps me around for cases like this…"

"Serial murders?" Noble asked when he realized Sanderson was not going to continue.

"No, that's not what I was sayin'," Sanderson said. "I mean

cases that might go south. Cases where he might need a scapegoat."

"I see," Noble nodded. "So let's make sure there's no need for a scapegoat."

"Agreed," Sanderson smiled. "And by the way, it takes three to be a serial killer."

"Sheriff Billie Hilton, Frank Nelson, Sam Wilson," Noble counted them off on his fingers.

"We don't have a solid connection with Billie Hilton," Sanderson argued. "We're just speculatin' that it's the same person because this killer uses a knife and cuts their throats. But we need to find a better link, especially since Billie was killed with a kitchen knife and these new murders have both been with tactical knives."

"Gut feelin'," Noble said.

"Won't stand up in court," Sanderson countered.

A green highway sign indicated that to reach Burneyville, a left turn was necessary just ahead. Sanderson slowed for the turn as Noble scanned the vehicles in the gravel parking lot of the combination gas station, convenience store, and restaurant. A couple of Hummers, three flatbed farm trucks, and several pickups told him the establishment was not lacking for business.

Sanderson made the turn. A pasture spotted with Texas longhorn cattle caught Noble's attention briefly, and then for a long stretch, a fence line overgrown with trees—most of them cedar—blocked the view on both sides of the truck. Noble stared at the blacktop ahead and waited for the next opening. As his mind wandered back to the case at hand, he thought it was a bit like traveling one of these off-the-beaten-path roads. A lot of the time, investigators drive around blind, waiting for the next clearing and hoping that in it will be a clue.

Lord, I hope this isn't a wild goose chase, Noble thought, as Sanderson slowed to navigate a sharp turn and then accelerated once more.

CHAPTER 12

Death stood beside Grandmother's grave. Sunlight glistened off dew that still clung to the ankle-deep grass. It would not be long until it needed to be mowed again. The morning silence was broken by the call of a lonely meadowlark. When he finished his call and received no response, he grew quiet once again, leaving the cemetery eerily still.

Death had come for a visit; he did not need a sign this time. He knew he could not chance the Crow escaping. He would have to be the next, and he would have to be soon.

"Grandmother, the *sinti* is dead," Death said aloud, "the *flva* is next."

In the distance, a train blew its warning whistle. Death flinched involuntarily. Even in life, he had never truly understood Grandmother. Now, what some would easily explain away with simple scientific reasoning, his mind speculated might be her way of communicating—her spirit's way of refusing to leave until they were all dead.

With a nod at her headstone, he muttered one simple word, "Soon."

"There it is," Sanderson said, pointing out the Muncy family residence as they turned a corner.

Noble had not known what to expect, but somehow this was a far cry from anything his imagination would have conjured. At least ten vehicles cluttered the front lawn, only one of which was jacked up and looked as if it would not run. The big two-story frame house looked like it was in good shape despite its need for a fresh coat of paint. It was surrounded by trees that had not been cut back, and whose branches now overhung the building, lying on its roof and crowding what looked to be a large balcony above the wrap-around porch.

Sanderson eased to a stop behind a red Chrysler 300. Noble gave Sanderson a questioning look.

"Yes, siree, Bob," Sanderson grinned, "That's Brucey's?"

Noble looked from the vehicle to Sanderson and then back again. "From the tow yard?"

"The one and only," Sanderson confirmed just as the front door screen flew open with enough force to drive it into the wooden siding with a resounding bang.

"This is harassment, you asshole!" shouted a tall, thin woman as she crossed the porch and came to a stop at the top of the steps, one hand on her hip the other pointing an accusatory finger toward Sanderson.

Sanderson swung his door open and stepped out but left the vehicle running. "What seems to be the problem, Linda?" he asked from behind the open door.

"You!! You're the problem, asshole!!" The rasp in her voice betrayed her two-pack-a-day habit.

"How do you figure?" Sanderson raised both hands above his head as if to say—no problem here.

"Yeah, right." Linda's response lacked the volume and intensity of her last; whether due to lack of air or Sanderson's passive demeanor, Noble could not tell. He watched as she removed her hand from her hip and retrieved a pack of Marlboro 100s from inside the left cup of her bra. "What the hell does Ed want now?"

"I wouldn't know," Sanderson lowered his hands as he spoke, "I'm not here for Ed. Noble needs to talk to you." He nodded toward Noble, indicating him without turning to look at him.

"Who's Noble?" Linda asked, seeming to notice Sanderson's passenger for the first time.

Figuring it was time for introductions, Noble opened his door and stepped out. With a gentle tip of his hat, he said, "I'm Noble, ma'am."

Shaking a small pink lighter out of the clear cellophane that surrounded the cardboard packing of her cigarettes, Linda eyeballed Noble as she worked on lighting her smoke. Noble watched as her expression moved through stages: disgust at another badge, curiosity as she scanned the mental facial recognition of her memory, a flicker of joy at a possible identification, and, once again, back to disgust at the badge.

"Noble, huh?" one nostril raised in a mixture of distrust and caution, "Wouldn't be Noble Harris that went to school with Carla, would it?"

"Yes, ma'am," Noble answered as he moved around the front of the vehicle and approached the porch.

Linda drew deep on the cigarette and blew the smoke out slowly. Noble watched as her eyes narrowed, studying him. He stopped just short of the bottom step, waiting for some sign that she had reached a decision on whether she approved of him or not. As the seconds ticked away, he realized that her approval meant more to him than it should, and it bothered him. *Nothing like hometown folks to make you feel seventeen again*, he thought.

"So, whatcha wanna talk to me about?" she asked, flicking the ashes from the end of her cigarette.

"Billie Hilton," Noble answered, watching carefully for her reaction.

It came quickly. A new level of disgust filled her features as she launched a glob of spit that landed in the dirt between the steps and Noble's boots. Reflexes took over, and his eyes followed the spittle to the ground. When he looked back up, Linda had turned and started back inside.

As she reached the door, it opened. "Now wait a minute, Momma," a woman's voice said, "Let see what this is about."

Linda spoke as she whirled around to glare at Noble, "It's about the same damn thing it's always been about. He wants to know if a Muncy killed that worthless son of a bitch. Ain't' that right?"

Noble heard the question float past him and down the road as Carla Muncy stepped out the door to stand beside Linda. The years had been kinder to Carla than anyone Noble had ever known. The foundation of someone beautiful had been there back in high school, but time had added a little here and a bit there in just the right amounts and in just the right places. She wore a brightly colored loose-fitting blouse with large red, yellow, and green stripes decorated with marijuana leaves. It reminded Noble of an old Bob Marley album cover he had seen somewhere. Faded Wranglers and a pair of scuffed western boots completed the ensemble. Her voice had not changed. It had just enough grit to be sexy but not so much as to sound masculine. "Hello, Noble." She smiled as she spoke his name.

Linda's question boomeranged back around, and he spoke as he tore his eyes from Carla. "No ma'am. Nothin' like that." Then back to Carla, "Hello, Carla," with a smile.

Linda steadfastly refused to discuss Billie Hilton. Carla, on the other hand, seemed open to conversation as long as law enforcement was not looking to take any of her kin to jail. Once it was established that neither he nor Sanderson was looking for anything but answers, the porch began to fill up rapidly. Virgil and Wyatt appeared first, followed by Bruce.

"Don't need no law snoopin' 'round here," Bruce snarled loud enough for all to hear from the back of the porch without making eye contact with either Noble or Sanderson.

"That's right, Cube," Virgil agreed, staring down Sanderson from behind Linda.

"Wyatt, take these two dumbasses back in the house before one of them ends up doin' somethin' stupid and gets hauled off again," Carla ordered as she stepped down from the porch.

"You can't talk about me like that," Bruce whined.

"Reckon she just did," Wyatt grinned, already heading for the door. "Come on, let's go finish our movie."

"Let's take a walk," Carla said, as she stepped off the porch and did not even bother to slow down as she passed Noble.

With a shrug at Sanderson, Noble turned and hustled to catch up. Carla held a steady, no-nonsense pace for a block until they reached a four-way in the road. She stopped long enough to look left and right and then stepped off again, this time at a slower pace. Fifty yards further along, the blacktop doglegged, and Noble knew without looking back they were no longer visible from the porch. Carla walked on, eyes ahead, back straight, with a seemingly clear destination. He was about to ask where that might be when she raised a finger and pointed at the entrance to the Burneyville cemetery just ahead. *Damn, she reads minds*, he thought.

A four-foot chain-link fence separated the faded asphalt of the road from the well-maintained resting place of those inside. Along the backside, five strands of barbed wire on faded orange T-posts kept livestock out. Carla turned into the first set of ruts that served as a roadway through the cemetery. Noble took the second rut. Near the far end of the cemetery, Noble noticed a pair of tables under a long metal pavilion set well behind the last row of headstones.

"Gotta phone?" Carla asked as they were nearing the first table.

"Yes. Why?" Noble asked.

"Let me see it," she said, putting her hand out, as they reached the pavilion, and she settled herself into a seated position on the edge of the table.

"Why?" Noble asked.

"Because that is the only way I'm goin' to have a conversation with you," Carla's eyes widened, and she extended her hand just a bit further toward him.

A half-smile curled the edge of Noble's mouth as he pulled the phone from his pocket using only his thumb and index finger. As he dropped it in her hand, he said, "A bit dramatic, huh, darlin'?"

"Just cautious," a flush of red colored her cheeks and then was quickly gone. "I've found it's best with the people I hang around."

"That's a helluva way to talk about family," Noble said.

Carla's began to slowly swing her legs. For a long moment, she stared at the ground, then raised her head to meet Noble's gaze. "You don't get to pick your family. And I reckon you don't have to like them all the time, but you gotta stick by 'em."

"That's a helluva personal philosophy," Noble raised an eyebrow.

"Don't be an asshole," Carla snapped. "You're the one who wanted to talk. So, go ahead and ask your questions before I change my mind."

Noble raised both hands shoulder-high, took a step back, and laughed. "Damn, you're just as mean and surly as I remember you from high school."

"I wasn't mean and surly in high school," she shot back. "I was quiet."

"Sure came off as mean and surly." Noble countered with another chuckle.

"Well, if you hadn't been so stuck on yourself, maybe you would have noticed I had a crush on you back then," she hissed, eyes narrowing as she spoke.

Noble could feel his face flush red as he opened his mouth. His brain refused to summon a response. With nothing to verbalize, it was his turn to stare at the ground.

"Well, I'll be damned," Carla chuckled. "Cat got your tongue, does it?"

"No," Noble answered, shifting his weight from one leg to the other before meeting her eye again. "And I wasn't stuck on myself in high school."

"And I wasn't mean and surly," she repeated with a smile.

A picture of Carla sitting on the edge of a table somewhere around his junior year began to form in his mind. This was one of the reasons he hated coming back to Love County. Here, he always felt like he was the same shy, awkward teenager who had sworn he would only return to visit Granny. His brain pushed the edge of the memory back, and suddenly the picture became a video. They were at a party down on the backside of Lake Murray. Damn, if he could remember whose house it had been. Everyone had a drink in their hand, mostly beer, but some hard alcohol here and there. Carla was holding a can of Busch in one hand and a joint in the other. It was the first time he had ever smelled marijuana or seen anyone smoke it. He must have been staring because when she looked over and caught him, she had winked, pursed her lips in a kiss, and smacked them at him. He wondered if she remembered.

"Agreed," Noble said. "Truce?"

"Truce," Carla agreed. "Go ahead, ask your questions."

Noble only had one. It was not a very nice one, and he realized he was not exactly sure how to phrase it. The question itself was simple: Did anyone in your family murder Billie Hilton? Asking it without seeming accusatory was going to be a bit tricky.

"I'm trying to get to the bottom of the recent murders," Noble said, "and I have a theory I'd like to run by you."

"Okay," Carla said as she moved from the tabletop to sit on its bench. "Why don't you have a seat?" she asked, pointing to the opposite bench.

The way she moved so fluidly derailed his train of thought, and he found himself staring blankly at the seat she had indicated. "What?"

"Sit down," her voice more forceful this time. "You look nervous, maybe it'll help."

"I'm not nervous," Noble argued, but slid onto the bench.

"Really?" Carla grinned. "Could have fooled me. You got that same look on your face, like the time I winked at you at that party."

And just like that, he felt the need to bolt. *Damn, what was it with this girl?*

"I'm just messin' with you," Carla giggled. "Now, come on, how can the Muncy family help you solve these murders?"

Noble stared at his hands for a long minute, then without making eye contact said, "Well, I think these murders are connected to the murder of Sheriff Billie Hilton."

"And you want to know if a Muncy killed the sheriff," Carla said.

"Actually, what I want to know is why folks around here think it was a Muncy," Noble tapped the aluminum beam of the table with his index finger. "And I'd like to know who you think did it."

Carla's brow furrowed as she asked, "Don't you remember when it happened? I had only been out of school for a year, so you had to have just finished high school yourself. Weren't you still around?"

"Yes and no," Noble answered. "I remember it happening. I think it was about a week after graduation, so I was still around, but my mind was on getting' everything ready to go to basic training."

"Well, it didn't take ol' Ed Hughes long to come callin' on MawMaw." Carla's lip curled at his name.

"Why?" Noble asked.

Carla shook her head, laid both palms down on the table, then said, "You really don't know much of the history of our county, do ya?"

"I guess not," Noble admitted. It had been a long time since he thought of Love County as his. For some reason, Carla's reminder of it caused a feeling of guilt.

"The Hiltons moved into the area west of here. I don't know for sure, maybe just before or just after us Muncys moved into Burneyville. I'm not sure if the Hiltons were over around Jim's Town or all the way out towards Rubottom. Anyway, our two families were in competition, and it got pretty ugly."

"Competition, how?" Noble asked.

"Goodness," Carla smiled. "You are clueless here, aren't you?"

"Absolutely," Noble said. "That's why I'm here."

"I don't know what actually started it," Carla stared out past the barbed wire at the trees momentarily. "I guess no one alive really does. Maybe MawMaw might… anyway, somewhere back during Prohibition, a feud started between the two families because they were both runnin' shine. Huntin' accidents were a common occurrence for a while, and I've heard a lot of vehicles ended up runnin' into trees over the years. So there has never been a lot of love lost between us and the Hiltons."

"I don't recall hearin' about any Muncys or Hiltons being killed around here for as long as I can remember, with the exception of Billie, of course," Noble said as he rubbed his thumb along the scar on his chin.

"That's because Billie was the last one," Carla shrugged.

"I don't think so," Noble shook his head. "I graduated with a guy whose last name was Hilton."

"Different family." Carla smiled and shook her finger at him. "Those folks moved in not too long before you showed up."

Noble sat silently, staring out across the land as he let his mind digest what Carla had told him. A car sped by, slowing just enough to navigate the curve at the end of the cemetery and then accelerated away out of sight. Intuition told him there was something here he was missing. Another part of his brain insisted it was a dead end and he was just grasping at straws. He reminded himself that it only took grabbing the right straw to break a case wide open and that one had to investigate every lead, especially when there were so few.

"So even after twenty years, Ed Hughes still comes around regularly buggin' your family about the murders, huh?" Noble asked.

"What?" Carla frowned. "Oh, no, that's not why the sheriff's been harassin' us. Hell, he's left us alone for the last twenty years for the most part. It wasn't until about six months ago he started comin' 'round again."

"Why?" Noble asked. "What did he want?"

"Well let's just say MawMaw and the good sheriff worked

out a deal a ways back to keep his family and ours from feudin'."
Carla's lip turned up in a half grin.

"And what kind of deal would that have been?" Noble
asked.

Carla gnawed at her bottom lip and stared into his eyes.
Noble stared back, wondering if she was going to answer the
question, and then realized she was deciding how far she could
trust him.

"The deal was…" Carla began, then stopped and cleared her
throat. "The deal was that my family would sell peanuts and his
would sell cotton candy, if you know what I mean. And neither
family would infringe on the other's business."

"I think I understand," Noble said. "So what changed? Why
is the good sheriff harassin' y'all?

"Because, it's just a matter of time before sellin' peanuts is
legalized in this state and cotton candy never will be," Carla
smiled. "So in a few years, my family's business will be legit and
his won't. So, you see, he wants to renegotiate."

"Are you tellin' me that the sheriff is dealin' meth?" Noble
shook his head in disbelief.

"I never said anything about meth," Carla declared. "I said
cotton candy. And no, he doesn't deal it. He just makes sure no
one interferes with his kinfolks who do, especially those who
aren't from around here."

"So, you keep your mouth shut about the cotton candy, and
he looks the other way when you sell your peanuts?" Noble raised
an eyebrow.

"Now you're catchin' on," Carla smiled.

"Still doesn't get me any closer to an answer on who killed
Billie Hilton," Noble sighed.

"Maybe we should go talk to MawMaw," Carla suggested.

"MawMaw?" Noble gave her a questioning look.

"MawMaw is my grandmother," Carla explained.

Noble raised an eyebrow. "And does she lives somewhere
close?"

"Of course," Carla giggled. "She's in the nursin' home in town."

Noble considered it briefly, then said as he pushed himself up from his seat, "What good would seein' your MawMaw do?"

"Maybe none," Carla admitted, rising to stand beside him, "but she did run the family business for a very long time. And she ran it very well because she made it her business to know everything that was goin' on in this county and even some of the surroundin' ones."

"And she might know somethin' about somethin' because she sold peanuts?" Noble smirked.

"MawMaw never sold anything," Carla laughed. "She just made sure the workers did what they were supposed to and kept the books."

"MawMaw was the manager of the peanut farm?" Noble surmised.

"Oh, hell no. MawMaw was the manager of our pot farm," Carla chuckled. "And she was damn proud of it, but she's retired now." And with that, she stood and started back toward the road they had come to the cemetery on.

Noble stood and watched her go, enjoying the natural way her stride exaggerated the sway of her hips now that she was not in a hurry. When she realized he had not followed her, she turned, put both hands on her hips, and said, "Stop starin' at my ass and come on. If we hurry, we can get to the nursin' home before MawMaw has lunch. If not, we'll have to wait until she gets up from her afternoon nap."

Carla waited for him to reach her side before turning to go, then said, "I hope you have change of clothes."

"Why?" Noble asked.

"Because what you're wearin' screams cop," Carla shrugged. "And MawMaw ain't likely to talk to you if she thinks you're a cop."

CHAPTER 13

The nice thing about places that employ large numbers of people is that not everyone knows everyone. Death walked in the front door wearing a white hard hat and toting an eight-foot ladder. He passed the reception desk without interference and wandered through the hospital until a shift nurse stopped him and asked if he needed help.

"Well, yes ma'am," he used his best hick accent and smiled, "I just got hired on to help with the renovations. I was told to show up this mornin', but no one told me exactly where I was to go."

"There's five different projects in the works at the moment," she smiled back, "do you know which one you're assigned to?"

Death took a chance, "The fella who hired me said to go to the terminal care facility." He shrugged.

"The kitchen remodel." The nurse nodded, "You are lost. Go back out the front entrance. It's across the parking lot. The building right next to the CVS. The kitchen is in the back, but you'll probably have to go through the front entrance."

"Thank you so much," Death smiled, "I sure appreciate it. I better get goin'. I'm already late."

Noble backed into a parking space directly in front of the walkway leading up to the nursing home. He was not sure which of the vehicles parked in front of the Muncy house had been Carla's and had been kicking himself for not asking her since he and Sanderson had left. His thoughts turned to the drive back into town. The first few miles had been a bit strained. Sanderson had queried him about his conversation with Carla. Unsure of how deep the corruption at the sheriff's office ran, Noble was not quite sure how to approach Sanderson with his newfound information.

Finally, as they reached Highway 32, Noble asked, "What do you know about meth distribution in this county?"

"Hmm…" Sanderson paused as if gathering his thoughts. "I know it's here. I suspect it's more rampant than we realize, but I can't prove that. It's just a feelin'. I've been with the department going on six years, and I can count on one hand the number of times deputies have busted a meth operation. Why?"

Noble had watched him closely for any telltale signs as he listened. Seeing none, he asked, "What would you say if I told you Ed Hughes may be involved or at least runnin' interference for the meth organization here in the county?"

He gave Noble a sideways glance and said, "I'd say I'm not surprised. I've suspected somethin' illegal was goin' on for a while now, but I don't think I would have ever guessed meth. I figured it was some kind of embezzlement or somethin' along those lines."

By the time they arrived back at Noble's truck, they had decided it would be best for Sanderson to proceed with his duties as if they had not had this conversation, but that he would also keep his ears and eyes open and begin to compile any evidence that presented itself. If Ed Hughes was dirty, it would only be a matter of time before he made a mistake.

Noble wondered what the chances were that Ed was somehow involved in the recent murders but had trouble justifying that train of thought. As he mulled it over, he fidgeted with the tab on the top of the empty Dr. Pepper can in the console of his truck. There was no doubt in his mind that if he shared what he had learned with Tom Jack, he would be spending a lot more time in Love County and while Granny would love the idea, he was sure he did not.

The metallic ting of metal slapping against metal filled the cab of the vehicle as in frustration he plucked the tab on the soda can one last time and then checked the time on his cellphone. Fifteen more minutes before the time he and Carla had agreed on. The day seemed to be one aggravation after another: lack of leads on the murders, the possibility of a dirty sheriff, waiting—which he always found irritating. Top that with having to go into an old folks' home, as his grandfather was so fond of calling what were now known as skilled nursing facilities, and he could not see how the day could get any worse.

The cellphone vibrated, followed by a long wolf whistle. Noble did not need to check the screen to know it was Jacqueline. He tapped the accept icon at the bottom of the phone and then the speaker symbol. "Well, hello, sweetheart." He grinned despite his foul mood.

"Hello yourself, sexy." She giggled. "How's your day goin'?"

"Let's just say it's goin' and leave it at that," he answered. "How 'bout yours? Everything okay?"

"All is good," Jacqueline assured. "I'm just callin' to remind you that I'm headed up to Tulsa for the night. I have trainin' up there all day tomorrow. I know we talked about it a while back, but I wasn't sure if you remembered."

"I'm glad you called," he said. "With all that's goin' on, it had slipped my mind. I think I'll crash at Granny's tonight since you're gonna be out of town."

"Okay, I've got to run." Jacqueline's words came quickly. "Donna is at the door, and I don't want to keep her waiting. See ya when I get back."

"Alright, be careful." And she was gone, leaving him to wonder if she had even heard what he had said.

All thoughts of Jacqueline disappeared when a red Ford Mustang GT convertible pulled into the space beside him, and Carla stepped out. He did not recall seeing the vehicle among those at the Muncy place and was wondering where it had been.

"You ready?" she asked as he eased the door open and stepped out.

"I reckon," he said and fell into step beside her as she started across the parking lot.

"Nice shirt," she grinned.

"You're funny." Noble shook his head as he caught a reflection of himself in a window they passed. He was just glad he and Jacqueline had caught a Texas Rangers game during his vacation, or he would have had to stop at the Dollar General and pick up a shirt of some kind.

"No, I'm actually a fan," Carla said as they reached the front door. She pressed the button on the intercom.

"It's the only thing I had that didn't look like a cop," Noble shrugged as they waited for someone to let them in. Standing close to Carla, he could smell a sweet tropical fragrance that he had not smelled at the cemetery. It made it hard for him to concentrate on the reason they had come, and he began to wonder if he had not agreed to meet Carla's MawMaw just so he could spend a little more time with Carla.

The automatic doors parted as Death toted his ladder toward the building's entrance. He had prepared himself mentally to work an entire shift if that was the only way he could gain access to the Crow. Neutral-colored tiling on the floor and the smell of freshly painted walls told him he had found the right building. A fluorescent bulb above the receptionist kiosk, nearing the end of its lifespan, had entered a perpetual cycle of flickering, shrouding the area in an eerie light show. Synchronized clicking grew louder as he approached the receptionist's counter.

"How can I help you?" the middle-aged woman behind the counter asked in a robotic tone as she looked up from a *People* magazine.

"I'm here…" Death began only to be cut off immediately when the receptionist noticed the ladder.

"Oh, thank the Lord!" she exclaimed, rising from her seat

and pointing up at the light. "I was beginnin' to think y'all had forgotten about that darn light. It's enough to drive a person to drinkin'."

He nodded as he made his way around to her side and waited as she rolled her seat back out of the way. It took less than five minutes for him to open the panel covering the fixture and find the problem. One of the four tubes inside was blackened on both ends. A quarter of a turn in the tube socket and the light went out, the flickering ceased, and the lady standing below him gave a little squeal of happiness.

"That was pretty simple," he said as he pushed the cover back up and locked it in place. "But I didn't bring a replacement bulb with me, so I'll leave that one there for now."

"Fine with me," she declared as he made his way down the ladder. "I'm just glad the strobing is over. I was beginning to feel like I was in a seventies disco nightmare."

"Glad to be of help," Death said as he began to close the ladder. "I probably ought to go ahead and check the rest of the lights while I'm here. No sense in havin' to make multiple trips if I don't have to."

"Makes sense. Oh, by the way, I'm Dorothy," she said offering her hand.

"I'm Larry," he said as he shook her hand. "Mind if I leave this ladder here while I get a count of the number of tubes I'll need?"

"Not at all," Dorothy smiled. "I'll keep an eye on it."

"I just started this job last week," he lied, "and I've never been to your building. Any rules I need to know about before I start lookin' around?"

"Oh, well let's see…" she pursed her lips. "Not really. Just try to be quiet if you check the rooms. Some of the patients might be asleep, and we try not to disturb them if we don't have to."

"I'll be quiet as a mouse," he winked as he turned to go - *or a panther* - he added to himself.

The aroma inside the nursing home took Noble back to the Sundays after church visits Granny had insisted on when he was in high school. He had never liked the smell, nor had he ever really understood the reason for the visits. When he had questioned Granny about why they had to go since they did not have family there, she had said it was part of the Lord's plan. Further questions were unnecessary at that point. He had learned from experience that when Granny said God had ordained it, there was no need to argue, and no further explanation would be forthcoming.

The squeak of rolling wheelchairs filled the hallway as he and Carla passed the nurse's station. The clunk-clunk of a walker added its rhythm to the orchestra, and somewhere further away, someone dropped something metal, which seemed to complete the ensemble. Noble had an overwhelming desire to turn around and leave.

"Breathe," Carla said as she laced her hand around his arm just above the elbow.

"Never really liked this place," Noble mumbled through a grimace.

"Really?" Carla gave him sideways look. "I would have never guessed."

"Sarcasm," Noble chuckled. "Now you're speaking my language."

While they waited for someone to acknowledge that they had signed in, Carla reached across the cluttered counter and swiped a newspaper. While Noble watched, she flipped it open to the obituary page.

"Lookin' for anyone in particular?" Noble asked.

"Yep, him" she answered, tapping a picture of Frank Nelson.

A young woman in light-green scrubs stepped around the corner and noticed them. "Oh, I'm so sorry to keep you waitin'," she said as she hustled over. "It's been one of those days, Carla.

We're short-staffed again, but y'all go right on back. She's finished eatin', but last I checked, she hadn't laid down for her nap yet."

"No worries, Jamie." Carla folded the paper as she spoke. "I'm gonna borrow this," she said and held it up. "I'll put it back on our way out."

"Don't bother," Jamie shot back as they walked away. "I've already read it."

Death strolled down the hallway stopping beneath each light fixture, studying each one as if his job depended on his proficiency. He had learned long ago that people were less likely to disturb someone who seemed to be hard at work. So, he played the part as he made his way down the hall, checking each room as he went.

The door to the first room was ajar. Beside the door, a clear plastic clipboard hung. Clipped to it was a single sheet of yellow paper with the patient's name and any requirements necessary to enter the room. The name did not belong to the Crow.

The second door stood wide open. The odor of slow decay crept from the room, a saddening combination of urine, sweat, infection, an indication of a slow demise. Death shook his head, hoping that when his time came, it would be quick, and continued to the next door.

A spark of anticipation, a quickening of the pulse, a heightening of the senses arrived with each new door. One after another, Death checked the names, eased the doors open as if checking lights, and moved on. The rhythmic click of some machine behind him seemed to match the beat of his heart. It annoyed him.

He stopped briefly and checked the corridor behind him. It was empty. He turned back to his task. Three doors left. Perhaps he was too late. He moved to the next door and then the next. The door was closed, but there it was, the Crow's name. With a sigh, Death relaxed and placed his hand on the latch.

CHAPTER 14

"MawMaw, what in the world are you doin'?" Carla asked as they stepped from the hallway into her grandmother's room.

Noble stopped just inside the door. MawMaw was seated in a padded armchair with a metal-framed walker turned upside down on the floor in front of her. She looked up as Carla crossed to her.

"This damn thing won't quit squeakin'," she fussed, "I cain't sneak up on anybody the way it squeals."

"I'm sure we can get it fixed," Carla assured her as she squatted down and began to inspect the walker. "Who ya tryin' to sneak up on anyway?"

MawMaw cut her eyes around toward Noble and with a nod his way, said, "I'd sneak up on him."

A half-smile turned up the corner of Noble's mouth as the color flashed across his cheeks. Carla's eyes widened as she looked from her MawMaw to Noble. Noble found comfort in her reddening face. At least he was not the only one who had been caught off guard.

"MawMaw! What's gotten into you?" Carla looked back at her grandmother. "Goodness, you'll be eighty-four next month."

"So what?" MawMaw shrugged, not taking her eyes off Noble. "I ain't blind, and I can still…"

"MawMaw!!!" Carla cut her off.

Noble chuckled, which brought a sharp look from Carla. "Do *not* encourage her," she warned.

"Are you gonna introduce me to your new boyfriend?" MawMaw asked.

"He is not my boyfriend," Carla said, then waved Noble closer. "MawMaw, this is Noble Harris. Noble, this is my MawMaw."

"Nice to meet you, Miz Muncy," Noble said as he stepped forward and offered his hand.

"It's MawMaw," she said, looking deep into his eyes and holding onto his hand with a grip that surprised him. "You can call me, MawMaw."

"Yes, ma'am," Noble smiled.

"Carla," MawMaw spoke without breaking eye contact with Noble, "if you don't want him, I'll take him."

"MawMaw!" Carla scolded. "He's…"

MawMaw cut her off. "I know who he is. He's the one you had such a crush on your senior year."

Carla's jaw dropped, and she refused to look at Noble. "Now you're just tryin' to embarrass me," she muttered.

MawMaw grinned and winked at Noble before looking back at her granddaughter. "Is it workin'?"

"You know it is," Carla rolled her eyes as she answered.

"Good." MawMaw released Noble's hand and pointed to the corner. "Pull that chair over here and have a seat. Carla, you can sit on the bed. I'll fiddle with this walker later. What is it y'all need?"

Noble moved the blue plastic chair to the edge of the bed and eased down onto it. Carla helped her grandmother move the walker out of the way and settled onto the bed as instructed. Noble did a quick scan of the room. The bed was covered with a hand-sewn quilt made of small squares in a simple pattern of diagonal lines. Two pillows perched against the headboard, and a crocheted comforter hung at the foot of the bed. A small nightstand with a lamp, several pictures in little metal frames, and a well-worn Bible, the chairs he and MawMaw sat in, and a rolling hospital tray finished the inventory of the furniture. The walls were bare, except for a clock above a set of doors Noble figured must be a small closet and a large corkboard attached to the left of the door. A collage of pictures, some recent and others faded from age, adorned the board.

"Have you seen the paper?" Carla asked extending it toward her grandmother. The obituary for Frank Nelson faced up.

"Sure have," MawMaw answered. "Is that the reason for this visit?"

"Since when do I need a reason to visit?" Carla countered.

MawMaw smiled. "You never need a reason to visit." Then the smile faded, and she said, "But little missy, don't you try to pull the wool over my eyes. I may be old, but I'm not stupid or naive. You cain't take the badge off a lawman, put him in a t-shirt, and think I won't know what he is. Besides, I hear more gossip in this place than I ever did out of it. And I know all about Agent Noble here and who he works for. What I don't know is what he wants from me."

Carla brought both hands up, palms out, then shook her head, and said, "You're right, you're right, I'm sorry. I just thought you might be able to help him with what he's workin' on, and I was afraid you wouldn't if you knew he was a cop."

"Maybe we should go," Noble offered and began to rise.

"You sit your ass right back down," MawMaw pointed in his direction, keeping her eyes on Carla. "I'll get to you in a minute."

Noble sat. Carla cringed. MawMaw spent the next several minutes on the topics of family, integrity, and honesty, mostly directed at her granddaughter, but Noble squirmed in his seat feeling like she was speaking straight to him. When the lecture had ended, she turned to Noble, raised an eyebrow, and asked, "And what makes you think I'd know anything at all about Frank Nelson's murder?"

"It's not Frank Nelson's murder I want to ask you about." Noble maintained eye contact as long as he could before glancing over at Carla.

Carla seemed to understand his need for help and said, "MawMaw, he thinks there's a connection between Frank Nelson, Sam Wilson, and Billie Hilton."

"I never liked Sam Wilson. Never trusted him," MawMaw

said, eyes still cold and hard. "And as for Billie Hilton, well… it ain't no secret I couldn't stand that man's guts."

"Now, MawMaw," Carla softly scolded.

MawMaw raised her hand, palm out, toward her granddaughter. Then her eyes softened slightly, and she said, "But Frank Nelson. I liked him. He was a kind man. Always careful about what he printed in his paper and never looked down on me when we'd pass in the grocery store."

"I think one person is responsible for the death of all three men," Noble said, "and I don't think they're done. I've got a feelin' there's gonna to be more before it's over."

MawMaw sat quietly, looking past Noble as if concentrating on something in the distance. Noble shifted in his seat and studied MawMaw's face for signs of what she was thinking. Carla sat perfectly still, staring at the floor. After a long minute, MawMaw shifted her gaze to her granddaughter and then to Noble.

"I liked Frank Nelson," she said. "So I'm going to tell you a story that I heard."

Noble nodded but said nothing.

"Once upon a time, there was an Indian maiden who came to this land with a young panther in her arms. The maiden's heart was broken, but the little panther made her happy. Then one day, the maiden went for a walk, and a dog, a nasty beast, attacked her and left her bleeding. The little woodpecker was sent out, and a council was gathered. The crow, the wolf, the snake, the shadow, and of course, the little woodpecker all confronted the dog. The dog denied any wrongdoing, said the maiden must be mistaken, and asked those gathered why a young maiden would wander around by herself in a place where so much danger existed. Was she not asking for trouble by doing so?"

Noble opened his mouth to ask a question, but before the words reached his lips, MawMaw raised a hand and gave him a look that warned against any interruptions.

"The council argued amongst themselves. The woodpecker wanted the dog punished. The wolf and the snake said there was not enough evidence. The little crow just wanted to go home, and the shadow could not decide what to do. In the end, they did nothing, and the Indian maiden died of sadness. Everyone thought it was over, but not the panther. The panther did not think it was over. He grew and he grew, and one day, when he was big enough, he caught the dog alone and he killed him. And one day, when he is ready, the panther will hunt down all of those who knew and did nothing, and he will kill them too."

When it became apparent that she was done with the story, and Noble had conjured enough courage to speak, he asked, "And you think this story has somethin' to do with the murders?"

"It's a theory, as they say," MawMaw nodded. "By my reckonin', the dog, the woodpecker, and the snake are all dead. I'm not sure which of the animals represents Sam Wilson, but if I was to guess, I'd say the snake. Never liked him much, and the more I think on it, the more he reminds me of a serpent slitherin' around causin' trouble. I guess I should say 'reminded me' since it looks like the panther took him out."

Noble decided to play along. "And just where did you hear this story, ma'am?" he asked.

MawMaw frowned. "Don't patronize me, young man. You're the one came to me lookin' for answers. I didn't come to you."

"Now, MawMaw," Carla chimed in. "I don't think Noble meant that the way you took it."

"Bullshit." MawMaw's voice was flat and hard. "I know when someone's pretendin' to play along, and his tone said that's what he was doin'."

"Fine," Carla said exasperated. "Then don't tell him where you heard the story. Tell me."

"I heard it right down the hall in the common area," MawMaw answered Carla and turned to glare at Noble.

Noble cleared his throat, wondered if he should speak at all, then asked, "Ma'am, would you mind tellin' me who told you that story?"

"Yes, I do mind," MawMaw snapped. "But because I liked

Sam Wilson, I'll tell ya." She paused and squinted one eye down in a scowl that reminded Noble of Clint Eastwood in an old spaghetti western, then said, "It was Nita Mosley, but everyone called her Grandmother Mosley or just Grandmother."

"Called?" Noble asked.

"Yes, called." MawMaw turned back to Carla. "She passed on last month."

Carla looked from her grandmother to Noble, then back again. MawMaw sat silently. Noble mulled over the name Mosley in his mind and found nothing. The visit had been a dead end. A dead end in more ways than one, he figured. He was no closer to finding the killer, and after the way he had upset MawMaw Muncy, he seriously doubted if Carla would want anything further to do with him. For some reason, that thought bothered him more than it should.

"I think I'm ready for my nap," MawMaw said suddenly. "Put the chair back before you leave."

"Okay, MawMaw," Carla said rising from the bed. "I'll walk Noble out and come tuck you in."

"I can tuck my own damn self in," she said, pushing herself up out of the chair and ambling over to the bed. "And Carla, next time you come, come by yourself."

"Yes, MawMaw," Carla said as she took Noble by the arm and started him toward the door.

"It was nice to meet you, Miz Muncy," he said over his shoulder as Carla ushered him out the door.

"Dammit, I told you to call me MawMaw," she hollered through the opened door. "And when you find Lincoln, you tell him he should not ought to have killed Frank Nelson."

Carla stopped so quickly that it caught Noble by surprise. "Holy shit!" she exclaimed.

Noble confused, stood and stared at her. She stared back with an expression that suggested she was waiting for the light bulb to switch on. When she realized it wasn't going to happen, she whispered, "Lincoln Burns."

"What about him?" Noble asked, visualizing the young man who had graduated with him so many years ago.

"He was Grandmother Mosley's grandson," Carla's voice still just above a whisper. "Don't you see? He's the panther. He's the killer. It all makes sense now."

"Not to me, it doesn't," Noble said.

Carla took his hands in hers and pulled him back into MawMaw's room. "I keep forgettin' you didn't grow up here," she said, her voice thick with exasperation and excitement. "Lincoln moved her with his mother, I don't know… sometime when he was really young."

"Okay." Noble leaned closer, trying to understand.

"When we were in grade school, his mother just up and disappeared," she continued. "I remember one day at recess a bunch of the girls in your grade were kind of babying him because of it. He was always kind of shy and awkward, but I guess one of them had heard somethin', or maybe he was just actin' sad… anyway, he didn't like them babying him. He got mad and started cussin', and I remember he got sent home for a few days. Ain't it crazy how you don't think about somethin' for years and then one little thing sparks a whole memory?"

"So, what are you sayin'?" Noble asked.

"I think Lincoln is the panther. His mother was the Indian maiden," Carla said, tapping a finger on his chest with each point she made. "The dog was Sheriff Hilton, and he did somethin' bad to Lincoln's mother. I think she killed herself somehow, and before he left town, Lincoln killed the sheriff. That's what I think."

Noble struggled, trying to fit the guy he knew into this new role. He had played football with Lincoln and had run track with him. Yes, he was different from most of the other guys, but then some would have said the same about Noble in those days.

"Guess it's worth checkin' into," Noble said, once again wondering if his agreeing had more to do with seeing Carla than it did catching the killer.

"Maybe y'all could check into it somewhere else," MawMaw's harsh suggestion reminded them where they were. "You're keepin' an old woman from her beauty sleep."

"Sorry, MawMaw," Carla said and turned Noble back toward the hall.

"Afternoon, ma'am," half-whispered at the door.

As the two of them stepped through the doorway, Noble heard MawMaw's parting shot, "It's a wonder anything ever gets solved as slow as menfolk are."

Noble couldn't help but smile.

CHAPTER 15

Death stood over Hal Spencer's sleeping body. He did not recognize the face of this man. The idea of killing someone he did not know did not bother him. He had killed strangers many times in the line of duty, but having no recollection of this man bothered him for reasons he could not fathom. Of the names on the list Grandmother Mosley had given him, Hal's and the Wolf's were the only two he had not been able to visualize. He had hoped that on seeing the Crow, his memory would recall him somehow. It had not.

Death strolled softly across the room to the door. A quick look to ensure no one was in the corridor, and he eased the door shut, then turned to survey the tiny room. The motorized bed took up a third of the space. A metal cabinet on rollers served as a nightstand, complete with drawers and a storage compartment. An adjustable overbed table had been pushed against the railing of the bed to allow easy access. A television remote, a pink plastic hospital cup half full of liquid, and a large-print Bible lay on it, all within arm's length of the Crow. Attached to the far wall on a movable wall hanger was a flatscreen television. Wrapped around the railing of the bed was a call button.

Careful not to awaken the Crow, Death eased the table back and slowly unwound the cable from the bed. He bent with care and placed it under the bed, out of reach. The Crow stirred restlessly and moaned. Death pushed himself back into a standing position and stood staring down at the dying man before him, knowing if he had waited any longer, the Crow would have escaped Death.

He thought of Grandmother Mosley and the disappointment she would feel had that happened. He had never considered himself a believer in fate, but now he found himself wondering if it had not been fate that had made this moment possible. Had fate and karma united to allow Grandmother Mosley's wish to be granted? He shook his head—*more likely just plain dumb luck,* he thought.

After a quick goodbye in the parking lot of the nursing home, Noble called Kent Davenport in Oklahoma City to see if the results had come back from the lab on the prints and blood samples from the Sam Wilson crime scene. The answer on both accounts was negative. Noble then filled Davenport in on his suspicions and asked him to see what he could find out about Lincoln Burns. As soon as he hung up with Davenport, he called Sanderson.

"What's up?" Sanderson sounded weary to him. "Did that lead pan out?"

"Maybe," Noble answered. "Won't know for sure until I hear back from Davenport, but it's definitely a possibility. Have you had dinner yet?"

"No, why?" Sanderson seemed to perk up a bit.

"I thought we might grab a bite and discuss the conversation I just had," Noble suggested.

"You buyin'?" Sanderson asked.

"Depends," Noble grinned. "What sounds good to you?"

"Ollie's," Sanderson chuckled. "And you're buyin'."

Death shook Hal Spencer gently. With an irritated moan of reluctance, Hal slowly moved his head in Death's direction and offered his right arm. Death waited while realization that he was not a nurse filtered through the grogginess, and as the patient's eyes widened, he placed a finger to his lips.

"Don't make a sound." He held the knife inches from Hal's face.

Death smiled as Hal's eyes remained locked on his. Hal's hand shot for the spot where the nurse's call button should have been. When it was not where it should be, he wheezed, "Had to try."

For a dead man, you sure seem to want to live, Death thought to himself before speaking low, "Understandable. In your position, I would have tried too."

"I told them it wasn't over," Hal sighed deeply.

"Told who?" Death's eyes narrowed and stayed the hand that would have slashed through Hal's throat had he not spoken.

"All of them." Hal moved in what might have been the beginning of a shrug. The motion brought a grimace to his face and a low groan, "Everyone who had anything to do with covering up your mother's rape. I told them it was you who killed the sheriff. I told them, but no one wanted to listen."

"How did you know I killed the Dog?" Death knew he should cut this man's throat and be done with it. He had worried for so many years that someone would figure it out and come looking for him, and now here was a man who knew it all the while.

Hal stared blankly, "The dog?"

"Sheriff Hilton," the name escaped as more of a hiss than words, "the Dog."

"I didn't know," Hal took a ragged breath, "I suspected. They said I was just paranoid. And even if it was you, they said Sheriff Hilton got what he deserved. But I told them… I told everyone who was involved, it wasn't over. I told them, you would come back one day."

"They didn't listen?" Death smiled once more, the question more to himself than to Hal.

"No," Hal answered, "They just laughed."

Death had heard enough. It was time he was going.

"You should not have killed Frank Nelson," Hal sucked air

in and slowly released it, "He did everything he possibly could have."

"And still, the Dog ran free." Years of pent-up anger rolled to the surface. Death's eyes narrowed. His nostrils flared. *Enough.*

"Billie Hilton deserved to die. I deserved to die." Hal struggled to speak, "Sam Wilson, Jason Hall, we all deserved what is coming to us, but Frank Nelson, him you should not have killed."

"The Dog raped my mother. He is dead. The Woodpecker and the Snake did nothing. They are dead. You did nothing, and soon you will join the others. The Wolf will follow you, and then the Shadow."

"I did what I was supposed to do," Hal's eyes narrowed, and his mouth thinned, "I did the rape kit. Your mother refused to talk. And by the time she told us who had raped her, Billie Hilton already had the rape kit. What could I do?"

Death did not have an answer. The man had done his job. He had done what he was trained to do. Death had been on more than one mission in the military where things went sideways, and he had done whatever he had to do. Perhaps this was a similar situation.

"What else could I do?" Moisture seeped from the corner of Hal's eyes, "It was her word against his and the evidence… he tricked us all. And he knew…"

"Knew what?" Death fought the urge to be gone.

"About our secret lives. About the affairs. About…" Hal closed his eyes, and when he opened them again, he forced a smile, "It doesn't matter now. I guess it never really did. It just seemed like it at the time."

Something new crept through Death's mind. Something he had never felt. He stood staring at Hal, knowing he had already spent too much time in the room, and yet unable to finish what he had come to do. *Pity.* His mind found the word and matched it to the emotion.

"Who is the shadow?" Hal's voice cut through the space between them like a bolt of electricity.

Death's knife flashed from left to right. The Crow was dead before Death reached the back exit and started across the parking lot toward his truck.

Ollie's Juke Joint & Cafe was nothing Noble had envisioned. Sanderson had driven east out of Marietta and into Marshall County. He turned south toward Lake Texoma before reaching Kingston. Ten miles of rural Oklahoma countryside passed before Sanderson pulled into the gravel parking area in front of a building Noble figured would fit perfectly into any backwoods swamp scene set in Louisiana. The structure was a patchwork of weathered wood and rusted metal siding. The front porch was wooden, the roof half shingle and half metal. A variety of metal signs—Marlboro and Authorized BUICK Dealer— along with a red and blue neon sign that announced the place was OPEN, adorned the outside of the building.

"You eat here before?" Noble questioned as Sanderson put the vehicle in park. Theirs was one of only three vehicles in the parking lot.

"As often as I can." Sanderson grinned, stepping out of the truck. "Don't judge a book by its cover."

"It ain't the cover I'm worried about," Noble countered over the hood as the two started across the parking area. "It's the food."

"No worries there," Sanderson nodded at him. "Best food you'll get west of the Mississippi."

"Now I know you're full of it." Noble shook his head as he stepped up onto the wooden plank porch.

"You just wait," Sanderson proclaimed as he reached for the latch. "In an hour, you'll be singin' a different tune."

"We'll see," Noble said as he stepped through the door Sanderson held open for him.

Once inside, he felt like he had been transported to a different time. To his left waitresses were coming and going out of what had to be the opening to a kitchen. To his right was a fully stocked bar complete with stools. A menagerie of tables and chairs spread out in front of him. Sanderson pointed past them to a doorway at the end of the bar.

"Right through there," he said, steering Noble toward the opening.

Noble noticed the door to a restroom to his left as he stepped through the entryway and into a much larger screened-in dining area. A small stage in one corner suggested the promise of a live band, but at the moment the music came from strategically placed speakers. Noble followed Sanderson through the room to a booth near the rear door. Sanderson slid into the seat on one side of the table, and Noble took the one on the opposite side. The mounted head of a white-tailed deer with an eight-point rack caught Noble's attention. It was adorned with long blonde dreadlocks, a bandana, and a string of pearls. Scanning the rest of the room's décor, Noble was surprised to find that the deer fit in perfectly.

"Whatcha havin' tonight, Dan?" a female voice brought Noble's attention back to their table.

"I'll have the usual," Sanderson answered, "but you better bring Noble here a menu. It's his first time."

"Can do," came the answer, and by the time Noble turned, she was gone.

Turning back to Sanderson with a grin, he said, "You weren't lyin'. You have eaten here a time or two."

"Sure have," Sanderson smiled. "And I bring Crystal out here at least once a month. It's our favorite spot. She loves the live music."

The waitress dropped a menu on the table as she passed with an arm full of dirty dishes headed back toward the kitchen area. Denim stretched tight across a well-rounded bottom caught Noble's attention. Sanderson chuckled.

"What's so funny?" Noble picked up the menu as he spoke.

Instead of answering the question, Sanderson jerked his head in the waitress's direction. "That's Rhae. And if you like what you just saw, you're gonna love the view when she comes back to take your order."

"Don't know what you're talkin' 'bout." Noble cocked his head to one side. "So what is the usual?"

"You're a liar." Sanderson raised an eyebrow. "And the usual is Catfish Susie Mae."

"Catfish Susie Rhae." Noble said as he searched for it on the menu.

Sanderson chuckled. "That's Mae, not Rhae."

"A man can hope, can't he?" Noble wiggled his eyebrows. "And what would Crystal say if she knew you were sizin' up another woman?"

"Well considerin' she was the one who pointed her out to me," Sanderson grinned, "she'd probably say, 'Did you see the ass on that woman?'"

Before Noble could respond, Rhae stepped around the corner and up to the table. "You know what you want, hon?"

"Um…" Noble tried to focus on her eyes, but being eye level with her bosom was a problem. Handing the menu to her, he stammered, "I'll just have what he's havin'."

"Two Catfish Susie Mae's comin' right up," Rhae turned to leave, then pivoted back quickly. "I'm so sorry, y'all don't even have drinks yet. Look at me, the night's just startin' and already I'm forgettin' things. Guess I should have taken that nap I decided to skip. I'm usually on top of things better than this. What do y'all want?" She placed a hand on Noble's shoulder and leaned a hip into him.

"Sweet tea," Sanderson answered, but his eyes were on Noble.

"Same for me, Ma'am." Noble stuttered, electricity shooting through his body.

Rhae stepped back quickly. "Oh no, Noble… it is Noble, right?"

Noble shook his head.

"Well, Noble," she shook a finger gently at him, "I'm Rhae, not Ma'am, not Miz, just plain ol' Rhae, and if we're gonna be friends, then that's what you'll be callin' me. We clear?"

"As Pappy's moonshine." Noble nodded.

"Good." She smiled and placed a hand back on his shoulder. "I'll be right back with your drinks."

The sensations that had rippled through Noble at the touch of her hand had just begun to dissipate when he turned his attention back to Sanderson. The knowing grin he received from the sheriff's deputy had him shaking his head. "So much for turnin' over a new leaf."

"What?" The confusion on Sanderson's face was immediate.

Noble chuckled. "Oh, Granny has been after me to get married and settle down. I figured if I was even gonna consider it, I'd better stop lookin' at other women and flirtin'."

"Wow." Sanderson's eyes widened. "I didn't know this thing with Jacqueline was gettin' that serious."

Noble shrugged. "I don't know if it is. Just testin' the waters, I guess, or maybe just testin' myself."

"You want my honest opinion?" Sanderson leaned forward, then without waiting for Noble to respond, continued, "You are not the marryin' kind. I think sometimes you would like to be but Noble…"

"You know," Noble held up a hand to stop him, "I think we should talk about the case."

"Oh, now you want to talk about the case," Sanderson chuckled.

"Yep," Noble shook his head. "Does the name Lincoln Burns mean anything to you?"

CHAPTER 16

Death squatted beside his grandmother's grave. Blood from the Crow had dried on his shirt and hands. He had driven straight from the hospital to the cemetery. The conflict in his mind threatened his sanity. He found himself wishing he had killed the Crow before he had spoken, but he had not, and now the questions would not stop. Did the Crow truly deserve to die? And the Woodpecker, should he have been killed? The Dog he had no doubt about, and for some reason, the Snake's death did not plague his mind, but the other two did. Was the Crow telling the truth? Why wouldn't he that close to death?

Death stared at the headstone. He had been so sure his actions were pure, were justified, right up until he had allowed the Crow to speak. Grandmother Mosley had prepared him well for what must be done. She had groomed him from his youth until he left for the military. On his few trips back to Marietta, she had reminded him that this was his destiny. She had given him the list. And when she passed over to the other side, she had walked in his dreams and told him it was time to begin. Now, for the first time since his mother had left, he was unsure.

"Lincoln Burns." Sanderson repeated the name. Noble watched as Sanderson's eyes narrowed, and he could almost see the wheels in the deputy's mind turning. After a long two minutes, he shook his head. "No, I don't reckon it rings any bells. Why?"

"Let's just say he is a person of interest in our case," Noble paused as Rhae delivered their drinks.

"Two sweet teas, gentlemen," she winked at Noble as she spoke. "Anything else I can get for y'all?"

Noble flashed her a smile. "Not at the moment."

"Think I'm good," Sanderson nodded.

"Be back with your food shortly," she spoke over her shoulder, already moving away from their table.

The case momentarily forgotten, Noble watched her go until Sanderson cleared his throat loudly. Noble turned his attention back to the deputy and shook his head. "Sorry, Rhae there is a bit of a distraction."

"I noticed," Sanderson grinned, then redirected, "Lincoln Burns."

"Yes, Lincoln." Noble explained who Lincoln was and how he knew him. He had barely finished telling Sanderson about his conversation with MawMaw when Rhae returned with their orders.

Sanderson picked up his fork and went to work on his food. Noble watched him for a second and then did the same. The instant the first bite hit his tongue, a symphony of tastes exploded in his mouth, leaving no doubt in his mind that someone in the kitchen damn well knew how to cook.

"Good stuff, huh?" Sanderson spoke around a mouthful of catfish.

Noble just nodded. Conversation would have to wait. He intended to thoroughly enjoy what was in front of him.

Head down, heart heavy, Death walked away from his grandmother's grave. He had asked his questions. He had hoped for an answer, a sign. A train whistle or a lightning strike would have been nice. He would have even settled for the call of a meadowlark—just anything to let him know he was still headed down the right road. None had come.

Had he angered Grandmother with his doubt? At the truck,

he stopped. There was no longer any reason to question who was to die next. The Shadow had to be last. That Grandmother had made clear so the Wolf would be next. But did they deserve to die? He considered turning around but knew it would do no good. If Grandmother was angry with him, he was certain that in death, as in life, she would refuse to speak to him. He had always hated that about her. She had never been one to lay hands on him. No, that was not her way. Silence had always been her choice of discipline, and Death had learned early in life that when she was angry, it was best to leave her to herself.

"Maybe tomorrow," Death whispered as he reached to open the truck door. "Maybe tomorrow, I'll try again."

"So, what's our next step?" Sanderson asked Noble as the two waited for Rhae to return with dessert.

Noble ran the knuckle of his index finger along the scar on his chin as he considered his friend's question. Before he could answer, Rhae set a plate in front of him with the deep-fried Twinkie on it that he had ordered, along with chocolate dipping sauce. After she placed Sanderson's slice of homemade buttermilk pie down in front of him, she turned back to Noble, "How'd you get that cute little scratch on your chin there, hun?"

Noble looked across the table at Sanderson, who rolled his eyes and picked up his fork. The deputy had heard too many stories about how the old chin had been injured, and Noble was not sure if he had actually told him how it really happened. It had become somewhat of a game for Noble to respond to inquiries about the wound with whatever outlandish fabrication came to his mind first.

"Well, my lovely Miz Rhae, it's like this," Noble began. Sanderson gave a rude snort. Noble ignored him and continued, "I did a bit of bull ridin' when I was in college, and one Friday night, me and some buddies of mine decided we needed more practice if we were gonna get better. Now mind you, we'd been drinkin' since noon, and all of us were totally shit-faced when we arrived at the rodeo arena."

"Oh, my," Rhae gasped, and Noble knew he had her hooked.

"We ran the chutes full and drew straws to see who got which bull. Of course, as luck would have it, I was the first ride. Demon Dawg was the bull's name, and he had these great big ol' long horns that came to a needle-sharp point."

"Oh, my," Rhae's eyes widened. "He got you with his horns?"

"I wish," Noble flashed a smile. "The boys opened the gate. Demon Dawg made one twistin' jump, and I went airborne. As I was comin' down, that damn bull did a spinnin' back kick that landed one of his rear hooves right against my chin. It spun me around like a figure skater on ice and launched me into the second row of the arena stands."

Rhae's eyebrows raised, and she looked from Noble to Sanderson before she spoke, "Is your friend here always this full of shit?"

Sanderson nearly choked on the piece of pie he had just swallowed. Before he could catch his breath and before Noble could say another word, Rhae turned and walked away, shaking her head.

Eyes watering, Sanderson took a drink of his tea and then, still chuckling, said, "I reckon she's got your number, smartass."

"You may be right," Noble picked up the Twinkie and dipped it into the chocolate.

Sanderson spoke as he scooped another piece of pie onto his fork, "So, before Rhae called you on that bullshit story, you were gonna tell me our next step."

Noble held the Twinkie over its plate as chocolate dripped from one end. "Davenport is the best researcher in the office. I figure by tomorrow he'll have everything someone can possibly dig up on Lincoln. If it turns out that he's our guy, then we'll start huntin' for him. I've got to tell you though, I'm sure hopin' it ain't him."

"Why's that?" Sanderson asked before he placed the last of the pie into his mouth.

"Lincoln was, well…" Noble paused. "Well, I don't know that I would say we were friends, at least not close friends, but we played football and ran track together. I don't know, somehow, huntin' someone I graduated with just doesn't sit right with me."

Sanderson swallowed the pie. "Do you want to turn the case over to someone else?"

Noble shook his head. "Not at all. If Lincoln is the bad guy, then it's my job to stop him. I've just never had to go after anyone I've had this close of a connection to, no matter how long ago it was. It's kind of the reason I never really had a desire to come back here. Some of the guys that show up in the court proceedings column of the newspaper are ones I partied with back in high school."

Sanderson laid his fork down and pushed the empty pie plate back. "Kinda hard to picture you as a partier."

Noble chuckled. "I wasn't, but that didn't keep me from ending up at them every once in a while." Thoughts of Carla surfaced. *Rhae, Carla, Maria—forget about turning over a new leaf; at this rate, I'm gonna have to uproot a whole damn tree,* he thought to himself.

"So, until tomorrow, we wait and pray no one else dies," Sanderson looked across the table at Noble. Noble could see the frustration in his friend's face.

"Yep," he nodded around a mouth full of Twinkie, chewed it, and swallowed. "When we signed on, we all thought that every day was gonna be wild car chases and gunfights twenty-four seven."

Sanderson laughed. "Yeah. No one tells you about the sittin' on your ass waitin' for forensics or research or the paperwork you have to do after the arrest. You don't find out about any of those things until after that first adrenaline rush, and then you're already hooked."

"Hooked on what?" Rhae appeared at Noble's side and asked as she laid a check on the table.

Noble picked it up as he answered, "Hooked on the fine food in this wonderful establishment and your lovely company."

Sanderson guffawed. Rhae looked down at Noble and smiled. "Hon, before you make a run at little ol' Rhae here, let me warn you I've worn down men heartier than you without even breakin' a sweat. But you and that little scratch on your chin do intrigue me, so any time you wanna back that flirtin' up, you just name the place and I'll see you there."

Noble's eyes widened, and he could feel the red as it crept up his neck. Not sure what to say, he looked at the bill, took out his wallet, pulled three twenties from it, and handed them to Rhae.

"I'll keep that in mind, Rhae," he managed a wink, "and you can keep the change."

Rhae winked back. "Until next time, gentlemen," she said, turned and headed across the room towards another table.

"Think maybe you bit off more than you bargained for there," Sanderson commented.

"You may be right, partner," Noble agreed, then, as he eased out of the booth and stood, "Come on. Let's go chase bad guys. I think that might be safer than me flirtin' with Rhae."

Death sat at the desk in his room and stared at the screen of his laptop. On the television mounted to the wall to his left, the nine o'clock news had begun. The five and six o'clock programs had not mentioned anything about the killing in Ardmore or any more about the murders in Marietta. He knew it was just a matter of time, though.

The Wolf was next. It had taken less than two minutes on his computer to pull up a picture of the man. Death did not recognize him. He had not really expected to since he had never had any run-ins with the law and so had never been to the courthouse. He studied the image in front of him. Even from the headshot beside his bio,

Death could tell he was a big man—not obese, but stocky and strong, like a wolf. Once again, Grandmother had chosen correctly. Death hoped his prey was not as keen as a wolf, but then it did not really matter. It was his job to kill. It was the Wolf's job to die. Whether or not Grandmother was right or not about the others, killing the Wolf was not a problem for Death.

The news finished with no mention of anything that concerned Death. Finished with his research for the night, Death shut the computer down. It was time for him to move. He had stayed longer than he had planned to, and he knew why - Candy. Each time he had visited the office to extend his stay, she had become a little bolder.

Last week, as she counted his change back to him, she had looked him in the eye and said, "If there is *anything* I can do for you, all you have to do is ask." The emphasis on "anything" had been more than clear.

What the hell, Death thought as he rose from the chair. In two days, his rent was up, and it would be suicide to stay. A good romp with Candy might just relieve some of the stress he was feeling and clear his mind. He knew her shift ended at eleven o'clock. She had let him know this on more than one occasion. A check of the time let him know he still had a couple of hours until she was available. He stepped into his bedroom and stopped. His eyes scanned the wall of newspaper clippings and notes he had tacked to it. Tomorrow, he would take them all down and get them packed up, but tonight—tonight, Candy.

CHAPTER 17

Granny tossed the television remote to Noble. "I'm headed to bed."

The two had watched the nine o'clock news together. Nothing had been said about Frank Nelson's or Sam Wilson's murders. Not even a mention of an ongoing investigation. Noble picked the remote out of the air. "Goodnight, Granny."

"Goodnight, grandson." She waved over her shoulder and disappeared down the hall.

Noble hit the off button on the remote, and the television faded to black. It always amazed him how quickly the social media platforms moved on. If it did not happen today, it was not important. Here today, gone tomorrow. He shook his head as he rose from his seat. Tomorrow was going to be a long day. Perhaps he should call it a night himself.

His cell phone rang as he laid the remote on the entertainment center in front of the television. The name on the screen indicated the call was from Kent Davenport.

"Already got something for me?" Noble asked as soon as he tapped the accept button and placed the phone to his ear.

"Yep, a whole shitload of stuff that can wait until tomorrow," Davenport answered in the smug voice that Noble had come to recognize as Kent's damn-I'm-good tone, "and one thing that you might want to get on tonight."

Noble looked at the antique clock sitting on the shelf beside the television and then longingly down the hall to his bedroom door. If he knew Davenport, it was going to be a long night.

"You still there?" Davenport's voice was accompanied by the dinging sound of an incoming text.

"I'm still here." Noble sighed. "Give it to me."

"Just did. Check your messages," Davenport laughed. Noble heard music in the background.

Noble took the phone from his ear, hit the speaker icon, and then his messages. It was an address to a hotel in Denton, Texas. Afraid the noise from his phone would keep Granny from getting to bed, he stepped into the kitchen.

"Got the text," Noble heard the volume of the background music increasing as he spoke. He stopped at the sink and stared out of the little kitchen window into the darkness. "I'm guessing this has something to do with Lincoln."

"And the winner is…" Davenport did his best impression of a game show host. "You got it partner. He paid with cash but used his Georgia driver's license and a military identification. If he's your guy and he's smart, he's already vacated, but it might be worth a look."

"Anything else I should know?" Noble's mind was already racing.

"He retired from the Marines just a few months ago," Davenport shouted to be heard above the background music. "So, I figure he's a badass."

"Wonderful, is that all?" The volume of Noble's voice rose to meet that of Davenport's.

"Everything else will have to wait until tomorrow," Davenport laughed above the music. "I'm off duty for the night."

"Strip club?" Noble shook his head, knowing the answer before Davenport responded.

"You know it," Davenport shouted. "Be careful out there, Noble, and happy hunting."

The call ended. Noble grinned down at the screen. "You, too, buddy, you, too."

"Who was that?" Granny's voice behind him caused him to flinch.

Noble whirled around. "Dammit, Granny, you nearly scared the liver out of me."

Granny grinned. "Still doesn't answer the question. Who was that?" she repeated.

"Davenport," Noble shrugged. "Looks like I'm gonna have to make a trip to Denton tonight."

With a humph, Granny spoke over her shoulder as she turned. "Don't be too loud when you get back. It's damn near impossible for me to get back to sleep once I wake up and I need my beauty sleep."

"Yes, ma'am," Noble did not even attempt to suppress a chuckle. He waited until he heard the door to her bedroom shut before he touched his phone screen. The light it gave off cast an eerie blue aura across half of the kitchen. Noble searched through his contacts until he found the name he was looking for and placed the call.

"What the hell you callin' me this time of night for, Noble?" The voice on the other end was a deep baritone with a gruffness that hinted at sleep, but Noble knew it was unlikely his counterpart in the Texas Rangers was in bed at this early hour.

"Howdy to you too, J.T.," Noble could hear road noise. "Hope you aren't headin' for that ole honky-tonk you love so much."

"What's it to ya?" came J.T.'s response. "I'm off duty."

"Maybe, maybe not," Noble corrected, then asked, "You still liaising for Denton County?"

Noble heard the crunch of gravel through the phone as J.T. pulled to the side of the road. He could almost picture the disgust on the big man's face. James T. Gilyard did not like to be kept from his favorite bar, especially on Friday nights. A hardened officer of the law and a regular Fred Astaire on the dance floor, his love for country swing had made him a bit of a legend south of the Red River. The first time Noble had met J.T., he had been two-stepping a young lady around the floor at one of the local watering holes. Noble suspected J.T. had been heading to that very watering hole when he had called him. For such a big man, J.T. moved like he was floating on air.

"Something tells me you're about to ruin my night, amigo." J.T. did nothing to hide his aggravation.

"Maybe, maybe not," Noble repeated with a smile. "Need to check out a motel room and maybe talk to the occupant if he's even still there."

A long pause ensued. Noble wondered if the connection had been lost and was about to remove the phone from his ear and check, when J.T. spoke, "Last time you needed to check a motel room, it led to a three-week chase across three state lines and earned me a good ol' ass- chewin' from my captain."

"Yeah, and now you have a story to tell your grandkids, if you ever settle down long enough to have any kids to have 'em for ya." Noble chuckled.

"Like you're one to talk," J.T. returned. "Where and when do you want to meet?"

"Race Trac, that little convenience store, on University just off Interstate 35," Noble answered. "Can you be there in an hour?"

"I can," J.T. did not sound happy to Noble, "see you there."

As the line went dead, Noble dug his truck keys from his pocket and smiled, "Sorry 'bout this J.T., but I'm graspin' at straws."

Death stepped out the door of his motel room and scanned the line of parked cars along his side of the motel. Nothing out of the ordinary. He walked briskly past several doors on his way to the office. Candy's shift would be ending in half an hour, and he wanted… All thoughts of Candy vanished as he made the corner and stopped. Not one, but two extended cab pickups were parked in front of the building.

Both vehicles screamed law enforcement. Death took a deep breath, walked to the edge of the building, and took a peek through the window. Two men flanked the desk in front of Candy. Even without hearing, he could tell from her demeanor she was troubled. Her lips moved, and the bigger of the two men pulled something from his jacket pocket. When he flipped it open for her to see, Death saw the metal flash and instantly knew it was a badge and that his time was limited.

Maybe, they're here for someone else, he thought as he turned quickly around and started back for his room. *Yeah, and maybe the Easter Bunny really can lay eggs.* He picked up the pace as he rounded the corner. To run would bring unwanted attention, so he kept to a fast walk while contemplating what he could grab from his room and still have time to get away before they convinced Candy to tell them which room was his. The laptop, of course, he would grab first. He had never really unpacked, so his clothes, except for what was dirty, were still in his duffle. Did he have time to take everything down from the wall?

He reached the door to his room and looked over his shoulder to see if anyone was following him yet. No one. He opened the door and stepped inside. The clock was ticking.

Candy felt like vomiting. She was not sure what she should do. The big man had shown her his badge and told her he was a Texas Ranger. He said she could call him J.T. Should she ask to see a warrant? She tried to remember her training. Had they said a warrant was needed to answer questions, or just to open the door to the room?"

"I'm sorry, but I don't think I'm allowed to tell you our guest's room numbers without a warrant," Candy fidgeted behind the counter. "Maybe I should call my boss."

"We're not askin' you to open the door," J.T. smiled. "You don't need a warrant to answer our questions."

Still unsure, Candy picked up her cellphone.

"Well, hell, Noble," J.T. turned and leaned against the counter. "I hope he doesn't kill anyone else while we're waitin' around for Ms. Candy here to ring her boss."

The man the Ranger had called Noble shrugged and shook his head. Candy could feel her insides squirming. Someone was dead, and the killer might be in one of the motel's rooms. Real-life shit right here in the same room with her. Suddenly, her wish for a little excitement was materializing, and she did not like it. If anyone died because of something she had or had not done, she would never forgive herself.

"Kill someone… did you say kill someone?" she stammered and nearly dropped the phone.

Noble spoke, "Yes."

Candy felt clammy and wondered if she was as pale as she felt. She set her phone back down and keyed up the computer. "Somebody is dead?"

"Yeah, a couple of somebodies actually," Noble shrugged. "Hey, don't sweat it. He probably won't kill again before you get your call made."

"Perhaps it won't hurt if you just knock on the door," Candy said, moving towards the computer. "But if they don't answer, I'm pretty sure you have to have a warrant."

Noble stepped back up to the desk. "That sounds reasonable."

"Who is it you are looking for?" Candy asked. "I'll see if they are here."

J.T. spoke over his shoulder. "Lincoln Burns."

Candy's knees threatened to buckle, and she grasped the edge of the counter for support. This had to be a mistake. She looked from the computer screen to Noble.

"So he is here?" one side of Noble's mouth turned up in a half-grin.

"Room eight," she answered just above a whisper.

At the intersection of Mesa and University Drive, Death stopped long enough to contemplate his next move. It had taken him less than three minutes to clear everything from the bathroom counter into a plastic bag, toss it and the few items of clothing not already packed into his duffel, grab it and his laptop from the desk, and step out the door. Luck had been with him. He had thrown everything into the passenger's seat and driven around the back of the motel without seeing a soul. And if his luck held, no one had seen him either.

But now, the clock was ticking. He ran the calculations in his head as he turned left toward the interstate. He had closed and locked the door to the hotel room. The key was lying in the truck's console. By law, when he did not answer the door, the officers would have to call for a warrant. Death knew how easily it was for some to bend the rules when it suited their needs. Prepare for the worst and hope for the best seemed like the best course of action in the current situation.

It was time for a different vehicle. He took a deep breath and let it out slowly as he maneuvered onto Interstate 35 and headed south. Dirty Dick's Bar was less than ten minutes away. His heart beat quickened as the adrenaline rush hit, and he laughed out loud. That had been close, too close. *And now the real game begins*, he thought, *two kills to go and now we're in hostile territory.*

CHAPTER 18

Candy watched as J.T. knocked on the door. The gold number eight just below the peephole caught her eye, and she remembered her comment about it being a lucky number. Her heart refused to believe Lincoln was a killer. Her mind, however, continued to remind her how little she actually knew about him.

"Looks like no one is home," J.T. stepped back from the door as he spoke.

Noble nodded and turned to Candy, "I don't suppose you would be willing to do a welfare check for us, would you? We would stay out here unless, of course, you found something out of the ordinary."

Her heart in her throat, Candy pulled a master key from her pocket. One way or another, she had to know, or she would never be able to sleep tonight. A quick walk-through, and she could send them on their way. The key turned in the lock, and she eased the door open a crack. "Mr. Burns, it's housekeeping," she lied, not wanting the officers behind her to think she was familiar with Lincoln.

When no one responded, she stepped inside, but left the door cracked. Nothing seemed out of the ordinary in the living area. A beam of light across the floor let her know the bathroom light had been left on. The door to the bedroom stood half open, and everything looked normal as she approached it. The bed looked like it had not been slept in, which seemed a little odd to her, but other than that, nothing struck her as out of place.

At the bathroom door, she listened for water running, and when she did not hear any, she knocked. No answer. She opened it. There were towels on the floor and a washcloth on the counter beside the sink, but nothing else. No toiletries, no comb, nothing she would expect to see. Still, she saw no reason to allow anyone in the room without a warrant.

She sighed and released the breath she had not realized she had been holding in. It was all going to be alright. All she needed to do was let the men outside know all was fine, and she could clock out and head home. She eased the bathroom door shut, turned to go, and stopped in her tracks. From her position, she could now see the bedroom wall that had been hidden by the partially opened door, and her heart dropped.

Where a picture should have hung, the wall was covered with papers. She eased the door open, reached over, and turned on the light. She had seen too many movies not to recognize… she felt the color drain from her face. Her stomach rolled. She swallowed hard and forced herself to walk. She stepped out into the night air and tried to speak.

Both officers stood staring at her. She had tried to seduce a killer. If she said it, it was real. Guilt choked her. She swallowed again, before she spoke, "You need to see the bedroom." It was all she could manage before she stepped to the curb and began to vomit.

Noble was the first one through the door. J.T. was right on his heels. Bits and pieces ran through his head as he looked at the wall. Newspaper clippings and handwritten notes created a macabre puzzle of sorts. Among the papers, Noble noticed several scribbled words he did not recognize.

Taking his phone out, he brought up the internet and typed in "*biskinik.*" The first item identified the word as the name of the monthly Choctaw newspaper published in Durant, Oklahoma. As he scrolled down, he found it was also the Choctaw word for a yellow-bellied sapsucker, which was a medium sized woodpecker. Still further down, a reference linked it to a Choctaw legend where it was referred to as "little *Chahta* news bird".

The word was scribbled in red ink on a newspaper clipping below a picture of Frank Nelson handing an award to a man. Maps of the cities of Marietta and Ardmore, and another of Love County, had several circles drawn in blue pen. The one of Marietta had a red X at the corner of Main Street near where the news office was located and another at the corner of the block where Sam Wilson had resided.

"Don't think you're gonna make it to the dance hall tonight," Noble did not look at J.T. as he spoke. "Sorry, amigo."

Death sat patiently watching the steady flow of traffic moving along the street. Dirty Dick's was busy. He had circled the block twice before a space had opened. He had already spotted a Ford pickup across from where he had parked. He knew it would be easy enough to take it, but once the officers talked to Candy, they would be on the lookout for a truck. If given the choice, he wanted a car.

With the window down, Death sat in the dark and waited. All his senses focused, he let his mind wander. He thought of Candy and smiled. It was time to move. Sitting still in one place for too long was a sure way to be spotted, and he had allowed himself to become complacent. A new vehicle and he would disappear, but to where?

The best place to hide a leaf is in a forest. The thought pleased him. He could head south, deeper into the Dallas/Fort Worth metroplex. The idea did not appeal to him. It was too far from his target, and for reasons he could not put his finger on, the thought of the Texas Rangers on his trail did not sit well with him - too many old western movies, perhaps. North, he would head north. Norman was not that much further from Marietta than Denton.

The doors to the bar opened and a middle-aged couple stepped out onto the sidewalk, breaking his train of thought.

Music from inside poured out into the street, and Death leaned further back behind the doorframe of his truck. The two staggered playfully along the sidewalk until they reached the Silverado Crew Cab parked beside the truck Death had been considering. The man pulled keys from his front jean pocket, and the lights on the vehicle flashed. The woman swung the back door open on the driver's side and giggling, stepped up into the truck.

"Hurry up and get in here," she laughed, already pulling her shirt off over her head, "I need a good…"

The man pulled the door shut behind him, leaving only the low hum of music and the road noise of another passing car to fill the night air. Death turned the key in his ignition - so much for the Ford. He shook his head as he pulled out of the parking spot. At the corner, he waited for a tan Honda Accord to pass and turned in behind it. Another turn, and the Accord pulled into an empty spot in the lot behind Dirty Dick's. Death eased past, pulled into the last space at the end of the lot, and watched as two young men in green North Texas T-shirts got out of the car and started across the lot for the bar.

Death waited five minutes after the door had closed behind the two men before leaving his truck. He walked quickly to the Accord, found the door unlocked, opened it, slid behind the wheel, and in less than two minutes backed the vehicle up and drove it to the rear of his truck.

A check to see that there was no one around, and he stepped out and moved his belongings from the pickup into the backseat of his new vehicle. Back behind the wheel, he started to pull away and then stopped. He reached into his duffle and pulled out a combat knife. A flat tire on the truck might buy him a little more time. The lot owner was less likely to call it in first thing in the morning if he thought someone would be coming back to fix the tire. Death smiled as he thrust the knife into the sidewall. Maybe it would work, maybe not, but it did not hurt to try.

Twenty minutes later, he passed the motel where he had been living. Even from the highway in the dark, he could see the growing collection of police vehicles around the building. If they had not known who he was before tonight, they did now. So be it; let them know. He had two more to kill, and his job was done. He would disappear into the night like he had done so many times before. He was not a man; he was Death, and Death could not be caught.

Noble watched as the forensic techs eased the door open and started to work. While J.T. had made the necessary calls, Noble had used his cell phone to take pictures of everything on the wall. A search of the rest of the room, the living area, and bathroom had turned up nothing more, not that anything more was needed as far as he was concerned. Now it was just a matter of hunting Lincoln down.

"I'll be outside," he pointed at the door as he spoke.

J.T., who was still on the phone, nodded, "Be along in a minute."

Noble eased past two techs on his way out and found Candy sitting on the curb not far from where she had been when they entered the motel room. A Denton County Sheriff's deputy leaned against his unit, visiting with her.

"Noble Harris with the Oklahoma State Bureau of Investigation," Noble identified himself to the deputy as he approached the two, "Mind if I borrow her for a few minutes?"

The deputy shrugged, "She's all yours."

Noble turned to Candy, "I need to ask you a few questions. Maybe we could do that back at the office, if you would like."

"Sure," she nodded and pushed herself off the ground, "Then can I go home?"

"That's not my call," Noble smiled, "J.T.'s in charge, so he'd be the one to answer that one."

"Okay," Candy started toward the front of the building.

The Candy that had greeted Noble and J.T. when they

arrived seemed to have disappeared. The girl that walked in front of him now was a lot less cheerful and sure of herself. Noble found himself feeling bad for her. "You gonna be okay?"

Candy shook her head, "Maybe, I don't know. I've never been around a killer before, at least, if I was, I didn't know it. I just can't quit wonderin' if I was ever in danger."

As they reached the office door, Noble stepped in front and opened it for her. "If Lincoln is our guy, I would have to say no. His targets seem to be very specific, and none so far have been women."

Noble let her mull the information over as they crossed the lobby. Normally, he would not have shared even the little bit he had with her, but she seemed to be struggling more than most. He followed her past the front desk and noticed when she gave a weak nod to the receptionist who had come in at shift change. In the office, she took a seat behind a small desk and looked up at him. "You said you had a few questions."

"Lincoln used his driver's license when he rented the room," Noble looked around the office. "Can I get a copy of it?"

Without answering, Candy turned her chair sideways and pulled the drawer of a metal file cabinet open. She shuffled through several folders before pulling one out. From it, she produced a single sheet of paper with an image of Lincoln's driver's license and his military ID.

"Is there any chance he's not the killer?" she asked as she handed it to Noble.

"I don't think so," he looked down at her and realized she was hoping for a different answer. "Were the two of you an item?"

"No, not really," she shook her head, but he could tell he had hit a nerve.

"Had he been coming on to you?" he pushed.

"No," Candy looked down at her hands. "I was coming on to him. I think that's why I'm so freaked out. What if…" She laid her head on the desktop and began to sob.

"What ifs will make you crazy," Noble squatted beside the desk and placed a hand on her elbow. "Don't do that to yourself. You're safe, and it won't be long until we catch him and put him away."

Candy raised her head and wiped at her eyes. "Do you really think so?"

"I do," Noble looked her in the eye and shook his head. She smiled, and he smiled back. Maybe she believed him. Maybe it would help her sleep a little better. Maybe, but he was not at all sure that he was convinced himself.

CHAPTER 19

Death pulled into a motel in the heart of Oklahoma City. The kind of place you locked the car doors and hoped the vehicle would still be there when you came out from checking in. The overflowing trash bin out in front of the dirty sliding door and the unconscious body covered with cardboard and newspaper on the rusty metal bench beside it told Death more than the sign advertising rooms for thirty-one dollars a night.

The clock on the Honda's dash indicated it was nearly three hours after midnight. He had not planned to travel this far north, but he had been unable to find a suitable place until now. Tired but glad to be free, he opened the door and stepped out to the smell of urine and used condoms. The place was perfect.

He left the car unlocked but grabbed his duffle from the backseat. If they took the car, he figured he could steal another, but his personal possessions were a different matter. A faded blue ball cap with a Texas Rangers' "T" on the floorboard caught his eye. He picked it up, put it on, and stepped to the office entryway. The glass door slid aside with a high-pitched squeal that suggested the track was in bad need of lubrication. Inside, a sign on the front desk instructed guests to ring the bell for assistance. Death pushed the tiny button on top of the metal dome causing a loud ding to echo through the room.

A pockmarked man with greasy hair and a scraggly beard stepped through an archway behind the counter and stifled a yawn, "Need a room?"

"One on the second floor, near the far end, if there's anything available," Death kept his head down using the bill of the cap to hide the features in the top half of his face.

"Just for the night?" The man stepped behind a computer screen.

"Not sure," Death shrugged, "Maybe, one night, maybe more."

"Check out time is eleven o'clock, so if you're plannin' on stayin' past that, you'll have to pay for two nights." He pressed his palm into his eye and rubbed it as he spoke.

"Better make it two," Death said, "Can I pay with cash?"

"Kinda prefer you did," the man smiled, revealing a space just left of center in his upper row of teeth. "Got any identification?"

"Nope," Death answered, "lost it."

That brought a chuckle, "Get that a lot around here. Have to charge you a little extra."

"How much?" Death asked, already pulling out his wallet.

"Fifty a night," the man punched buttons on the keyboard as he spoke, "A hundred total, tax included."

Death pushed five twenties across the counter and waited for the man to hand him a key. "Better lock your car. The motel ain't responsible if someone breaks into it."

Death nodded and shouldered his duffle. The man handed him his key and turned toward the archway from which he had appeared. "Welcome to Oklahoma City," he said over his shoulder as he disappeared.

The glass door squeaked open once more to reveal the Honda still parked under the portico. Death passed the unconscious person on the bench. The slow rhythmic movement of the cardboard covering rising and falling was the only indication the being was not dead. Death figured if he did not get up to the room soon, he might be in the same situation. He needed a long sleep and a shower. The shower could wait until tomorrow. Tonight, he would sleep. Tomorrow, a shower and then he would plan. *Sleep well, Wolf,* he thought, *Death is coming for you.*

The buzzing of his cellphone vibrating woke Noble. He picked it up. Nine o'clock, his muddled brain calculated, four hours of sleep. Not enough to satisfy his aching body, but enough to get him through the day, he hoped. It does not really matter one way or the other, his thought pattern decided on its own path; the bad guy is still out there and it is our job to catch him. Noble shook his head, knuckled the sleep out of his eyes, and typed the passcode into his phone.

Five missed phone calls and a dozen messages. He tossed the cell onto the bed and stood. They would all have to wait until he had showered. He grabbed a fresh shirt and jeans from the closet, clean underwear from the second drawer of the antique dresser beside the bed, and made his way down the hall to the guest bathroom.

He turned the water on in the shower and allowed it to heat up while he undressed and urinated. The reflection in the mirror caught his attention as he turned back around. Rough was the first word that came to his mind. Bloodshot, sleep-deprived eyes stared back at him. The salt-and-pepper stubble seemed whiter today than it had yesterday. What was it Jacqueline had told him on his birthday? Forty was the new thirty. Normally, she was right, but this morning, he felt like forty might be the new eighty. Damn, Lincoln. Damn, him to hell.

He pulled back the curtain and stepped over the side of the tub. The water was too hot. He adjusted the temperature as he pushed the curtain against the back wall and made sure it was in place. He stepped into the warm water and let it cascade over his body. Head down, eyes closed, he replayed the prior night in his mind. His gut told him that they had missed Lincoln by mere minutes. As far as he knew, there was no way to tell for sure, but something nagging at the edge of his mind had him believing it. He opened his eyes, shook his head, and reached for the soap.

Ten minutes later, showered and freshly shaven, he stepped out of the bathroom. The air in the hallway felt light and crisp on his skin. Two steps from his bedroom door, he stopped. That was it. The air in the motel bath had been heavy, weighty, like someone had recently taken a shower. Noble backtracked and stepped back into the bathroom. It had been roughly five minutes since he turned the shower off and opened the door to let the steam out. There was still condensation on the mirror, except where he had wiped it away to shave.

He returned to his room, picked up his phone, and checked to see whose calls he had missed. The first name on the list was Sanderson. He tapped the screen and then the speaker icon.

"We got another body," Sanderson sounded tired. Noble stared at the screen, trying to process. "You there?" Sanderson's voice jarred him back.

"Who was it?" Noble braced himself as the question escaped his lips.

"Hal Spencer," came Sanderson's answer, and Noble relaxed. He did not know that name.

"Who was he?" Noble turned and wandered back up the hall as he spoke.

"A doctor," Sanderson sounded angry. "He used to work out at the clinic and, Noble, he was terminal. They figured he had less than a week to live, and the son of a bitch cut his throat anyway. Who does that?"

"Lincoln Burns." Noble sighed as he stepped into the bathroom. The condensation was gone. He looked at the time on his phone. Noble figured he had missed him by less than fifteen minutes.

"Are you sure?" The sound of Sanderson's voice and the click of the switch as Noble turned off the light coincided.

"Yes, I am," Noble said, already headed for the front door. "Did he leave the knife?"

"Yes, he did," Sanderson responded. "Same kind of tactical knife from the other two murders."

As Noble pulled the door shut behind him, he asked, "Where are you now?"

"At the station," Sanderson answered.

"Be there in fifteen," Noble picked up his keys as he spoke.

Death popped a stale cheese cracker into his mouth and began to chew. Not exactly brain food, but it would do until he had a chance to watch the midday news. The flat screen television mounted on the wall was as dusty as the rest of the room, but it worked. Death's duffel sat in a corner. His laptop was beside him on the bed, propped on a pillow. He had checked the local news websites but had not done any specific searches for fear they might be traced back to him.

He worried that the news of a murder in south-central rural Oklahoma would not be of enough interest to reach the metro area. Having slept through the early morning broadcast, he hoped the twelve o'clock airing might give him an idea of how he should proceed.

The last cracker from the pack fell from the cellophane wrapper and into his hand as the anchorman on the screen announced breaking news out of Ardmore, Oklahoma. Death grabbed the remote from the nightstand and increased the volume.

"A man dying from terminal cancer was brutally murdered in his hospital bed yesterday," the reporter stared straight into the camera as he spoke, "this from our associate network…"

Death placed the cracker in his mouth and followed it with a sip from a half empty bottle of Sprite. The screen shifted from the suited anchorman to a uniformed official behind a set of microphones. The man identified himself as the Sheriff of Carter County and asked the public for help in solving the heinous crime. He then introduced Oklahoma Bureau of Investigation officer, Noble Harris, who stepped up to take his place. Death smiled.

Noble fought the urge to throw down the gauntlet. He hated dancing around, playacting, especially since he knew that

Lincoln Burns was their guy. Noble's ego would have him flash a picture of Lincoln across the screen with the message "This is the son of a bitch we are looking for" written below it. He wanted to look into the camera and say, "I'm coming for you."

Instead, he stuck to the script they had agreed on. It was the right thing to do. Lincoln had killed and disappeared before, and even though it was unlikely he would be able to do it again, it was not an impossibility. Tom Jack had suggested caution. Sheriffs from both Love and Carter Counties had agreed, and so Noble repeated the message that anyone who had information should come forward.

"Do you have any leads at all?" a young man's voice questioned from somewhere in the back of the crowd.

Noble shook his head as the sheriff stepped back up to microphones, effectively cutting Noble off. "We cannot discuss the specifics of an ongoing investigation," he said as Noble stepped back. "All we are asking is that if you have information or think you saw or heard something that might help, please call the number on the screen below. That's all we have at this time."

As soon as he finished speaking, he turned and motioned for those around him to exit through the door behind them. Noble fell in with the rest of the group. The door to the outside shut, and the sheriff turned. "Do you think he bought it?"

"I sure hope so," Noble inhaled deeply through his nose, then relaxed as he released the breath from his mouth. "Your supposed interruption was perfectly timed. He would have seen me shake my head no just before you stopped me from sayin' anything further. Yeah, I think if I were him, I would have bought it."

"So, what's our next step?" Sanderson asked as the group continued down the hallway and deeper into the building.

Noble stopped and stepped to one side, allowing the others to separate from Sanderson and him before answering. "We need to figure out who the Wolf and the Shadow in Grandmother Mosley's story are," he kept his voice low. "And we don't need every Tom, Dick, and Harry, knowin' what we're doin'. If too many get involved, Lincoln will sense it."

"Really," Sanderson looked skeptical. "You don't think you're givin' him too much credit, do you?"

"Not at all," Noble shook his head. "I don't know how he did it, but somehow, he saw us comin' at the motel. I'd say we missed him by less than fifteen or twenty minutes. It was that close."

"But now we know who he is," Sanderson smiled. "That should count for somethin'. Bits and pieces and all."

"We know his name," Noble did not smile. "Who he is, that's an altogether different matter. I went to school with this man. If you had asked me a week ago if I thought he was capable of murderin' four people in cold blood, my answer would have been a solid no. So, you'll have to forgive me if I'm not jumpin' for joy. I need to know who this man is now, then I can figure out how to hunt him."

"And how do you do that?" Sanderson was no longer smiling. "How do you figure out who he is?"

"I'm hopin' that Davenport can help me with that," Noble's eyes narrowed as he pulled his phone from his pocket. "As a matter of fact, I missed a call from him this mornin'. Everything's been so crazy, I haven't had time to call him back."

Noble tapped the phone and waited for it to awaken. Another series of touches followed by a short wait, and Davenport answered.

CHAPTER 20

"Hello, old friend." Death spoke aloud with a smile.

It had taken him two days of careful and painstaking surveillance to finally locate Noble Harris in person. A computer search had turned up fragments of his career, but no home address. After the initial broadcast in which Noble had lied about not having any leads, there had been no additional mention of the deaths of the wretched men Death had removed from society. Grandmother Mosley had been right. Death regretted doubting her. The narrow escape showed him that fate was on his side. The lie that Noble told had made it clear that there were none within the traditional justice system who could be trusted. Two more, and then justice would be served. It would be done, complete, over, and he, Death, could move on with his life.

He watched as Noble and a short, stocky man walked down the sidewalk towards the line of parked cars in front of the building. The short man said something before stepping onto the Harley Davidson Death had been eyeing while he waited. Noble nodded, turned, and opened the door to the truck next to the cycle.

"Let the games begin," Death smiled as Noble's vehicle backed out of its space and Death turned the key in the ignition of the white SUV he had stolen the night before.

Noble asked Siri to call Sanderson and then waited as the ringing of the phone sounded through the speaker system in his truck. On the third ring, Sanderson answered. Exhaustion and frustration were evident as he spoke, "I hope you've got something on your end, 'cause nothin' down here is pannin' out. I was just headed over to where the old, or should I say ancient, file cases are stored in the basement of the courthouse. I thought maybe I'd get lucky and find a case that… oh, hell, I don't know, I guess I just need to stay busy. So, please give me some good news."

"Got a few things, but none of it gets us any closer to catching him," Noble admitted as he made the loop at Sixty-Third Street and accelerated onto the highway.

"Humor me," Sanderson almost sounded as if he were begging.

Noble understood the feeling. Sometimes, when chasing leads, the simple act of repeating what was already known could take the edge off feeling like you were spinning your wheels and getting nowhere fast.

"DNA came back from the Wilson crime scene. It took some doing, but we have a match from his military records," Noble repeated what Davenport had told him earlier, "no doubt it's Lincoln."

Noble paused as he switched lanes to pass a semi. A little red sports car jetted out from in front of the truck, and Noble braked hard to keep from colliding with it. "Son of a bitch."

"What?" Sanderson's voiced his confusion.

"Nothin'," Noble cleared the front of the truck and eased into the right lane, "just another example of the wonderful driving skills of your average motorist."

Sanderson chuckled, "So, are you headed this way?"

"Not today, partner," Noble watched as the red car disappeared from view in front of another vehicle, "I'm headed up to Edmond. Got some personal business to take care of, but I'll be down your way tomorrow."

"Tell Jacqueline, I said howdy." The sound of mirth in Sanderson's voice caused Noble to visualize the smile on his friend's face.

"Will do, smartass," a smile spread across Noble's face as

he spoke and he realized he had not smiled much in the last couple of days, "so, I take it you're not havin' any luck figurin' out who the Wolf and the Shadow are, either." Noble changed the subject as he switched lanes and pulled around the truck in which the red sports car disappeared. It was no longer there and looking up the road, he could not see it anywhere. Somewhere, it had taken an exit, and he had missed it.

"No more luck than you're…"

"That's it," Noble interrupted Sanderson before he could finish his sentence.

"What's it?" Sanderson asked.

Noble collected his thoughts, then explained, "We're at a dead end looking backward. We know the story but not who is who. Looking forward, all we can do is wait until he kills again, and I'm tired of waiting around for that to happen. So, that leaves the present."

"Okay," Sanderson interjected, "but how does that help?"

"I don't know if it does," Noble confessed, "but it gives us a new perspective and maybe a new direction to go. Maybe that will shake somethin' loose. I don't know about you, but I'm tired of feelin' like I'm chasin' my own tail."

Noble passed the ramp for the John Kilpatrick Turnpike. As he passed the Toyota and Chevrolet dealerships, another light bulb flashed brightly across his brain. Stolen cars. In the few minutes before he pulled into the real estate office Jacqueline owned and operated, he outlined his thoughts for Sanderson. He figured it was a long shot, but at least it would give them something more to do.

"Oh, I almost forgot," Noble said as he pulled into the parking space in front of Jacqueline's building, "Davenport is headed to McAlester to talk to Lincoln's grandmother. Turns out the one in the nursin' home down there was actually his great-grandmother."

"Sounds like me and Davenport are gonna be carryin' the load today, while you go frolic with Jacqueline," Sanderson joked.

"Try not to sound so jealous," Noble chuckled as he opened the door and stepped out of his truck.

A white SUV caught Noble's attention as it pulled to a stop in front of the kitchen remodel shop at the far end of the parking area. Noble watched the back of a man's head disappear from view as the driver leaned over to pick something up in the passenger floorboard. He said goodbye to Sanderson, slid the phone into his pocket, and reached for the door handle.

Death turned back in time to see the door slowly shut behind Noble. This was closer than he had planned, but the guidance system he was using had not given him much choice. All he could see on the screen was a labyrinth of dead ends and cul-de-sacs. His patience had worn thin, and he did not want risk losing Noble and have to spend two more days waiting around Noble's work again.

He considered stepping just inside the kitchen remodel store but business in the place looked slow, and he did not want to be tied up with some pushy salesperson when Noble returned to his truck. He was in the middle of contemplating his best course of action when the door Noble had disappeared into opened, and a woman came out dragging Noble along with her. Noble pulled her in close and kissed her soundly before opening the passenger door of his truck and helping her inside.

Death watched and smiled; *the Wolf is mine.*

"You are absolutely beautiful," Noble whispered in Jacqueline's ear as he pulled the chair out for her.

Hidalgo's Mexican Restaurant and Cantina was a little over half a mile from Jacqueline's office and one of her favorite lunch spots. "You're just sayin' that 'cause you think you're gonna get lucky tonight." She grinned up at him as he settled into the seat across from her.

Noble smiled, "Well, am I?"

"That remains to be seen," Jacqueline giggled, "I'm way behind at the office, and from what I've seen on the news, you have a bad guy to catch."

The smile vanished from Noble's face, "I didn't know you were keepin' up with the case. There hasn't been a lot on television or social media, so I was kinda hopin'… well, I hate to worry you."

"I'm datin' a cop," Jacqueline reached out and placed her hand over his, "Cops chase bad guys. Bad guys sometimes shoot cops. I knew what I was gettin' into when we started dating. And it's okay if I worry."

Death crossed the John Kilpatrick Turnpike headed south. If he didn't hit any traffic, he would be in Marietta in two hours. His need to visit Grandmother Mosley had grown daily, and now that he had the Wolf in the palm of his hands, he could not wait to tell her.

Killing the Wolf was never going to as easy as killing the others, and now that law enforcement knew who he was, it would be even harder. Harder, but not impossible. Thankfully, Death had many tricks, and if necessary, he would use all of them to bring down the Wolf.

His thoughts turned to Grandmother Mosley. The last time he had visited her, she had reminded him that he had a mission in life and had told him once again the story of the woodland creatures who had wronged his mother. Even as he had listened to her that day, he had begun to plan.

Now, as he drove, he thought about the Wolf. Of all the men in Grandmother's story, he was not only the largest, but also the most powerful. Through his research, Death learned that even as far back as when Death was in school, the Wolf had been a big man in the county, and now the Wolf was even more powerful.

Several scenarios ran through Death's mind as he made his way toward Marietta. He toyed with the idea of surveilling the Wolf at his house. He knew where the Wolf lived. Once, after a long day of following the Snake around town, he had even driven past it on his way back to Denton. It was a big house - one might even say a mansion - set well back from the road between Marietta and Thackerville on the old highway. Death mentally went over what he remembered from the drive-by and knew it would not be his first option.

The nearest neighbor was a quarter of a mile away, but like the Wolf's house, it was also large and looked like money. As he let his mind wander, he realized it would be no easy feat to hide himself in the open area around the house, and there was no place to park his truck that would not be easily spotted and reported as suspicious. The Wolf's house might be a no-go.

At his work? Death smiled at the thought. Now that would be justice. The smile widened as Death continued to contemplate the best place to kill the Wolf.

"Have you heard from Davenport yet?" Sanderson's voice coming through the speaker of Noble's cellphone sounded loud. From his desk, Noble looked around the room to make sure it was empty before answering.

"Nope," Noble leaned back in his chair, "I figure he's probably on his way back. I reckon I could call him. Why?"

"No particular reason," Sanderson answered. "I found a file this afternoon. It kind of raises more questions than answers, so I thought if Davenport had checked in, maybe between his interview and this file, we could make some sense of…I don't know. I feel like there's something here, but I'm not sure."

Noble ran his thumb along the scar on his chin as he listened.

When Sanderson finally paused, he leaned forward, "Well, I haven't heard from Davenport, but that's no reason not to discuss this file you've found. What's in it?"

"Not much," Sanderson's voice sounded odd. "I don't think this was ever supposed to be found. I feel like I'm lookin' at someone's insurance policy, if you know what I mean, like in case somethin' went south, they slipped this into the file room knowin' they could find it again if they needed it. There are two statements in the folder. Both of them have been marked up, like when they redact stuff on classified paper. Names and dates have been scribbled through with what I figure was a ballpoint pen and then a Sharpie was used to cover that up. They even went the trouble to do both sides of the paper. But it's pretty clear from what is left that whoever gave the first statement was some kin of a rape victim."

"Anything else in the file?" Noble asked.

There was a sound of papers being shuffled before Sanderson answered, "Yes. If I had to guess, I'd say this is from someone in the medical field. Maybe the doctor that did the exam."

"Where exactly did you find the file?" Noble could feel the hair on the back of his neck standing on edge as he asked.

"That's what's strange," Sanderson responded loud enough for Noble to hear him, but almost as if his desire was to whisper, "I was movin' boxes of files. They were stacked three and four boxes high on the shelves. I wasn't even sure what I was lookin' for or which boxes I should be lookin' in. Anyway, I had several stacks moved over to a makeshift table and had picked up another set of three when a snakeskin caught my eye. I don't like snakes at all. It startled me, and I stumbled back and hit the table. I dropped the boxes in my hand and knocked all the others over. When I got myself calmed down, I started tryin' to put the files back into the boxes I figured they should be in. That's when I noticed one folder had slid all the way across the room. It was this folder, and unlike the others, it had no tab or any kind of markings on it."

"Where are you now?" Noble asked.

The sound of Sanderson breathing in deeply then letting it out came before his answer, "I'm sittin' in front of my house."

"Does anyone else know about the folder?" Noble asked.

"No," Sanderson answered, "just you and me, and Noble, even if this has nothin' to do with Lincoln Burns, I have a feelin' someone out there might not have wanted it found."

Noble's phone buzzed, letting him know he had an incoming call from Kent Davenport. Before he hit the icon to switch to Davenport, he told Sanderson. "Find a safe place to put the file, and I'll pick it up next time I'm down your way. Davenport is calling, so let me see what he's found out, and I'll call you back in a bit."

CHAPTER 21

Death squatted beside Grandmother Mosley's headstone. An overcast sky that threatened rain matched his mood. He had been trained to listen then do; nowhere along the way had he ever thought to question. Now, he had questions and no one to give him answers.

Decisions like where to kill the Wolf he could figure out himself. Even why each man had been placed on the list no longer mattered to him. What he should do with his life after the mission was over had begun to plague his mind, and he found himself wishing he could have one more visit with Grandmother Mosley.

Far off, he heard the whistle of a train. The wind carried the sound to him. It did nothing to answer the question in his mind, but it did give him an idea of how he might get into and out of the Wolf's house without being noticed. The answer to what he should do once the Wolf and the Shadow were dead would have to wait; for now, he had things to do, and a plan was forming in his mind.

As soon as Noble broke the connection with Sanderson, he realized he had missed Davenport's call. He brought Davenport's number up on his phone and tapped it, then the speaker button. The sound of ringing filled the office, followed by Davenport's voice letting Noble know he was not available and to leave a message. Noble waited for the beep that followed and started to speak when the office door flew open and Davenport hollered, "What the hell do you want now?"

"I was returnin' your call," Noble answered as he turned towards Davenport.

"I saw your truck out front," Davenport explained. "Didn't see any sense in answering the phone when we could talk in person."

Noble waited for Davenport to cross the room and sit down at his desk before speaking. "It's been a long day. I hope you found out something we can use."

Davenport leaned back in his chair and shook his head before speaking. "Don't know if anything I learned today will help catch him, but man, is his family history a real bitch."

"How so?" Noble leaned forward as he asked.

Davenport exhaled long and slow before answering. "Well, to start with, Grandma Mosley was one racist old lady."

"Grandma Mosley?" Noble cocked his head to one side. "You mean Grandmother Mosley, the woman who raised him?"

"Yes," Davenport nodded his head. "She was actually his great-grandmother. The lady I visited earlier today was his actual grandmother."

"Did she have any information about Lincoln that might help?" Noble asked.

Davenport chuckled—not a ha-ha that's fun sound, more of a yea-right before he answered, "She had very little information about Lincoln. She had never met her grandson."

"How can that be?" Noble eyes narrowed as he asked.

Davenport pulled a piece of paper from his front shirt pocket and studied it for a moment. "I made some notes. I didn't want to miss anything, so here goes. When Lincoln's grandmother, Issi Mosley, graduated high school, she left Marietta to attend college in Durant and earn a degree in elementary education. Both of her parents were full Choctaw, and in high school, she was an exceptional student. Not straight A's, but close. Grandmother Mosley, as you called her, did not want her daughter to attend college. It seems, in Grandmother's mind, that was not a woman's place, and that is where the rift between the two started.

By the time Issi graduated, she had become Mrs. Burns. You see, during her second year of college she met Randy Burns, who would become her husband and the father of Lincoln's mother…but I'm getting ahead of myself."

Davenport paused, and Noble interjected, "This still doesn't explain why Mrs. Burns never met Lincoln."

"I'm getting there," Davenport held up his hand. "Much to Grandmother Mosley's disgust, Randy Burns was white. The fact that he was a good man did not make up for his skin color. The fact that he finished the aviation program at Southeastern Oklahoma State University and was going to make a more than decent living for him and his new bride did not matter. Grandmother Mosley disowned her daughter and refused to acknowledge the wedding."

"Wow," Noble interrupted. "That's harsh."

"Oh, it gets better," Davenport looked up from his notes and then back down again as he continued. "Mr. Burns got a job with the airport, mainly flying out of good old Will Rogers right here in Oklahoma City. Mrs. Burns got a job teaching, and the two settled in Nichols Hills."

"Nichols Hills?" Noble did not try to hide the shock in his tone. "You mean Lincoln came from money?"

"Not Lincoln, but his mother did," Davenport answered. "Her name was Rita, and from birth they gave her anything and everything she wanted. Only it backfired when she got into drugs at fifteen and started running with the wrong crowd. At the beginning of her junior year in high school, Rita told her mother she was pregnant. When asked who the father was, she laughed and said, 'You take your pick. It could be any one of a number of guys.' I guess mom and pop had finally had enough and tried to put their proverbial foot down. That too backfired. Our little pregnant Rita left."

Davenport paused long enough to turn the paper in his hand over. "Two weeks later, the Burns filed a missing person's report, and six months later they were notified by an officer that Rita was living with Grandmother Mosley in Marietta. A phone call was made, and Mrs. Burns was informed that Rita was fine; she had arrived with her infant son, Lincoln, and they would be living there. When asked if they could visit, Grandmother Mosley said no and hung up."

Davenport folded the paper in half and pushed it across the desk towards Noble. Noble stared down at the paper for a long second before asking, "That's it?"

"That's it," Davenport nodded. "It seemed to me that Mrs. Burns was afraid of her mother. Did you ever meet this Grandmother Mosley person?"

"No," Noble answered with a shake of his head. "Like I said before, me and Lincoln weren't close like that. We played sports together, that's all."

"Did you know he was Native American?" Davenport asked.

Noble thought about the question for a minute before answering. "You know, I don't think I did. His skin wasn't much darker than mine. I guess I just thought we both tanned well in the sun, and between his work at the feed store and playing sports, he spent a lot of time outside."

Davenport traced imaginary figures in the air in front of himself as he spoke, "So Grandmother Mosley and her husband were both full Choctaw. Lincoln's grandmother, Mrs. Burns would then also be full, but Issi, the daughter, would be half, making Lincoln a quarter depending on who his father was." He looked at Noble, and with a shrug, added, "Don't know if that helps much, but there it is."

Noble wasn't sure any of the new information was helpful, but at least they had it now. He had learned long ago that having information was much better than not having it. More than once, some bit or piece he thought insignificant had turned a case around.

Noble picked up the single sheet of paper Davenport had taken notes on and studied it briefly before asking, "How did the Burns end up in McAlester?"

"I asked Mrs. Burns the same question," Davenport grinned. "Didn't really seem like the answer would help the case but since you ask…Mr. Burns graduated from high school there and still had family in the area. When the two of them retired, they decided to relocate."

Noble placed the paper back on the desk. Three animals from the story were still in play. Well, two animals: the Panther and the Wolf, and the Shadow. Lincoln was the Panther, that Noble was sure of, but who were the Wolf and the Shadow?

Death backed the stolen Accord into a spot behind an Ardmore restaurant called Café Alley. It was situated near the railroad tracks that ran through Ardmore. He had no doubt that the Accord would be found sooner rather than later, but at this point in the game, it did not matter.

His duffel was packed with only the essentials. If it was not needed to survive or to finish the job, he had tossed it into one of the dumpsters behind the local mall. He shouldered the pack, pulled the Texas Rangers cap low on his forehead, and started for the train tracks. The streetlights blinked on along Main Street, announcing the coming of night. A train whistle and the squeal of metal on metal told him his ride was about to arrive.

Huntin' time, Death thought to himself as he stepped onto the tracks and made his way slowly along the train, looking for an open boxcar.

CHAPTER 22

Noble could feel the tension in his friend as Sanderson handed him the file folder. There was something eerie about it. Noble had never been spooked by material things. He had seen too much of the evil that mankind could do to believe in haunts and spells. Holding the folder now, he felt unnerved. He told himself he was simply channeling Sanderson, or the excitement of where the reports inside might lead was getting to him. Somehow, he was having trouble believing either.

"Did you happen to take another look at the report?" Noble asked as he flipped the folder open.

"I did not," Sanderson shook his head.

Noble took the three pieces of paper out of the folder and laid the folder on the dash of his truck. He began to read the words that had been left on the first. Even with the redactions, it was clear that a rape had taken place and the person writing the report had knowledge of the events that transpired following the rape. The more he read, the more he began to suspect that the author of the report was none other than Grandmother Mosley.

When he finished the first report, he placed it behind the second. The first thing he noticed about the second was that the handwriting was similar, if not the same. Reading between the blacked-out portions, he realized that this report was a brief statement taken from the person who had been raped. When he reached the bottom of the page, he felt as if he might vomit. Even with the redactions, there was enough to paint a picture of the atrocity that had occurred.

"See what I mean?" Sanderson's voice broke the silence in the truck. "I believe you're as pale as I was after I read through those." He pointed at the files in Noble's hands.

"Maybe so," Noble agreed. "I think there might have been more in this file at one time."

"How do you figure?" Sanderson looked from Noble to the statements and then to the file folder on the dash.

"Gut feelin'," Noble answered. "My gut also says you're right about someone hidin' this as an insurance policy."

The two men sat silent for several minutes. Noble mulled over what he knew and what he did not in his head.

"Do you think Billie Hilton left it there?" Sanderson interrupted Noble's thoughts.

Noble shook his head. If Billie Hilton was the rapist, his leaving evidence did not track.

"Then who?" Sanderson asked.

Noble placed the statements back in the folder and shut it. Turning in his seat, he stuffed the folder into a satchel lying on the backseat. As he turned back, he said, "That's the six-million-dollar question."

"Any idea on how we're gonna find the answer?" Sanderson asked.

Noble nodded. "If there's a statement, then there was an investigation. If there was an investigation, then it is highly likely that the district attorney was involved."

Sanderson smiled. "So we need to find out who was the district attorney at the time the rape occurred."

"First, we need to find out when the rape occurred," Noble stated. "You up for a little ride? I think I know who can help us narrow the time frame."

Death lay on his stomach and, through field glasses, watched the Wolf sitting on the porch drinking from a large brown mug. He considered walking across the yard and killing the Wolf, but that little voice of caution, he had ignored with the Snake spoke, and this time he listened. When the Wolf finally stood and went back inside, Death slowly pushed himself into a seated position. It had been a long night, but a productive one.

Twice raccoons had set off motion sensors, causing light to flood across the backyard. In addition to the motion sensors, Death had spotted five game cameras attached to various trees around the property. Once he knew where the cameras were, it had not taken him long to find the weakness in the Wolf's security system. He was confident that he could reach the house without being seen, but that would have to wait. Never one to believe in luck, he figured if there were such a thing, it had been with him last night, and he saw no reason to push it.

He had managed to find a place on a southbound train out of Ardmore where he could comfortably ride without fear of falling off. The train he was on had met another one headed north as it entered Marietta. Had it not been so, Death's train would not have slowed, and he would not have been able to jump from the train. He wondered what his chances were of it happening again.

The gurgle of water running in the creek behind him threatened to lull him to sleep, so he stood and slowly moved deeper into the overgrowth. The game trail he had used the night before materialized, and he took it to the edge of the creek. Squatting, he splashed water on his face and then ran wet fingers through his hair. While the Wolf was at work, Death would find a place in the woods and get a few hours of sleep. He smiled at his reflection on the water's surface. Tonight, he thought to himself, tonight the Wolf dies.

"Who is it we are goin' to see?" Sanderson asked as Noble turned onto Main Street.

"My Granny," Noble answered with a smile.

The two men rode in silence for the next several minutes. Noble made his way through town to the interstate and headed north. He reminded himself that some pulled strings lead to nada, then chided himself for being pessimistic. His gut told him this was a break, but his head refused to let him celebrate just yet.

"So, who's left?" Sanderson finally broke the silence.

Noble considered the question before answering. "Well, according to the story Grandmother Mosley was so fond of telling at the nursing home, Billie Hilton was the dog. That left five additional characters in the story that the Panther was supposed to kill. He's managed to take out three so far; that leaves two."

As Noble slowed for Exit 21, Sanderson spoke once more. "Tell me again the five characters."

Noble stopped at the end of the off ramp and looked both ways before making a left turn onto Oswalt Road. As they passed the Valero station, Noble said, "Woodpecker, Crow, Wolf, Snake, and Shadow."

Trees and tall grass crowded the narrow road as Noble made his way west. After several minutes, he glanced at Sanderson, who seemed to be lost somewhere deep in his own mind.

"Did I lose ya?" Noble chuckled as he spoke.

"Nah," Sanderson looked at him. "Just tryin' to put the pieces in order. Any idea which animal belongs to which person? And what the hell does a shadow have to do with the animal kingdom? Seems damn odd to have it in the story."

"Carla's MawMaw thought Sam Wilson might be the Snake. The collage we found on the motel wall had the word *biskinik* scribbled below Frank Nelson's picture. According to the internet, *biskinik* is Choctaw for news bird. I'm pretty sure Frank was the Woodpecker. That leaves the Crow and the Wolf as far as animals are concerned, and your guess is as good as mine as far as the Shadow goes."

"Humph," Sanderson tapped his finger on the center console. "Let's say this rape is connected. If the victim was Lincoln's mother and he's checkin' off the characters from his grandmother's story… damn, Noble, I feel like I've got more questions now than I did before."

"Like?" Noble raised an eyebrow and glanced across the cab of the truck as he asked.

"Like," Sanderson held up a finger as he spoke, "how does an ex-mayor and the owner of a newspaper get involved in a rape case? The doctor, I can understand, but not those two."

Noble slowed and turned into the drive leading Granny's house. "According to Granny, Sam Wilson, your ex-mayor, has…or had a habit of knowing everyone's business, so it's not a stretch to think he caught wind of the rape somehow. Frank Nelson…that's a bit harder for me to connect."

As Noble pulled to a stop, Sanderson asked, "What's your best guess as to who the last two on the list are?"

Noble turned the key in the ignition, killing the engine before answering, "Whoever the district attorney and the judge were at the time of the rape."

"I hadn't considered the judge," Sanderson admitted, "but it does make sense. Those judicial robes do cast a big shadow."

"Well, let's go see if Granny can help us narrow down the timeframe," Noble opened said as he opened the truck door.

"My goodness, Noble," Granny Harris shook her head, "you think I remember every bit of this town's history since the day it was founded? You must really think I am busybody."

Noble shook his head, "That's not what I'm sayin', Granny."

"Good," Granny snapped, "because if memory serves me correctly, you and I were just over that road recently."

From the way Granny's eyes narrowed, Noble knew he was skating on thin ice. "Now Granny, it's not like that. Me and Sanderson need some information, and we need to get it without makin' a big fuss about it at the courthouse."

"And why is that?" Granny asked.

"Because there are some folks that we aren't sure if we can trust," Noble answered quickly, hoping his answer would take some of the fire out of her eyes.

When she did not respond, Noble shot Sanderson a wide-eyed glance that suggested a little help might be nice. Sanderson smiled and shrugged as if to say "You're on your own, buddy."

"Well, I suppose if you need my help," Granny cocked her head to the side and squinted one eye, "and you're not callin' me a busybody, then we can have a chat. Either of you want something to drink?"

"I wouldn't mind a glass of sweet tea if you have some made," Sanderson spoke up. Noble shot him a so-now-you-can-talk look and then turned back to Granny, "I'm good for now. Thanks anyway."

Granny grinned at Sanderson and shuffled towards the refrigerator. "Y'all pull up a chair there at the table while I get you that tea. Think I'll have a glass myself. Noble, you sure you don't want one?"

"No, Granny, I'm good," Noble repeated.

Noble watched as she took a gallon pitcher and set it on the kitchen counter. She opened the cabinet, took out two jelly glasses, and turned back towards the fridge. Noble shook his head as she filled each of the glasses half-full of ice and returned to the counter. He knew if he asked her a question now, she would not answer it until she was done with her task and seated at the table. He smiled and remembered how frustrated her actions had made him when he was a teenager. If he was honest with himself, he still found it a bit aggravating, but as he had matured, he had learned that an inkling of patience went a long way with Granny.

Granny sat one of the glasses on the table in front of Sanderson and then seated herself, and said, "So, you want to know if I remember anything about a rape."

"Yes, ma'am," Sanderson spoke up.

"And when might this rape have happened?" Granny asked.

"That's what we're tryin' to figure out," Noble answered.

"I don't suppose you can tell me who it was that was raped," Granny looked from Noble to Sanderson and back again.

"Not with any certainty," Noble answered, "but we think it may have been Rita Burns."

The furrow in Granny's brow let Noble know she was running the name through her memory. She picked up her tea, then set it back down and said, "I don't know that name."

"How 'bout Rita Mosley?" Sanderson asked.

Granny's eyes widened, and for a long minute, she was silent, then in a hushed tone, she said, "That would explain a lot. It would indeed."

CHAPTER 23

Just before noon, unable to sleep any longer, Death rolled out of his makeshift bed and stretched. Cautious as always, he stood silently, listening to the woods around him. The sun had begun to warm the air, and it felt good on his face, but it was the smell that made him feel alive. Dirt and cedar tried to mask the scent of other odors, but if he concentrated, he could detect a faint aroma of damp moss that lined the shadowed places of the small creek. The fragrance of honeysuckle floated along on the soft morning breeze, and for the briefest instance, he almost forgot about the Wolf.

With a smile, he gathered his few belongings and started down the trail toward the Wolf's house. Somewhere in the recesses of his mind, he wondered if he would truly be able to quit killing. After the Wolf and the Shadow were gone, and he had fulfilled Grandmother's wishes, would he—could he—retire? With a chuckle, he shrugged; *only time would tell.*

"Man, I didn't sleep for shit last night," Sanderson rubbed his eyes as he complained.

"Good mornin' to you, too," Noble grinned and handed Sanderson a cup of coffee.

The two leaned against the side of Noble's truck, blowing across the top of the hot bitter liquid that would eventually bring a degree of alertness to their brains. At least, that was the hope.

Sanderson stopped blowing long enough to say, "So, what's the plan?"

Noble watched the steam rising from the top of the black liquid as he blew across his cup once more. The plan was simple, but to speak it aloud would put it into play, and he wasn't sure he was ready to do that yet. Staring at the surface of the coffee, he found himself wondering if death was nothing more than an eternity of constantly looking into a long black, abyss. He shook the thought from his head. This case was getting to him.

"The plan?" Sanderson repeated.

"The plan is to make a visit to each of the judges," Noble continued to stare into his coffee cup as he answered, "and I think it would be better if we did it separately. I feel like Judge Winchester had no hand in any of this, maybe not even any knowledge, but in case he did, I don't want him and Judge Hall callin' each other to get their stories straight, if you know what I mean."

"I do," Sanderson nodded.

"So, which judge do you want to question?" Noble raised an eyebrow as he looked Sanderson's way.

After a second's thought, Sanderson answered, "Truth be told, I'd rather not question either of them, but if I must, I'll take Judge Winchester."

"Why Winchester?" Noble asked.

"When this is all done and behind us," Sanderson shrugged, "I'll still have to work with Judge Hall. Judge Winchester is retired, so it'll be less awkward in the long run."

"Makes sense, I guess," Noble shook his head as he spoke.

"When do you want to make these visits?" Sanderson asked.

"If we're right and Judge Hall is the Wolf and Judge Winchester is the Shadow, then the sooner the better," Noble answered, then with a smile added, "but I reckon we can finish our coffee first.

At ten-thirty, Noble stopped by the courthouse. Judge Hall's secretary informed him that the judge would not be in until after lunch. Seeing no need to cause alarm, he told her he would be back later. On his way back to his truck, he called Sanderson.

"Change your mind about something?" Sanderson asked as soon as he answered.

"Nope," Noble assured him. "Just hit a bit of a snag and need your help."

"Should I turn around and head back to town?" Sanderson asked. Noble could hear the change in the phone's background noise as Sanderson's unit slowed down.

"No, I just need some directions," Noble answered and smiled as he heard Sanderson's vehicle accelerating.

"Directions to where?" came Sanderson's next question.

"Judge Hall's home," Noble answered, then explained, "he's taken the mornin' off and I don't want to wait around for him, so I figured I'd…" The sudden end of highway noise on the line let Noble know Sanderson had hit a dead spot.

After several seconds, the highway noise returned, followed by Sanderson's voice, "Head south on Highway 77 toward Thackerville. Just before you hit Shady Dale Road, turn left on Fossil Creek Drive. His place backs up to the railroad tracks, but I don't know the exact address. I've only been out that way once to drop off paperwork. If memory serves me, there's one of those couple swings made of heavy pine logs out in the front yard."

"Got it," as Noble spoke, once again the road noise disappeared from his phone, and he hoped Sanderson had heard him.

At his truck, he stopped momentarily and watched two squirrels chasing each other around one of the trees in front of the historic building. It was funny how the world kept moving forward no matter what was happening in it. Noble shook his head. He was chasing a killer, and as far as the two squirrels were concerned, this sleepy little Oklahoma town was the perfect place to call home. With a chuckle, Noble opened the door to his truck and climbed in.

A white Chrysler 300 pulling into the parking spot next to his truck caused him to pause before backing out. He waited patiently for the driver to make her way out of the car and onto the sidewalk and then watched her walk toward the courthouse steps. Mesmerized by the sway of her hips beneath the tight beige skirt she wore, he forgot he was in neutral and pressed the gas pedal. The truck engine roared, and the young woman turned. Noble, feeling like the proverbial kid with his hand stuck in the cookie jar, did the only thing he could do, shrug his shoulders and smile.

The young woman smiled back and winked before continuing on. Noble shifted the truck into reverse and slowly backed into the street. At the end of the block, he stopped briefly and then turned left onto Main Street. In his mind, he blamed the squirrels. Logically, he knew they had nothing to do with his inability to look away when a well-stacked female walked by, but to hell with logic; today it was the squirrels' fault.

Before Death made it back to his nest, he heard a vehicle and wondered if the Wolf was returning home for lunch. From the cover of the woods, Death watched as a black truck pulled to a stop in front of the Wolf's house. Even before the driver's door opened, he felt the slow burn of heat in his abdomen. Noble Harris stepped from the vehicle, and the slow burn exploded. Like a bomb blast, Death felt anger and frustration radiate from his core until it encompassed his entire body.

How?! Only he and Grandmother knew the names on the list. Was Noble guessing, or had he figured it out somehow? The answer did not matter. It did not change anything. The Wolf would die. Maybe not tonight, but the Wolf would die!

With effort, Death took a deep breath and let it out slowly. Then he repeated the process. As he inhaled and exhaled, he watched Noble scan the area and then approach the front door. The sound of Noble knocking floated across the clearing, and Death waited.

The Wolf opened the door, and after a short exchange, Noble entered the Wolf's home. Death gritted his teeth and slowly backed into the woods.

"What exactly is this urgent business that couldn't wait?" Judge Hall asked the question as he led the way through an archway into what Noble figured was the formal living room.

He waved Noble toward an overstuffed leather chair and seated himself in one that matched it. Noble waited until he had seated himself before answering, "I suppose you could say, it's about a theory."

"A theory?" The judge shifted in his seat, and Noble could sense the beginning of irritation as the judge spoke.

"Bear with me, please." Noble raised a hand, then lowered it as he continued, "I believe the recent murders are all in response to a specific incident that happened nearly forty years ago." Noble paused briefly, then added, "And I think you're next on the list."

The judge's eyes narrowed, and he glared hard at Noble. Noble held his gaze until the judge looked away. "Fuckin' Billie Hilton," he snarled. "I knew this was gonna to come back to bite us in the ass one day. I told them it would. I told every single one of them."

An eerie silence filled the space between Noble and the judge, and for a long minute Noble let it linger. When it became apparent the judge was not going to elaborate, Noble asked, "So, why didn't you charge the sheriff with the rape of the girl?"

The judge turned back to Noble. The anger was still there, Noble could see it in his eyes, but there was also fear. Noble wondered if it was fear of Lincoln or fear of what this was going to do to his reputation if word got out. "It was his word against hers. The evidence was lost." The judge shrugged and shook his head as he spoke.

"Like I said before, I have a theory, but there are a lot of holes that need to be filled in," Lincoln ran a finger over the scar on his chin. "I think you may be the only person alive that can fill in those holes. So, if you don't mind, let's start at the beginnin'."

The judge looked from Noble to the floor. When he looked back up, several seconds later, he said, "I had just been appointed assistant district attorney for Love County, and, as they say, I was green. One day, I'm in my office doin' paperwork when my secretary tells me there is someone who wants to see me. I didn't have any appointments but from the way my secretary looked at me, I figured I'd better see what was goin' on. Anyway, she ushers in this woman. Her name was Nita Mosley, and she wanted to know why Sheriff Hilton was not in jail."

"How long after the rape was this?" Noble asked.

"Nearly a week," the judge answered with another shrug of frustration.

"What did you do after you found out?"

"Somethin' I should not have done," Judge Hall shook his head. "I called the mayor for advice. Together we had a meeting with Sheriff Hilton, who of course denied the accusations. He claimed that the young woman was unhappy with him because he didn't tip enough when he ate at the restaurant where she worked."

"What about the rape kit?" Noble leaned forward and studied the judge's eyes as he asked.

Once again, the judge's gaze returned to the floor in front of his chair. He inhaled deeply, then exhaled quickly, raising his head and looking at Noble as he did so. "Sheriff Hilton was the one who picked it up from the hospital. At the time, the young woman, Rita Burns, had not identified her assailant. It was her grandmother, Nita Mosley, who was forcing the issue, and since no one knew who had raped her granddaughter, no one knew not to hand the rape kit over to Sheriff Hilton. It wasn't until after he left the hospital with it that Rita told the doctor that it was the sheriff who had raped her."

"Did you ever get results back from the rape kit?" Noble asked.

The judge stared up at the ceiling and exhaled through his nose before saying, "Yes. It was inconclusive."

"So, you covered it up and hoped it would just go away?" Noble's tone was harsh, and he meant for it to be.

"What would you have had me do?" the judge shot back in a tone that matched Noble's.

"Your job," Noble stated flatly, then asked, "What did the good sheriff have on you?"

"Have on me?" Judge Hall repeated the question, but not before Noble caught the glint of guilt in his eyes.

Noble waited.

With a shake of his head, the judge answered, "I was married to my first wife at the time and having affairs with my secretary and the woman who would eventually become Mrs. Hall number two."

Rising from his chair, Noble crossed to a large bay window that looked out across the judge's yard. In the distance, he could see railroad tracks above a line of cedar trees. He scanned the tree line as he considered how best to handle the situation.

"Judge," he began, his voice less harsh but still firm, "the woman who was raped had a son, Lincoln Burns. I went to high school with him, and after we graduated, he just disappeared. Turns out he joined the Marines and became a sniper. As I understand it, a damn good one. Since his return to the area, he has killed Frank Nelson, Sam Wilson, and Hal Spencer. It is my belief that you are next on his list."

"Frank Nelson and Sam Wilson, I know, but who is Hal Spencer?" the judge asked.

"The doctor who performed the exam on Rita Burns," Noble answered, "and then handed it over to Sheriff Hilton."

"Oh," the judge said, and Noble got the impression he was searching his memory for the doctor's name.

"How did Frank Nelson figure into..." At a loss for the

correct word to use, Noble raised his hands in front of himself, half in frustration, half in anger.

"The Mosley woman went to the newspaper office trying to get him to print somethin', anything, that would help get an investigation goin'," the judge explained. "Frank went to Sam Wilson, and the mayor explained the situation. Frank wasn't happy about it. He wanted somethin' done, but… well, as you know, nothin' got done, because there was nothin' that could be done, at least not without bringin' heartache to a lot of folks. That was the beginnin' of the end of Frank and Sam's friendship."

Noble mulled over what the judge had offered so far. The bits and pieces were starting to add up, and a good portion of the puzzle was visible, but he still needed to know the identity of the Shadow.

"Daniel Winchester was the presiding judge at the time of the rape," Noble turned from the window as he spoke. "Did he know about the rape?"

"Not that I'm aware of," Judge Hall answered. "I never took it to him, and even though Nita Mosley tried to press the issue, it was only a matter of a week or so before everyone seemed to have moved on."

"Everyone except Nita Mosley and Lincoln Burns," Noble stated flatly.

"Lincoln Burns was a toddler," the judge rose as he spoke. "I doubt he even remembers…"

Noble interrupted, "That's where you're wrong. Nita Mosley remembered for him, and he's not a toddler anymore."

CHAPTER 24

Death waited a half hour after Noble's girlfriend entered the real estate office before stepping out of his vehicle. It was a dark blue van with an A-to-Z Electric Services decal on both of its sides. He had picked it up in Ardmore on his way to Edmond.

He scanned the parking lot one last time before approaching the door. The chance that something would go wrong was minimal, but as he had learned from past experiences, it was never zero. The plan was simple. Simple plans were less likely to go sideways. He chided himself at the thought. It seemed like everything was going sideways lately.

Opening the door, he stepped inside expecting to be greeted by Noble's girl. He was not. Instead, he found himself in a small reception area. A desk was situated so that it had a view of the front door. It faced four empty chairs that lined the far wall. Death crossed to the desk, half expecting to find a little bell with a note that read "Ring for service."

There was no bell, and before he had time to study the various bits of paper and sticky notes littering the desk, a female voice from somewhere in the back directed him to have a seat and she would be with him in a second. Instead, he stepped around the desk and made his way down the hall. There were three doors along the left side of the hallway, only one was open. He stepped through it quickly and pulled it shut.

At the sound of the door closing, Noble's girl whirled. The shock on her face did not escape Death as he held a finger to his lips. He hoped she would follow the silent instruction and stay quiet.

"Hey, you were supposed to wait up front," the woman's eyes narrowed as the shock faded.

"Yes, I know ma'am," Death smiled, "but I couldn't wait. I'm on a bit of a timetable, you see."

Death could see why Noble had chosen this one. She was not only beautiful, but she had a strength about her that Death liked. He wondered if that strength would be enough to get her through the next twelve hours.

"Oh my," she took a step backward, "you're…you're…"

"I'm Lincoln Burns," Death smiled, "an old friend of Noble's. I believe you know him. And you are?"

Eyes wide, she instinctively reached for the business cards on her desk and then pulled her hand back. "I'm Jacqueline."

"Well, Jacqueline," Lincoln continued to smile, "I need you to take a little ride with me."

Jacqueline shook her head and took another step toward the back corner of the room.

"Now, Jacqueline," Lincoln shook his head, "I really don't want to hurt you, but if you don't cooperate, things could get a bit messy."

Once again, she shook her head, but this time instead of moving farther away, she stepped forward quickly and made a grab for her purse. Her hand disappeared inside. Before she could find whatever it was she hoped would save her, Lincoln crossed the room, pulling a tactical knife from his waistband. A quick, sharp strike to Jacqueline's head with the butt of the weapon, and she crumbled onto the floor.

"Well, I guess this means you're not willing to cooperate," Lincoln shrugged as he bent over, lifted Jacqueline's body from the floor to his shoulder, and opened the office door."

Noble checked the time on his cellphone. It was almost noon. He stood in the judge's driveway, waiting for Sanderson to arrive. The previous night had been uneventful, as had been the longest morning Noble could remember. The judge had called in for another sick day. Noble had spent the night watching over him. After a short discussion with Sanderson, it was decided that it would be best if Sheriff Hughes was not informed of the situation yet. That left the job of babysitting the judge to Noble while Sanderson carried on with his normal deputy's duties.

Noble badly needed a shower and a long nap. He leaned back against his truck and wondered about the identity of the Shadow in Grandmother Mosley's story. Judge Winchester, the presiding judge at the time of the rape, was still his best guess. In his mind, he pictured a judge standing tall against a forested backdrop with his chamber robes spread wide. At dusk or on a moonlit night, he could see why one would consider him a Shadow.

He shook his head to clear the image and thought about calling Davenport to see if he was on his way. Noble had decided to call him in as reinforcements. In his mind, he cursed Ed Hughes. This would be so much easier if he could trust the sheriff and the sheriff's department.

The sound of a train approaching from the south floated across the yard, and Noble turned to watch the tracks. As the engine came into sight, Noble wondered how one became acclimated to the sound of it passing multiple times day and night. The steady clanking of the wheels against the rails threatened to lull him to sleep. He decided a short walk might get the blood flowing and help him stay awake.

As the last car of the train disappeared and its rumbling receded into the distance, Noble heard the faint trickle of water and remembered the small creek he had crossed on his way to the judge's house. For no particular reason, he wandered toward the sound.

The rustle of Jacqueline rousing caused Lincoln to glance briefly over his shoulder. Interstate 35 had a steady flow of traffic, and Lincoln found it necessary to pass a semi hauling cattle before chancing another look at his prisoner.

Jacqueline had rolled onto her back and was studying the zip ties that held her wrists together. The look of confusion on her face caused Lincoln to smile.

"What the hell?" Jacqueline's raspy voice was filled with equal parts of doubt and anger.

"Good mornin' sunshine," Lincoln spoke in his most pleasant tone. "I hope you had a good nap."

In response, Jacqueline kicked the metal screen between them and shouted, "You son of a bitch!"

Lincoln laughed. "Now, sunshine," he chided. "Does this mean we aren't going to be BFFs?"

"What do you want with me?" The volume of Jacqueline's voice had decreased, but the anger behind it seemed to increase with each word.

Keeping an eye on the traffic in front of him, Lincoln reached up and adjusted the rearview mirror so he could see Jacqueline without having to look over his shoulder. She had worked herself into a seated position. Lincoln had used a zip tie to bind her legs together at the ankles and a second to secure her wrists. The combination of restraints and the movement of the van, as he shifted from one lane, to another had Jacqueline swaying back and forth as she tried to stay upright.

Glaring into his eyes in the rearview mirror, Jacqueline raised her voice and repeated, "What do you want with me?" When Lincoln did not answer quickly enough, she shouted, "Answer me, you son of a bitch!"

With a quick jerk of the steering wheel, Lincoln switched lanes once again, this time watching as Jacqueline toppled hard. The sound of her body slamming against the floor made him wince. It had never been his plan to do her harm. She was a means to an end, nothing more, nothing less, but verbal abuse was not something he was willing to endure.

"Since you asked so nicely," Lincoln smiled into the

rearview as he spoke, "what I want from you is your help getting Noble to give up the Wolf."

Lincoln watched as Jacqueline worked her way back into a seated position. This time she managed to get her back against the van's side.

"The wolf?" Jacqueline snarled the question.

"The Wolf, *nashoba*," Lincoln shrugged, "or Judge Hall, take your pick."

The expression on Jacqueline's face told Lincoln that she had no idea of what or who he was speaking. He considered this as he passed the first exit for Purcell.

"We've got time," Lincoln smiled. "How about I tell you a story?"

"How 'bout, not?" Jacqueline answered.

Lincoln chuckled, "Sunshine, that was a rhetorical question."

Jacqueline mumbled something he did not understand, and he chuckled again before speaking. "When I was too young to remember, a man hurt my mother. A man who was supposed to be protecting people, a sheriff. My grandmother tried to get help from the men in the community, but none of them would help. When I was ten years old, my mother left town, and I never saw her again. I spent the next eight years living with my grandmother, and she spent those years helping me to understand my purpose on this earth."

"And what purpose might that be?" Jacqueline asked.

Lincoln smiled into the rearview, "Righting the wrong."

"So, vengeance," Jacqueline scoffed. "You must be so proud of yourself. Huntin' down old men to avenge something that, by your own admission, you don't even remember."

"It's not vengeance or revenge that I'm huntin'," Lincoln felt his ire rising as he spoke.

"Then what is it?" Jacqueline snarled.

Lincoln took several seconds before he answered, "Justice, sunshine; I'm huntin' justice."

The gentle gurgle of running water grew louder as Noble approached the tree line north of the judge's house. Noble found the sound almost mesmerizing. *Mesmerizing*, he thought, and his mind wandered back to a high school English class. If memory served him, it was Mrs. Sanders' class, in his junior year of high school. A discussion of Homer's *The Odyssey* had taken quite a turn.

"What's the difference between harpies and sirens?" Trevor Block asked from the back row. "I mean, they're both women, right?"

"Yes, Trevor, they are both women," Mrs. Sanders confirmed, "but harpies are half-bird, half-woman, while sirens are more like what we think of as mermaids. In addition, harpies were ugly creatures whose screeching was tormenting, while the sirens were portrayed as beautiful creatures with enchanting voices who lured sailors to their deaths."

"So, Lisa is a siren and Dianne is a harpy," Trevor announced, "and the only difference between them is how they're gonna kill ya?"

"Trevor!" Mrs. Sanders' voice had an edge to it.

Trevor reddened, but a grin spread across his face as the classroom erupted. Several of the guys in the room slapped their desktops and shook their heads in agreement. Every girl in the class turned to glare at him. Both Lisa and Dianne were out of their desks and moving toward Trevor.

"Girls!" Mrs. Sanders' voice stopped both girls in their tracks.

"But Mrs. Sanders," Lisa whined.

Dianne glared at Trevor. "Just wait 'til lunch," she threatened.

Noble stopped at the edge of the tree line and shook the memory from his head. From where he stood, he could hear the running water clearly but was still unable to see it. A quick look back at the judge's house, and he began to work his way west toward the railroad tracks.

As he walked, his mind worked. Was the memory of Mrs. Sanders' class some kind of subconscious warning? And if it was a warning, what was the warning? He shook his head and looked back at the judge's house once again. This case is gettin' to ya, man, he thought.

He took several more steps and was about to surrender to the cedar trees and the underbrush that barred his access to the creek when what appeared to be a game trail emerged. Bending low, he pushed aside a tree branch and stepped into the woods. Two steps in, he froze. At the edge of the bare dirt was the imprint of the heel of a boot. Drawing his weapon, he moved carefully past it and made his way to the edge of the creek. There, at the water's edge, he found another partial heel print.

Lincoln had been here. The thought hit him like a punch in the stomach, and he mentally winced and cursed aloud. Holstering his weapon, he turned and started back. If Lincoln had been here, and Noble was nearly certain the heel prints were Lincoln's, then something must have spooked him. Something, or someone, and Noble figured that someone was himself.

Noble felt the disgust rise from his abdomen and work its way up until he spat it out in the form of a string of obscenities. *He knows you're on to him,* played over and over in Noble's mind. Noble stood at the edge of the trees and looked at the judge's house.

"Where are you?" he asked the question aloud. "And what's your next move?"

CHAPTER 25

Lincoln opened the rear doors to the van and smiled at Jacqueline. It had been a long day, more so for her, than for Lincoln. The trip from Edmond to Love County had gone without incident. After the brief conversation they had as they passed the Purcell exits, Jacqueline seemed to retreat into her own little world for the next hour. She refused to even look Lincoln's way.

As they passed the exit for Marietta, she turned and announced that she needed a bathroom. Lincoln chuckled, "You're gonna have to hold it, sunshine. There's no way we're stopping before we get to the Brown Springs Road."

"And how far is that?" Jacqueline snarled.

Lincoln glanced up at the rearview mirror. The hate and defiance in Jacqueline's eyes nearly made him laugh out loud. Instead, he answered, "Ten, maybe fifteen minutes. Twenty at the most."

"And what if I can't hold it?"

"Well, I guess that depends," Lincoln half-chuckled.

"Depends on what?" Jacqueline asked.

"Whether what you have to do is solid or liquid," Lincoln replied with a smirk.

Lincoln watched as confusion furrowed Jacqueline's brow. It took several seconds for the meaning of his answer to register. When it did, Jacqueline's expression shifted from confusion to outright anger, and she hissed, "I need to pee, asshole."

"Well, in that case," Lincoln paused and smiled into the rearview before continuing, "if you can't hold it, then you're gonna smell like piss for the rest of the day."

Jacqueline had indeed held it until they pulled to a stop at the end of one of the dirt roads that led from Brown Springs Road to the Red River. She had cursed him when he refused to unbind her hands so she could relieve herself. She had cursed him even harder when he refused to allow her privacy. He had pointed at a tree, walked ten feet away, and stood so that he could see her in his peripheral vision.

That had been hours ago, and now the sun was slowly making its descent toward the western horizon. Lincoln motioned for Jacqueline to move, and when she did not, he said, "It's time."

"Time for what?" she asked. Her tone, while still defiant, lacked the energy that had been there earlier in the day.

"Time for you to get out of the van and walk with me a little way," Lincoln answered and gestured once again for her to move.

Jacqueline shook her head and scooted further away. Lincoln pulled a black tactical knife from its sheath in the middle of his back and stepped up into the van.

Noble stepped out of his truck and walked to the front door of Granny's house. Sanderson had been called to the other side of the county at the last minute, so Noble had spent the afternoon and most of the evening at the judge's, waiting for him to return. During the wait, he realized that the job of babysitting the judge was going to take more than three people and had called Davenport. Davenport was still finishing up paperwork on a case in the office but said that he would head south as soon as possible.

Frustrated and still unsure of whom to trust, Noble opened the door and stepped inside. Granny's house had always been his safe haven. When life got too hard, it was the one place he could run to and feel like all would be well. Tonight, even Granny's house did not remove the sense of impending doom that had encompassed him all day.

"That you, Noble?" Granny hollered from the kitchen.

"It's me," Noble answered as the aroma of homemade rolls found its way to him.

"You hungry?" she asked as he passed through the living room and stepped into the kitchen.

"Not really," he answered, "just weary and in need of a shower."

Granny turned from the oven with a pan of the rolls, and Noble was glad to know his sense of smell was still intact. It sure seemed to him like all his other senses were failing him lately.

"Looks like more than weariness etched across that forehead of yours," Granny commented as she set the pan of rolls on a hot pad beside the sink.

"Really?" Noble forced a smile.

"Really," Granny stepped close and studied his eyes as she spoke. It was something she had done since he had come to live with her those many years ago. Now, as always, he could feel her searching his very soul with her gaze. When he was young, it made him uncomfortable, but over time it had become therapeutic. Now, as he stood in the kitchen surrounded by the smell of hot rolls, he couldn't help but smile at how this simple act made him relax.

"Weariness and worry don't mix well," Granny's tone was soft and caring, "and I can tell you're worried about something."

As always, Noble found himself amazed at how easy it was for Granny to read his emotions. With a shrug, he agreed, "You're right, I'm a bit worried."

"Wanna talk about it?" Granny asked.

"Maybe later," Noble answered, "but first I really want a shower."

As he turned to go, Granny said, "Worry is not a good bedfellow. It'd be best if you got it off your chest before you go to bed."

Noble knew she was right, but a long, hot shower was what he desired most at the moment. As he made his way down the hall toward the bathroom, he wondered to himself where Lincoln Burns was.

It had always surprised Lincoln at how little pain it took for most people to become instantly compliant. A quick slash of his knife had left a three-inch wound halfway down on the outside of Jacqueline's left arm. It was not a deep cut, just enough to break the skin, but blood ran steadily from it and dripped off her elbow onto the floor of the van.

"Why?" Jacqueline half-whined as she looked from Lincoln to her bloody arm and back again.

"I needed to get your attention," Lincoln shrugged. "Needed you know I was serious."

"But why are you doing this at all?" Jacqueline's tone was almost childish.

Lincoln's brow furrowed as he answered, "I think we've already been over this. I'm righting the wrongs done to my family."

Jacqueline shook her head. "And you think this is your purpose in life?"

"Yes, I do," Lincoln answered.

"Why?" Jacqueline asked. "Because your grandmother told you so?"

"Yes."

"What if she was wrong?" Jacqueline stared into his eyes as she asked the question. Lincoln felt the flush crawl from beneath the collar of his shirt. That this woman, that any woman or person, for that matter, would question grandmother… he felt the edge of guilt as it cut deep. Had he not himself questioned grandmother after killing the Crow?

"She was not wrong," he hissed. "I was wrong to ever doubt her."

As Lincoln picked up a length of rope from the floor of the van, he asked, "Are you going to cooperate or do I need to cut you again?"

Jacqueline shook her head. "Please don't cut me. I'll do whatever you want."

"Alright then, sunshine," he smiled and cut the ties that bound her feet together. "Now move to the back of the van."

Jacqueline did as he asked. He was glad she did. Cutting her had given him no pleasure.

"Are you going to kill me?" Jacqueline asked as she stepped out of the van.

Lincoln smiled at her. "Well, sunshine, that kind of depends on you. If you play along, no…but if you don't, well then…"

"I already told you, I'll do what you ask," Jacqueline reminded him.

"Yes, you did," Lincoln nodded. "Now, if you would please turn around for me, I'm going to tie this rope around your ankle."

"Why?" Jacqueline asked already turning.

"Because, sunshine, we're gonna take a little walk up the road to a special place I know," Lincoln answered. "A place your beloved Noble knows too. And by tying this rope around one of your ankles, I can, if you decide to run or cause any trouble, simply give it a little tug, and well, I think you get the picture."

"I do," Jacqueline said as he tied the rope to her left ankle.

"Good," Lincoln chuckled as he stood. "Then let's get started.

The hot water felt good on Noble's skin. As good as it felt, it was not washing away the feeling that something bad was on the horizon. The first thing that came to Noble's mind was a tornado, massive unpredictable destruction. Everyone running to storm cellars, and those without finding a safe spot to shelter in place. Somehow, this analogy did not ring true. This was not like a tornado; this was more like a hurricane.

Hurricanes were more predictable, and they had a name. There was no sheltering in place when you were in their path. It was best to pack what you could and get to higher ground. Higher ground—Noble's thoughts turned to the judge's house and the train tracks that ran along behind it. Why did Lincoln feel the need to use a knife? He was, after all, a Marine sniper. Why not set up in the wooded area above the judge's house and shoot him when he stepped out the front door to go to work?

Because, Noble thought, a hurricane is predictable and unpredictable at the same time. Depending on the variables driving it, a hurricane might move in one direction, and it might move in another. Trying to understand where it was going to go was about as easy as trying to understand why Lincoln did the things he did.

As Noble turned the water off and stood with his head bowed, he decided the situation he was in was more like a hurricane. He pushed the shower curtain aside and reached for a towel. Hurricane Lincoln ran through his mind. Where it would make landfall, he was fairly certain, but when—was today's six-million-dollar question.

"Where is your grandmother?" Jacqueline asked as she walked in front of Lincoln.

At first, Lincoln thought about not answering her, but after several more steps, he spoke, "She died. Her *shilombish* is at the cemetery, I think, but her *shilup*, it's on its way to *Shilup lyakni*."

"I don't know what any of that means," Jacqueline turned far enough for him to see the outline of her face as she spoke. "What is this *shilombish*?"

"You are not Choctaw," Lincoln said in explanation, "so you do not understand the shadow and spirit."

Jacqueline stopped and turned, "Explain it to me."

Lincoln looked westward. He could not see the sun above the trees, but he knew from the color of the sky that it had almost reached the horizon. It would not be long until it was too dark to see clearly.

"Keep moving and I will tell you," he nodded his head, indicating he wanted her to move again.

"When a Choctaw person dies, the *shilombish*, or shadow, stays here on earth, while the *shilup*, or spirit, travels on a long journey westward to the *Shilup Iyakni*, or the Land of Spirits." For the next several steps, Lincoln wrestled with his thoughts before continuing, "At least that is how Grandmother explained it to me. I'm not sure I really ever understood it all."

"So, you are Choctaw?" Jacqueline asked.

Lincoln chuckled, causing her to turn and look at him. Lincoln shook his head and pointed forward, silently instructing her to continue moving before speaking. "No, I am not Choctaw. I am nothing. I am only purpose."

"What does that mean?" Jacqueline asked. "If your grandmother was Choctaw, then you must be part Choctaw."

Lincoln shook his head. "Grandmother said that one was either Choctaw or they were not Choctaw. There was no in-between. My mother was not Choctaw even though she was Grandmother's granddaughter. My mother's father was white. Because she was not all Choctaw, Grandmother said that was why she had so many of the white man's troubles. Because my mother was not all Choctaw, she had me, and I was also not all Choctaw. I was less Choctaw than my mother, but at least I was born for a purpose; at least that's what Grandmother told me. So, as I said before, no, I'm not Choctaw. I am nothing. I am purpose."

"You are not nothing," Jacqueline stopped once again and turned toward him. "You are a human being. Whether or not you are Choctaw, you are someone. Being part Choctaw does not make you nothing."

"Grandmother said people would tell me this," Lincoln smiled. "She said they would try to tell me this so I would not believe in the purpose I was born for, and they would try to stop me from completing it."

"But..." Jacqueline began.

"No, buts," Lincoln interrupted her. "We are here. We have reached our destination."

He watched Jacqueline as she turned and looked around. The instant her body tensed, Lincoln knew she had seen the weathered headstones that marked the graves of this ancient cemetery.

"You said you were not going to kill me," Jacqueline's words came in a terrified half-whisper.

Lincoln tightened his grasp on the rope tied to her ankle. With his other hand, drew his knife from its sheath.

CHAPTER 26

Noble sat across the table from Granny. After a brief conversation about the case and the need to babysit the judge, Granny sat silently sipping her jelly jar of Gentleman Jack. The hot shower had taken the grim and the edge off but had done little for Noble's sour mood. He hoped that a good night's sleep would help.

"How long do you think you can keep this from the sheriff?" Granny asked between sips.

Noble shook his head. "I have no idea. My gut tells me, Lincoln will make a try for the judge long before I have to worry about the sheriff finding out."

"You know, grandson, it's a dangerous game you're playing here," Granny set her glass on the table as she spoke, "and I'm not just talking about the sheriff. I think maybe you've met your match with Lincoln Burns, and I'm more than a little worried for your safety."

"I've been doin' this for a long time now and I'm pretty good at it," Noble offered, not sure if he was reassuring Granny or himself.

"Yes, you are," Granny agreed. "But even the best loses now and then. Just promise me you'll be careful."

Noble shook his head. "I promise."

"Good," Granny smiled as she retrieved her glass. "Now off to bed with you."

Brown Springs Cemetery in Lincoln's high school days had been a favorite spot for kids to visit, especially around

Halloween. The older boys, mostly, would tell stories of how haunted the place was and then convince whoever was willing to go with them to see if they could spot ghosts. Lincoln had gone on more than one of the 'ghost hunting' excursions but had never seen anything beyond the old gravestones and the eerie moving shadows of tree branches caused by the little wind that found its way through the area.

It was not a pleasant place to visit during the daylight hours, and darkness made it even less appealing. However, it was an excellent way for high school guys to get high school girls' emotions and hormones racing.

Lincoln picked a tree not too far from one of the upright headstones and ordered Jacqueline to sit down against it. Eyes wide, she shook her head and repeated, "You said you weren't going to kill me."

Lincoln smiled. "If all goes well and your boyfriend does as he's told, you might live to see the sun come up. I can promise you this: it will not be me that kills you. Now, please, sunshine, sit down with your back against the tree." Still smiling, he pulled the slack from the rope tied to her ankle, letting her know that if she did not comply, one jerk from him and she would go down hard.

With care, Jacqueline eased herself to the ground. Her hands still bound behind her back, she leaned awkwardly against the tree.

"I'm going to cut one of the ties from your hands. Then I'm going to move your hands so they are in front of you." Lincoln watched her expression as he explained, looking for any signs that she might be thinking of trying to escape. He saw none.

"Please, don't make me hurt you," he spoke the words softly as he cut the zip tie from her left wrist.

The rope held securely in his left hand and the knife in his right, he readied himself, prepared for resistance. None came. Jacqueline moved her hands from behind her back and held them out for him. Quickly he secured them, then removed the rope from her leg and used another zip tie to bind her ankles together. With that done, he used the rope to secure her firmly to the tree. Stepping back, he surveyed his work.

"What now?" Jacqueline looked up at him and asked.

"Now, sunshine, we see what your boyfriend is made of," Lincoln answered.

Noble's cellphone vibrated on the bedside table as soon as his head hit the pillow. He picked it up in time to see Jacqueline's face and number flash across the screen. Guilt oozed from somewhere in Noble's core. He had been so busy with the case that he had not called to let her know he was still in Love County and planning to spend the night at Granny's. Tossing the covers aside, he sat up and tapped accept.

"Hey there," he said into the phone.

"Hey there yourself," a man's voice returned.

Confused and shocked, Noble removed the phone from his ear and checked to see if he, in his exhausted state, had been mistaken about who was calling. Jacqueline's face and number were still on the screen.

"Who the hell is this?" Noble asked as he hit the speaker icon.

A series of beeps followed before the man spoke again. "Check your texts. I've sent you a very special message. We'll talk after you've watched the video."

"What?" Noble knew his mind was playing catch-up and losing.

"Check your messages and watch the fucking video," the man's voice was harsh and filled with irritation. "I'll wait."

Noble did as instructed. Once he had video up, he watched and listened.

The video began with what appeared to be a cemetery. An old, weathered headstone lit by what seemed to be a flashlight filled the frame. As the light moved, the frame widened and shifted to another headstone and then another.

"Hello, old friend," the same voice that had ordered him to watch now accompanied the video. "If you haven't figured it out by now, it's me, Lincoln Burns and it appears we have a bit of a situation. You see you're keeping me from completing my mission, and while the cat-and-mouse game was fun for a little while, I now find it tiresome. So, here's the deal. You bring me the Wolf, and I'll give you back Jacqueline." The camera nearly blurred the image as it swiftly shifted from a downed headstone to a bloodied Jacqueline tied to a tree. "I believe you know the place." And with that, the video ended.

"You son of a bitch," Noble hissed.

"Now, now," Lincoln chuckled. "Is that any way to talk to an old friend?"

"If you hurt her, I'll kill you," Noble snarled.

"I have no desire to hurt her," Lincoln assured him, "but the wild hogs that roam these woods have probably already caught the scent of her blood. I can't promise you what they'll do when they arrive, but I can promise you this: if you don't get here first with the Wolf, I will watch them tear her apart. I'll even record it and send it to you."

"You son of a bitch," Noble repeated.

Lincoln's tone turned hard and serious. "And Noble, if you don't bring the Wolf or if you don't come alone, I will cut her throat from ear to ear. You have one hour. See you soon, buddy." And the line went dead.

Frantic, Noble called Jacqueline's phone. It went to voicemail after two rings. He called again, same result. Heart pounding, he grabbed clothes from the closet and began to dress. Somewhere in the far recesses of his brain, a voice was shouting for him to slow down and think things through. He ignored it.

Jacqueline was in trouble. He knew exactly where she was but not how long she had been there or how badly she was hurt.

There had been blood on her forehead, arms, and down the front of her blouse. He thought about watching the video again but decided against it. Get dressed, drive fast, save Jacqueline, kill Lincoln—his mind seemed to be playing the loop over and over.

Dressed and ready, he started down the hall for the living room and met Granny coming from the kitchen. The confusion on her face asked the question before she could.

"Lincoln has Jacqueline," Noble stated flatly. "I've got to go."

The speedometer on Noble's truck registered one hundred miles per hour as he passed the Valero station on Oswalt Road. He slowed to sixty and barely managed to keep the truck on the southbound ramp for Interstate 35. The little voice was back, now, and in addition to warning him to think before acting, it was also telling him that he would be no good to Jacqueline if he rolled his truck. He ignored the voice and accelerated onto the interstate.

His mind raced. He had seen what wild hogs could do to a body. It was not pretty. Panic-stricken, he shouted above the roar of the engine, "Siri, call Sanderson."

Sanderson picked up on the second ring. "Lincoln's got Jacqueline at Brown Springs Cemetery," Noble shouted as soon as he heard the click. "He wants to trade her for the judge."

"What do you need from me?" Sanderson asked, the shock in his voice did not escape Noble.

"You're closer," Noble answered. "Head that way, and I'll meet you there."

"You want me to bring the judge?" The confusion in Sanderson's voice was clear.

"No," Noble replied. "Davenport should be on the road by now. I'll call him and tell him to get his ass to the judge's quick. We can't trade the judge for Jacqueline, but we can't let

Jacqueline…" Noble's voice trailed off. He could not speak the words.

"Got it," Sanderson said. "I'm on my way out the door now."

"Good," Noble accelerated around a slow-moving semi truck. "And, Sanderson, tell the judge to arm himself just in case."

Noble tapped the end icon without waiting for Sanderson's response and shouted, "Siri, call Davenport."

"What's up?" Davenport asked after the third ring.

"Lincoln Burns has Jacqueline," Noble knew he was shouting but could not seem to help it. He knew it was the adrenaline.

"Where?" Davenport asked, his voice louder than usual now.

"Brown Springs Cemetery," Noble answered. "But I need you to go to the judge's house and make sure this isn't a trick."

"Got an address?" Davenport inquired.

Noble shouted the address and then asked, "How far out are you?"

"South of Ardmore," Davenport responded. "I've got it floored. I'll be there as quick as I can."

"Thanks," Noble hit the end icon as the lights of Marietta came into view.

Lincoln smiled as he watched a deputy run from the judge's house, get into his cruiser, and speed away into the night. True love and friendship—two vices that can make even the most professional of people screw up. Lincoln laughed at the thought, then shook his head. Tonight, he was not Lincoln; tonight, he was Death, and this was no laughing matter.

Quickly he moved from the edge of the woods to the side of the Wolf's den, for that was how he thought of the structure. Inside was the Wolf, no doubt armed and ready but now was not the time for fear. After all, he was Death, and what was there for Death to fear?

Slowly, Death worked his way around to the rear of the house. The back door was solid, with no window. He continued past a set of curtained windows, careful to stay low, made the corner, and squatted near the corner of a large, solid plate glass window he figured must either belong to a den or the living room. With caution, he eased his head up far enough to see inside. Instantly, there was movement in the shadows at the rear of the room. Instinctively, he dropped to the ground as two shots rang out. Glass rained down on him as a section of the window exploded outward.

Quickly, he pushed himself from the ground and sprinted toward the front door. Another bullet cracked the middle of the window behind him. At the door, he grabbed the knob and turned. As he had expected, it was locked. Two more shots pierced the door as he turned and retraced his steps to the window. Now the question was: did the Wolf's pistol, for he knew it was a pistol by its sound, hold five shots or six? He hoped it was five as he circled wide and launched himself through what was left of the shattered window.

He hit the window solidly, and it gave way. Momentum carried him into the room, and he rolled to a stop, covered in glass, knife in hand. The glint of light hitting moving metal answered his question about how many rounds the Wolf's gun held, and a split second before the revolver erupted, he rolled to his left.

The sound of spent cartridges hitting the hardwood floor told Death all he needed to know. Still in a crouched position, he took three long strides toward the sound and launched himself at the shadowed figure holding the gun. Whether the Wolf saw or sensed him, he did not know, but the Wolf threw his hands up to protect himself. The movement would be the Wolf's last. Death slid his knife between the upraised hands as the full weight of his body hit the Wolf. The tip of the knife entered the Wolf's throat below his Adam's apple, and momentum pushed it well into the cranial cavity.

Both Death and the Wolf hit the floor hard. Death jerked the knife free and, in one swift motion, sliced the Wolf throat from ear to ear. As the Wolf's body spasmed, Death rolled away into the darkness and listened for any further danger. He heard none.

A minute passed, and then two. When his eyes had adjusted to the darkness and he was satisfied that all was good, he stood and surveyed the room. Bits of glass covered the floor, sparkling now and again as light from some unknown source hit them. The legs of a piece of furniture, possibly an end table, stuck out from a dark corner. Death smiled. It was done. The Wolf was dead.

Stepping back to where the Wolf's body lay, Death knelt and drove his knife deep into the hardwood floor near the Wolf's head. With a smile, he laid Jacqueline's cellphone next to the knife and made his way slowly through the house to the back door. Beside the door, he found a panel of light switches. Hoping one of them was for the security lights, he flipped them all before opening the door and stepping into the darkness.

CHAPTER 27

Noble slowed just enough to take Exit 1. At the top of the ramp, he turned left without stopping at the stop sign. Luckily, the traffic light on the east side of the interstate was green. The Chickasaw Travel Stop was little more than a blur as he passed it and slowed just enough to make the turn onto Brown Spring Road.

Almost instantly, the paved road ended. Caution outweighed panic in Noble's mind as he drove south. He slowed slightly. It had been years since he had driven down the dirt road to Brown Spring Cemetery, and he was afraid he would miss the path that led from the road to the cemetery.

The road curved to the east, and he slowed more. Heart racing, mouth dry, he swallowed hard and stared at the edge of the road, looking for the pull off and hoping it was not so overgrown he would not recognize it.

A break in the trees ahead of him came into view, and at the same time, a vehicle with its high beams on braked hard behind him. Praying he was right, he made a hard left as the trees cleared. The truck came to a stop inches from the trunk of a large scrub oak. The car that had nearly rear-ended him pulled to a stop right behind his truck. Noble threw the door open and stepped out, gun leveled at the driver's window.

Hands raised, Sanderson stepped out of his vehicle. "Hey, partner, it's me! It's me, Noble! Don't shoot!"

Noble lowered his weapon but did not holster it. "Let's go," he said, turning and reaching into his truck for a flashlight as he spoke.

Together, the two started up a narrow, well-worn footpath. Noble led the way.

"What if it's a trap?" Sanderson asked in a half-whisper.

Without turning around, Noble answered, "Then shoot anything that moves, just make sure it's not Jacqueline."

The little voice in his head was back. Rushing in as he was doing was rash and stupid. He knew that already; he did not need it to tell him. It reminded him that it was not only his own self he was putting in danger's way. Sanderson had a wife who needed him to come out of this still breathing. He tried to shake the voice from his head; it would not leave.

Several more steps, and he shut his flashlight off and stopped. Sanderson stepped up close and did likewise.

"I don't know what we're walkin' into here," Noble half-snarled through clenched teeth. "It could be nothin'. It could be shots in the dark or a knife in the back, so keep your head on a swivel."

"Got it," Sanderson nodded. "What about Jacqueline?"

"I'll take care of Jacqueline," Noble answered. "You cover me."

Sanderson nodded again, and after allowing his eyes to acclimate to the darkness, Noble started up the trail once more. The distant sound of traffic on the interstate floated through the night air. The earthy smell of decaying vegetation mingled with cedar trees encompassed Noble as the adrenaline coursed through his body, heightening his senses. The sound of a twig breaking off to his left caused him to pause briefly. Eyes wide, he stared into the darkness. Nothing there, only the shadows of trees and underbrush. He started forward again.

The trail ended. Shapes of what Noble knew to be grave markers appeared. He moved quickly to the nearest tree and motioned for Sanderson to do the same in the opposite direction. Eyes straining, heart beating loudly in his ears, he surveyed the shadows from left to right. Something rustled in the underbrush to his left. He could see nothing. The sound grew closer and then he heard it—a whimper.

It came from his right, and without thinking or caring, he

moved from one tree to another in the direction from which it had come. Whatever, or whoever, was to his left, moved again, and the whimpering stopped. Noble squatted, gun ready, and waited.

Minutes passed. Quietness all around. Nothing moved. The air felt thick and stagnant. Slowly, the subtle sounds of the night began again. Every muscle in his body tensed as Noble fought the urge to turn on his flashlight and shoot the first thing that moved.

Again, a whimper. Very soft, but closer this time. He moved, stopped, listened, moved again. What appeared to be the shape of legs and feet stuck out from behind a tree fifteen feet away. Staying low, Noble moved quickly.

Five feet, ten feet, and he was there. Jacqueline's eyes, filled with terror, looked up at him as he rounded the tree. The long piece of cloth gagging her had been tied behind her head and then used to tie her head firmly to the tree. He raised a finger to his lips as he holstered his weapon and pulled a pocketknife from his pants. Carefully, he cut the cloth that held her head and then cut it again and removed it from her mouth.

"Where is Lincoln?" Noble asked as he cut the zip ties from her hands.

Her voice coarse and raspy, she mumbled, "Don't know."

"Is he here?" Noble asked as he cut the ties from her ankles.

"Left," Jacqueline choked as she answered.

Noble prayed she was right as he screamed into the night, "Sanderson, I've got her. Gonna turn on my light. Don't shoot."

Death stood at the edge of the Wolf's house. Caution was his ally, and while he had seen the deputy leave, he wanted to make sure the Wolf's gunshots had not aroused any nosy neighbors. He studied the space between where he stood and the wooded area at the edge of the property. A hundred-yard sprint and he would be back under cover at the tree line. From there, it was a half-mile jog through the trees along a game path and then up an incline to the railroad tracks. One last scan of the area, and he darted from his hiding place toward the trees.

Ten yards, twenty yards—all seemed well—then he heard the roar of a motorcycle engine. It sounded like it was getting closer. He picked up the pace. Thirty yards, forty yards, and a single beam of light passed over him. Fifty yards, and now he was in full sprint.

Above the roar of the cycle's engine, he heard a man yelling but could not make out the words. Sixty yards, and once again the light found him, only this time it stayed with him. Seventy yards, and the light became brighter. The damn fool rider was off-road, trying to run him down. Eighty yards, and he broke hard right out of the light and back into the darkness. Another twenty yards, and he would be in the trees.

The sound of a shot rang out, and the whistle of a bullet screaming past him caused him to duck and roll. He came out of the roll running and dove for the space between two trees just as a second shot rang out and something hit him in the left shoulder hard enough to spin him mid-air.

He hit the ground hard. Light from the motorcycle's headlamp flooded the area to his left. He belly-crawled twenty feet to his right and then rose into a half-crouch, pushing through the underbrush until he found the game trail. The sound of two more shots cut through the night, but neither of the projectiles came close enough for him to hear.

His shoulder ached. He knew he had been hit, but now was not the time to worry about how badly. One step in front of the other, he raced along the edge of the creek until he reached the railroad embankment. A quick look back, and he started up it. His wounded shoulder refused to support his weight, and twice he slid several feet before regaining his footing. Laboring for breath, he reached the top and prayed that no trains were scheduled. He turned north and began to run.

The sound of distant sirens let him know he needed to hurry. His lungs ached, his shoulder throbbed, and still, he ran. The lights of a vehicle crossing the tracks in front of him let him know he was nearly there. McGehee Road, it had not been the ideal spot, but timing had left him few choices. Parked thirty yards south of the road on the gravel below the tracks, it had been a gamble. Anyone could have seen it and called it in. Death sighed with relief when the van appeared.

Breathing heavily, he slowed to a walk and listened for any sign of trouble. At the van, he opened the door, cringed when the dome light came on, stepped up into the driver's seat, and closed the door quickly. He was fairly certain the motorcycle rider had not followed him, but he saw no sense in taking a chance on it. When no shots came, he started the vehicle and prayed he could make it to the interstate and be out of the area before the cavalry arrived.

"I think I've got to call it in," Sanderson looked nervously at Noble as he spoke.

Noble looked up at him from where he sat on the ground holding Jacqueline. "I know," he nodded his head in agreement. "I'm sorry."

As Sanderson turned to walk away, Noble pulled Jacqueline closer and whispered softly, "It'll be okay."

Jacqueline shook her head against his chest but said nothing. A black nothingness formed in the pit of Noble's stomach and slowly began to spread outward. He was going to kill Lincoln Burns. The voice of reason emerged from the recesses of his mind long enough to remind him that he was an officer of the law and, as such, should not think such thoughts. Noble sent the voice away with two simple words—"Fuck that."

Jacqueline snuggled closer. Noble's flashlight lay on the ground beside the couple. The beam of light widened as it stretched out into the darkness. A dozen yards away, it illuminated an ancient headstone. Noble stared at it, not really seeing it. The world that had once been a large, exciting place had quickly closed in around him. A darkness that he could not explain pushed away every thought but two—get Jacqueline to the hospital and kill Lincoln Burns.

He heard the sirens long before anyone arrived.

Death pulled the van onto the road and drove west. Highway 77 and Interstate 35 seemed like bad ideas. From the sound of sirens wailing, every law enforcement officer in the county was out. He tried to remember the area and roads west of the interstate, but it had been too many years. Highway 32 was north, of this, he was sure. An intersection appeared, he rolled to a stop at the faded red, bullet riddled sign and looked both ways. No vehicles appeared, so he turned north. What seemed to be a rural road quickly ran into a more heavily populated neighborhood as soon as he passed a wrecker yard.

His heart nearly exploded when the lights of a police vehicle came to life several hundred feet in front of him. Slowing, he reached for his bag in the passenger seat. Before he could retrieve the gun from it, the vehicle backed into the road in front of him and, siren wailing, took off. He held back until he saw the lights turn east.

At the intersection where the police car had disappeared, he found Highway 32. Turning west, he grimaced. The Wolf was dead, but all had not gone as planned, and now he was injured. He told himself he was lucky to be alive. The pain in his shoulder suggested otherwise. It looked and felt like the Shadow was going to have to wait a bit longer than scheduled. He hoped Grandmother would be understanding.

The silhouette of three oil storage tanks appeared north of the highway. Death checked his rearview. No headlights as far as he could see. He slowed, and when he was sure there was no locked gate, he turned and crossed the cattle guard leading to them.

Putting the van in park, he shut off the headlights. He hated to stop at all, but the bullet wound in his shoulder needed checking. With effort, he pulled his bag closer, took the gun from it, and laid it on the passenger seat within reach. In the bottom of the bag, he found one of the two flashlights he had packed, pulled it out, and clicked it on. In the light from it, he examined himself. The bullet had hit him in the back to the right and just below his left armpit. It had exited half an inch below his collarbone. Blood covered the front and side of his shirt and had soaked the top portion of his pants. The pants would have to wait, he thought to himself as he started to pull off the bloodied shirt. It was more painful than he planned, and he screamed aloud.

Once he regained control, he slowly eased his right arm out, then his head, and finally pulled the shirt down over his left arm and tossed it on the floor of the van. Checking the wound once again, he began to laugh. Adrenaline and pain mixed to form an emotional cocktail of chaos and relief.

Still laughing, he tore a clean shirt into strips and made a temporary bandage for his shoulder. Later, when he was miles away, he would do a better job of it. Right now, he was alive, and that was all that mattered. That and getting well enough to kill the Shadow.

CHAPTER 28

Noble sat across the desk from Tom Jack and Sheriff Hughes in the Love County Sheriff's office. Sanderson sat to his right, Davenport to his left. Hughes was seated, Tom Jack stood slightly to the left of Hughes, a scowl on his face and arms folded across his chest.

"And you decided that I didn't need to be included in the loop?" Hughes repeated the question again.

Sanderson reddened and looked at Noble, who began to explain, "We had very little to go on. It was more of a gut…"

Hughes shifted his glare to Noble long enough to say, "I was talkin' to my deputy, not you."

Noble pushed himself up out of the chair he was in, intending to leave. With his face a dark crimson red and his jaw clenched down hard, he told himself not to say anything and not to swing. Before he had taken a step, Tom Jack bellowed, "Noble, you set your ass right back down." Without even watching to see if his order was followed, he turned on Hughes, "And you sir, will show some fuckin' respect. You asked for help from my department, and I sent Noble down here to this backwater hick town, and from what I've heard and seen, he and Deputy Sanderson have been cleanin' up a mess you should have handled twenty-some-odd years ago."

Hughes was on his feet facing Tom Jack before Tom Jack finished his last sentence. The two faced off like two old bulls out on the range. Noble, who had returned to his seat, stood once again. The office was small, and Noble did not want to be stationary if fists started flying. For a long minute, time stood still.

The only sound was the hum of the air conditioner. The musky smell of anger filled the room, and Noble realized both Sanderson and Davenport were on their feet.

"Screw you and screw your department," Hughes looked down on Tom Jack and snarled, "I've got a dead judge here to go along with a dead barber and a dead newspaper editor."

Noble watched and waited for Tom Jack's response. In his mind, he wondered who would win if the two decided to throw down. Hughes had a good three or four inches on his boss and probably outweighed him by at least eighty pounds, but Hughes was soft. Tom Jack was solid as a rock, and Noble seemed to remember someone saying Tom Jack had boxed in the Army.

"Like I said," Tom Jack snarled back, bits of spittle shooting from the edge of his mouth, "something you should have handled twenty years ago. Now we can all sit down and be civil, or…" his brow narrowed, and he let the 'or' hang in the air for several seconds, "me and Noble and Davenport can drive north, forget this godforsaken county even exists, and leave you to clean up your own mess."

Tension hung in the air. Noble watched as Hughes moved through a series of emotions. The angry squint of his beady eyes faded, and concern furrowed his brow, then wrinkled his forehead. Noble had seen too many bullies in his time not to recognize the signs of one folding under pressure. Concern turned to something akin to fear, and Hughes took a step back. Noble could almost see the wheels of Hughes's pathetic little brain turning. If he and Tom Jack left, there would be no one to shuffle blame onto except Sanderson, and this was too big a mess to pin on one sheriff's deputy.

"No need for that," Hughes returned to his seat as he spoke, then looked up at Noble. "You were saying?"

Noble looked from Hughes to Tom Jack. Tom Jack nodded at the chair Noble had been seated in. With a shrug, Noble sat down. Sanderson and Davenport followed suit.

"I was sayin' the reason we did not include you and your

department was the same reason I did not contact my own boss. We just weren't sure if we were on the right track. After we talked to the judge, it became clear that we were on to somethin', but before we could get all our proverbial ducks in a row…well, the shit hit the fan."

"How long ago was this talk with the judge?" Hughes asked.

"Less than forty-eight hours ago," Noble answered. "Had Lincoln not kidnapped my girlfriend, we would have filled you in." That was an outright lie, but Noble knew Sanderson was the only other person who knew it was a lie and figured Sanderson was not going to oust him.

"So, your story is it just happened so quick that you didn't have time to fill me in?" Hughes directed the question at Sanderson. Noble turned to his friend and waited.

Sanderson nodded, "That's affirmative. We talked to the judges late in the evenin' the night before last. It seemed like we might be on to something, but it also didn't seem important enough to get you out of bed for…in hindsight, it was."

"You think?" Hughes huffed.

Tom Jack pulled air between his teeth, making a sucking sound. Hughes did not turn or look up at him, but the expression on his face told those in front of him that he had received the message.

"And how do you fit into this cluster?" Hughes looked at Davenport as he spoke.

"Granny Harris's biscuits," Davenport answered, drawing heavily on his New Jersey accent. "I believe she makes some of the best damn biscuits I've ever tasted. Gravy and biscuits with three or four fried eggs and a couple of slices of thick-cut bacon, yes sir, it may be the only thing worth coming to this county for."

Even as exhausted and irritated as Noble was, he found himself fighting hard to suppress a grin at Davenport's response and Hughes's confused look. A quick glance at Tom Jack told Noble that his boss failed to see the humor. As usual, Davenport did not seem to notice, or if he did, he did not care.

"Me and Noble, here," Davenport indicated Noble with a nod of his head as if Hughes might not know the Noble he was speaking of, "well, we work together sometimes. Mostly we work on our cases alone, but sometimes we work together. And even when we work cases alone, we kind of bounce thoughts and ideas off each other. Anyway, Noble promised me a warm bed and one of Granny Harris's fabulous breakfasts if I'd come down and bounce some ideas around with him. I guess that's the long answer as to how I fit into this cluster. If you want the short answer, I guess it would be that I'm the Tigger."

Noble was not sure where Davenport was going with his response, but he had a feeling it was not going to end well. Tom Jack's brow was furrowed so hard his eyes were squinted nearly shut. Noble chanced a glance at Sanderson, who looked as confused as everyone else.

"The Tigger?" Even as Hughes asked the question, Noble head began to shake.

With a smile, Davenport answered him in a sing song voice, "The wonderful thing about Tiggers is that Tiggers are wonderful things. They bounce and bounce and bounce. Oh, it's lots and lots of fun. And all the bad guys go to jail when all the bouncing is done."

Noble stared at the floor and shook his head. Sanderson tried but failed to suppress a laugh, then attempted to cover it with a cough. Tom Jack roared, "Davenport out!" and pointed at the door.

With a smile, Davenport stood up, gave the red-faced Hughes a smug half-smile, turned, and walked from the room. Sanderson managed to get his fake coughing fit under control as Tom Jack turned his attention to Noble, "Paid leave until after a full investigation. You can hang on to your badge and gun, but consider yourself off duty until further notice. Now, unless the sheriff has any more questions, I think it's time for us to go."

His face still red, Hughes shook his head, then turned to Sanderson, "Same goes for you. Paid leave, but you can leave your badge and gun with me until after the investigation."

Pissed, Noble stood too quickly and sent the chair he had been seated in skidding across the floor. With a shake of his head and one last glare at Hughes, he headed for the door. The sound of Sanderson's badge and gun hitting the desktop echoed in his ears. He was pissed. Pissed at Hughes. Pissed at Lincoln Burns. But mostly, pissed at himself for putting Sanderson in a bad situation. He vowed to himself he would find a way to make it right.

Lincoln Burns sat naked on the edge of the bathtub in the Big Falls Motel in downtown Wichita Falls, Texas. The medical supplies he had stolen in the middle of the night from a veterinarian's business in Nocona, Texas, were laid out beside him. There was a late-model two-tone Ford truck parked outside his motel room door. He had picked it up in the early morning hours as he passed through Ringgold, Texas. It had been parked in the yard of an old gray-weathered house along with about two dozen other vehicles. He had parked the stolen van as far as possible from the highway at the end of a row of cars in various stages of decay.

Now with care, he tested his shoulder. Throughout the night, he had forced himself to move it, knowing that if it stiffened up, it would slow down his ability to use it for a longer period. A doctor might well have disagreed with his logic, and when he had removed the temporary bandage and saw the amount of blood that was clotted to it, he wondered at his own thought process.

Gritting his teeth, he leaned forward and poured the antiseptic soap down the back of his shoulder, cleaning the entry wound as best as he could with a wet washcloth. The pain was intense. Standing, he turned the shower handle to adjust the water's temperature, pulled up on the diverter valve, and stepped under the showerhead. The warm water flowed over his body, causing a pinkish-brown liquid to careen down his body and into the tub drain.

When he was satisfied that he was clean, he pressed a hotel hand towel against the exit wound with his left hand and a dry washcloth against the entrance wound with his right hand. Still dripping water, he stepped from the shower and walked to the counter. He looked at himself in the mirror and cursed aloud. The image staring back at him reminded him of the Twister game he had seen played at parties when he was a kid. Left hand to left shoulder, right hand behind the back to…he was exhausted and nearing delirium.

He turned so that he could see the entrance wound in the mirror and pulled the washcloth away from it. A trickle of blood ran from the wound. He ignored it and readied a large waterproof two-by-two bandage with antiseptic ointment. When he had it ready, he used the washcloth to quickly wipe away the new blood and placed the bandage over the wound.

Blood had soaked through the hand towel held against the exit wound. He found himself wishing a bandage would take care of it as well. He knew it would not. He had seen the wound. It needed stitches. As much as he hated to, he picked up the curved needle. Thankful that the sutures were pre-threaded, he pressed the point of the needle through the skin and as deep as possible into the muscle, then worked it to the other side, up through the skin. Sweating profusely, he managed to tie the first stitch in place.

He repeated the process until he was satisfied that the wound would not bleed. Dropping the needle in the sink, he reached for a second bandage, and his knees buckled. Grabbing the edge of the counter for support, he steadied himself and willed himself to finish the job. He loaded the new bandage with antiseptic ointment and placed it over the stitches, as the edge of his vision began to blur.

He stepped out of the bathroom and started for the bed. Blackness closed in around him, and he felt himself falling.

CHAPTER 29

Noble found Davenport at the bottom of the courthouse steps. He was sporting his usual shit-eating grin.

"Guy's an asshole," he stated flatly as Noble reached the bottom step.

Noble nodded his agreement, "Can't argue with you on that one, partner. Man, I'm sorry I got you into this shit."

Davenport laughed, "Like I've never got you into shit before. Don't sweat it. It'll pass."

Footsteps on the stairs behind him caught Noble's attention, and he turned to see Tom Jack glaring at him and Davenport. Noble knew Tom Jack was a creature of habit. His boss rolled out at five-thirty every morning, Sunday being the exception, and jogged a three-mile loop around his neighborhood. After which, he had breakfast and got ready for work. He drove the same route to work, parked in the same spot, and ate the lunch his wife had made him while sitting at his desk in his office. Noble also knew that having to alter his habits in any way would have put Tom Jack in a nasty mood, but having to come all the way to Love County for a meeting about the cluster he and Davenport found themselves had elevated that nasty mood to a whole new level.

"What the hell is wrong with you?" Tom Jack started on Davenport from halfway down the steps.

Davenport shrugged, "The guy's an asshole."

"Asshole or not, he's the sheriff of this county and deserves some respect," Tom Jack glared as he reached the bottom of the steps.

"Asshole deserves to be shot and quartered," Davenport returned.

"Now you listen here…" Tom Jack began.

"Do you respect him?" Davenport interrupted him.

Tom Jack's lips moved, but no sound came. His eyes narrowed, and he stared hard at first Davenport and then Noble. He inhaled deeply as if to gain control and then exhaled.

"I'll need your weapon," he stuck his hand out toward Davenport as he spoke.

"What?" Davenport drew back. "Why?"

"You fired it," Tom Jack answered.

"I fire it multiple times a week," Davenport replied, "and you don't take it from me."

Hand still outstretched, Tom Jack's tone hardened, "Yes, but last night you shot at someone."

"Not just someone," Davenport argued, "and I didn't just shoot at him. It was Lincoln Burns. You know, the guy that killed the judge, and I didn't just shoot at him. I hit him."

"Exactly," Tom Jack responded. "And because you shot and hit the suspect, I need your weapon. It's procedure. You'll get it back when…"

"Yeah, yeah, yeah," Davenport interrupted as he took his department-issued Glock still holstered and handed it to Tom Jack.

Tom Jack took it, stared hard at Davenport, and pointed north, "I think you should forget about Granny Harris and her biscuits and gravy. It's time for you to head back to the office. I'm sure there's some paperwork you can catch up on, and I don't need you and Noble down here stirrin' up more of a shitstorm." Turning to Noble, Tom Jack asked, "What's your plan?"

Noble shrugged, "Grab a few things from Granny's, pick up Jacqueline from the hospital, and head home."

Tom Jack's tone softened, "Give her my best. You take the day off and come see me in the office tomorrow." Then he turned on his heels and started down the walkway toward his vehicle.

"Right behind you, boss," Davenport shouted after him, then turned to Noble, "What's the plan, partner?"

Noble shrugged, "I'll let you know when I know. I'm havin' trouble wrappin' my mind around anything right now. I need to make sure Jacqueline's okay and then…" He shrugged again.

"And then we kill the son of a bitch," Davenport finished the sentence for him.

"Which son of a bitch?" Sanderson, who had approached silently from the other side of the building, asked.

Both Noble and Davenport turned and answered, "Lincoln Burns."

Sanderson nodded his agreement.

"Anything I can do to help?" Granny Harris asked from the doorway of his bedroom as Noble tossed items into his overnight bag.

Noble shook his head. His body was running on autopilot. The adrenaline that had kept his brain functioning through the night had cleared his system before sunrise, and since then, he had been running on sheer determination. He kept telling himself that if he just put one step in front of the other, sooner or later, he would make it through the current shitstorm, and then he could rest.

"Are you sure?" Granny asked. "You look rough, grandson."

"I'm sure," Noble answered. "And I feel pretty rough, but I'll be okay."

He looked around the room, double-checking to see that he had not missed something, then zipped his bag. Hoisting it, he turned to face his grandmother. He knew that she was able to read every emotion etched on his face, so he did not try to hide them from her. Frustration had deepened the lines in his forehead, but anger was the cause of the clenched jaw and fire in his eyes.

"Where to from here?" Granny asked.

"Gonna pick up Jacqueline from the hospital and take her home," Noble answered.

"Your apartment or hers?" Granny asked.

"Whichever one she wants," Noble answered.

"Alright then," Granny stepped aside as she spoke. "I know she's important to you, but you need to know you're important to me, so take you take care of my grandson. Okay?"

Noble forced a smile. "Okay."

Granny followed him to the front door and insisted on a hug before he left. It wasn't until he was halfway to the interstate that he realized he had not told her Davenport had shot Lincoln.

Sirens wailed outside Lincoln's motel. Lincoln fought the officers who had crashed through his door and were trying to subdue him. He kicked. He punched. He bit. But there were too many of them. His gun was inches away on the bedside table, but he could not reach it for the weight pressing down on him. He managed to get free and roll onto his stomach. Pain exploded from his shoulder and shook him to the core. He fought nausea as he reached for his weapon. His hand wrapped around the grip and his finger found the trigger. He fired once, twice, three times. The sound was deafening.

Again, the sound—once, twice, three times—this time, followed by a female voice, "Housekeeping. Do you need service this morning?"

Lincoln fought through the curtain of darkness, grasping for reality. The pain and fever threatened to drag him back under, and he knew if the voice from the other side of the door opened it, he was done. Summoning everything he had, he answered, "Not today!"

"Alright then," the voice returned, "if you change your mind or need anything, call the front desk."

It was only a dream, he reassured himself as he looked around the dimly lit room—only a dream. He thought about sitting up but could not find the strength, so instead, he grabbed the edge of the thin comforter, pulled it over himself, and drifted back into the darkness.

Noble made his way down the second floor hallway of the hospital. The receptionist at the front desk had been kind enough to give him Jacqueline's room number, and he found himself hoping that it would not be long before a doctor released her. He was about as fond of hospitals as he was of "old folks' homes," and in his present mood, he was not sure he had the patience for a long stay. He knew this was more about Jacqueline than himself, but lack of sleep and frustration seemed to be pushing all the wrong buttons.

The door to Jacqueline's hospital room was cracked, and he could hear voices coming from inside as he approached. Maybe his luck was taking a turn, he thought, hoping the additional voice was a doctor letting her know she was being released.

Easing the door open, he found Jacqueline seated on the edge of the hospital bed, signing papers, with a nurse standing beside her, waiting to take them from her. As he stepped into the room, he was surprised to see Donna, Jacqueline's friend.

"All done," the nurse said as Jacqueline handed her back the clipboard with the signed papers attached. "Would you like a wheelchair?"

"No thank you," Jacqueline answered. "I can walk."

Jacqueline stood and seemed to realize for the first time that Noble had entered the room. Their eyes met briefly before she looked quickly away. Noble felt like he had been sucker-punched in the stomach but was not sure why.

"I called Donna to take me home," Jacqueline stated flatly without looking at him.

Noble looked from Jacqueline to Donna, but Donna had busied herself searching for something in her purse. Was this the beginning of the end? Noble wondered.

"I can take you…"

Jacqueline shook her head, stopping him in mid-sentence. "I don't want you to take me. I want Donna to take me. I need some space, some time to think. Don't contact me. When I'm ready, I'll get in touch with you."

Noble stood motionless, trying to decide what he should do. Nothing came to mind, so he stepped back against the wall and watched as the two women walked past him and disappeared down the hall. The nurse followed them out and left Noble standing alone in the room.

Exhausted, frustrated, and confused, he stared just inside the door and considered his options. It was a twenty-minute drive back to Granny's and an hour and a half to his apartment in Oklahoma City. Mentally, he was too far gone to make the drive home. Granny's it would have to be.

As he made his way down the hall toward the elevator, he thought to himself, if I didn't already hate hospitals, this would sure enough put them on the list.

Lincoln woke tangled in a sweat-soaked comforter. His entire body ached, but the fever seemed to have passed. With effort, he managed to move from the bed to the bathroom. In the mirror, he checked his bandages and found them still in place and holding. He looked around at the bloodied towels littering the floor and was glad there were still places one could stay that did not require identification and where blood on the floor was normal.

Turning the shower handle halfway, he stepped into the bathtub and leaned against the wall as the warm water cascaded over his body. His brain felt too big in his head, and his mouth felt like a scorched desert. He chalked it up to dehydration.

"*Impa Shilup* is still alive," Grandmother Mosley's voice called from somewhere in the recesses of Lincoln's mind. "The Shadow is still breathing."

"Not for long," Lincoln promised. He spoke the words aloud, his voice little more than a rasp.

"Your work is not done," Grandmother's voice continued to nag.

"I know this," Lincoln tried to shout, but his voice broke, and it came out as more of a squeak. Frustrated, he turned the water off and reached for a towel.

One more, and he was done. His mind worked much slower than usual, but it still worked. As he dried himself, he considered his next move. Staying in one place too long was not a good idea. He turned the television on, found the guide channel, and checked the time. It would be dark in a couple of hours. He would leave tonight.

Digging a fresh change of clothes from his duffel, he considered his options. The Dallas/Fort Worth area was out. He had already stayed there. He had no desire to return to the Oklahoma City metroplex. Moving further west or south did not seem to him like a good idea, and it was too soon to return to Love County. If he remembered correctly, Lawton was only an hour away to the north.

A couple of days in Lawton, he thought, two maybe three. He needed to be able to think clearly before returning to Marietta for the Shadow. He removed the comforter from the bed and tossed it onto the floor. His eyes felt heavy again, so he stretched out atop the stained sheets and closed his eyes.

"Soon, Grandmother, soon," he promised as he drifted off to sleep.

CHAPTER 30

Noble sat across the table from Granny Harris. He had slept poorly, partly due to several dark and strange dreams. Each dream was slightly different, but all shared the same theme: a figure cloaked in black, a dark wooded area, and knives—Noble definitely remembered the knives. He woke from each dream drenched in sweat just before the cloaked figure plunged a knife into his chest.

He had called Tom Jack to update him on the Jacqueline situation and ask him for a few days off. Tom Jack had approved his request and offered his condolences for Noble's relationship problems. At the end of the conversation, Noble had hung up feeling more down than he cared to admit. Now he sat across the kitchen table from Granny, nursing a glass of iced tea.

"Logic tells me the Shadow is Judge Winchester," he swirled the iced tea in his glass as he spoke, "but my gut tells me no."

"I'm not sure there's anything about this case you can call logical," Granny gave a little humph at the end of her statement.

Noble nodded in agreement and took a sip from his glass. Granny had allowed him to sleep until almost noon. That would have been enough to show how worried she was about him, even if he had not noticed her bloodshot eyes.

"Can't disagree with you there," Noble nodded, "but Lincoln is still out there, and as much as I would like to believe being shot will deter him from further killin's, somehow that doesn't ring true."

"So, if not Judge Winchester, then who?" Granny asked.

Noble shrugged, "I'm at a loss."

The two sat quietly. Noble drank his tea. Granny sipped her coffee.

"You know," Granny finally broke the silence, "maybe you should go see Lucille Muncy."

"Carla's MawMaw?" Noble was not sure where this idea was coming from. "Why?"

Granny sipped her coffee the way she always did when she was trying to put the thoughts in her head into words. Noble recognized the tactic instantly and waited.

"Well, I'm thinkin'," she began, then paused to take another sip. "I'm thinkin' that story of Nita Mosley's that Lucille told you kind of broke the case open."

"And?" Noble asked after a long pause.

"And maybe you missed somethin' or Lucille forgot to tell you somethin'," Granny gave a little shrug. "I don't know I'm just brainstormin' here."

Noble thought about it for a minute before saying, "That's not a bad idea, Granny."

"Too bad you're off the case," Granny sighed.

Noble finished the last of his tea and gave his glass a whirl. The half-melted ice clinked loudly.

"That is too bad," Noble agreed. "I guess it's a good thing that visitin' the elderly at the old folks' home doesn't qualify as workin' the case."

Granny hmphed again, "I'd call that splittin' hairs."

Noble grinned, "Call it what you like. I think I'll give Carla a call."

Lincoln parked the truck in front of room number seven at the Rancher's Motel in Lawton, Oklahoma. The desk clerk had been more interested in the late-night rerun of Family Feud than checking Lincoln in. A quick swap of cash for an old-style door key, and he had returned to the show. As far as Lincoln could tell, the only way anyone would know someone was in room seven was that the key was not on the hook behind the desk.

The room itself was small and dingy. A bed, a side table, and a wall hung desk were the extent of the furnishings. A small flat-screen television was mounted to the wall. A remote for it lay on the side table. A door on the far side of the room stood open, allowing Lincoln a view of the tiny bathroom behind it.

Lincoln locked the door, tossed his duffle in the corner, undressed, and crawled into the bed. The hour drive from Wichita Falls had done him in. He was beginning to wonder if two days of rest would be enough to get his strength back. As he drifted off, a picture formed in his mind of his knife against the Shadow's throat. Soon, he thought, soon.

"Got any plans today?" Noble asked when Sanderson answered his phone call.

"Not really. Why?" came the reply.

"Wanna go visit some elderly people at the old folks' home?" Noble asked.

A long silence followed, and Noble did a visual check of his phone to make sure he had not lost service. "You hear me?" he asked when Sanderson still had not responded.

"I heard you," Sanderson answered. "I'm just tryin' to figure out why you would be goin' to talk to Carla Muncy's grandmother again when we have both been told we were off the case."

Noble forced a laugh. "Who said this was about the case? Isn't it our spiritual duty to visit the widows and the sick?"

Once again, there was silence.

"Look partner, I'm sorry things went sideways," Noble sighed aloud, "but I can't just sit back and let Lincoln kill again, and you know as well as I do that he will."

"Hughes has someone babysittin' Judge Winchester day and night," Sanderson stated flatly.

"I don't think Judge Winchester is the Shadow," Noble said.

"Why?" Sanderson asked.

"Gut feelin'," Noble answered.

Another long pause. Noble decided to wait it out instead of pushing this time.

"Okay," Sanderson finally spoke, "anything's got to be better than sittin' around here starin' at the walls. When and where do you want to meet?"

"Two o'clock at the nursin' home if that's good with you," Noble answered.

"Sounds good to me," Sanderson agreed. "Carla gonna be there?"

"Nope," Noble answered. "I called her, but she said her MawMaw—that's what she calls her grandmother—told her not to bring me back again, and she's scared of her MawMaw."

"So, I wasn't even your first choice for this date," Sanderson feigned disgust.

Jokes had always been Noble and Sanderson's way of communicating, but somehow with all that had happened, even the jokes now seemed forced. Noble hated it and hoped in time things would return to normal, whatever normal was.

"Sometimes life just be like that," he tried to joke back.

"Yeah," Sanderson agreed, "I feel ya. See ya at two."

Noble had to press the buzzer twice before anyone came to open the nursing home door. Sanderson stood beside him, still shaking his head over the flowers Noble had brought with him. To Noble, it had seemed like a good idea right up to the second Sanderson said, "Really, Noble, flowers? Is this an interview or a date?"

Once inside, he thought about leaving the bouquet at the

front desk, but the thought of the money he had spent on them got the better of him. Flowers in hand, he made his way through the front foyer and into the common area, Sanderson following close behind. A quick scan of the occupants told him Carla's grandmother was not present.

As Noble turned to go, a silver-haired lady in a wheelchair stopped him. "Oh, my," she smiled up at him as she spoke, "Is it my birthday?"

Caught off guard, Noble began to stammer, "I don't know… maybe… oh, the flowers… no ma'am, these are for somebody else."

The little lady pouched her lower lip out in a pout, and before she turned her wheelchair around, she held up her right fist then slowly extended a long, bony middle finger. Noble's eyes widened. Sanderson chuckled behind him. Noble ignored him and started down the hall that led to Lucille's room.

"I'm thinkin' you should have given that little lady the flowers," Sanderson whispered, just loud enough for Noble to hear.

Noble continued to ignore him as he made his way to Lucille's room. When he got to the door, he found it half-open. He knocked on the door frame and said, "Miz Muncy."

Lucille's raspy voice shouted back, "Who's there, and what the hell do ya want?"

Sanderson chuckled behind him as Noble answered, "It's Noble Harris and a friend, and we'd like to visit with you."

"You have got to be kiddin' me," came her response.

"Not at all," Noble assured her.

"Really? Really?" Noble heard her say. "The things I do…" Her voice trailed off.

"Really," Noble said, not sure if he should step into the room or not.

"I wasn't talkin' to you," Lucille sounded even more irritated than before.

Even more confused, Noble apologized and waited.

"Whatever. Fine," he heard her say and then in more pleasant voice, "Come on in."

Not sure what to expect, Noble pushed the door fully open and stepped into the room. He found Lucille sitting on her bed with a worn Bible opened in her lap. As he stepped aside to allow Sanderson room, Lucille closed the Bible and laid it on the nightstand beside the bed.

Noble looked around still confused, and said, "I'm sorry, Miz Muncy, but it sounded like you were talkin' to someone in here."

"I was," Lucille shrugged. "Don't you talk to the Lord?"

"The Lord?" Noble repeated, and then in a moment of clarity said, "Oh, you mean God."

"Yes, God," Lucille nodded. "And if memory serves me right, I told you to call me MawMaw last time you were here."

Noble felt himself redden. "Yes, ma'am."

"So, Noble who is this fine lookin' fella you've brought to meet me?" she asked.

Happy to defer attention from himself, Noble made introductions, "Miz Luc...I'm mean MawMaw, this is Dan Sanderson. Dan, this is MawMaw."

Grinning Lucille, looked Sanderson over before saying, "Well now, Dan, my man, ménage à trois is not usually my thing, but since Noble brought flowers, if you play your cards right... mmm... who knows?"

"Now, MawMaw," Noble knew his face was bright red, "you know that's not why we're here."

"Really?" Lucille feigned a shocked expression. "Well, the Good Lord told me to let y'all in, but He did not make the purpose of your visit clear."

"We need your help," Noble explained.

"Oh, I see," Lucille shook her head, "you wanted to ask me if I thought Carla would like the flowers. Oh, silly me, and here I thought you brought them for me."

"But they are for you," Noble spoke before thinking, stepped forward, and offered the bouquet to her.

"Oh, for me," Lucille clutched them, then as Noble stepped

back, she tossed them stems-first at the plastic trash can in the corner of the room. As the blossoms disappeared below the rim of the trash can, she glared up at the two men, staring first into Noble's eyes, then into Sanderson's, and back to Noble's again. "I thought I made it clear the last time you were here that I don't like cops. You showin' up with a bunch of dollar-store petunias tied up with a pretty ribbon is not going to change my mind. Oh, and to make matters worse, you brought another cop. Why the Good Lord wanted me to let you come in here is beyond me." She paused long enough to shake a finger in Noble's direction, then pointed it toward the ceiling. "Mister, you had better give Him thanks because if this damn nursin' home didn't have rules about havin' weapons, I'd have already shot your ass and probably Dan's too."

"I think I'll wait outside," Dan turned to leave.

"You will do no such thing," Lucille stopped him before he got to the door. "You get your ass right back where it was. You wanted to see the lightnin', now you get to hear the thunder."

While Lucille waited, Dan returned to Noble's side. Noble took the opportunity to speak. "MawMaw, I apologize for comin' around and upsettin' you, but last time I was here, you told me and Carla a story that really helped with the case. Now another man is dead, and I think he won't be the last."

"Another man," Lucille scoffed. "I suppose you mean the esteemed Judge Jason Hall?"

"Yes, Judge Hall is dead," Noble confirmed.

"You say that like I didn't know it," Lucille gave him a look of disgust. "I'm in a nursin' home, moron, not somewhere in the middle of B.F.E. We have televisions here, get the news and everything. Oh, and referrin' to Jason Hall as esteemed is about like stickin' a dildo up your ass and callin' it a popsicle stick."

Shocked, Noble stood and waited until she had finished then looked at Sanderson. Sanderson was staring at Lucille, eyes wide, mouth slightly open. Noble could see he would get no help from him.

"So, you don't…didn't like the judge?" Noble rephrased what he had heard Lucille say.

"No, I did not," she confirmed. "He was a bully and an ass, and he caused me and mine nothin' but grief."

"Well, that was kind of his job," Noble spoke before he thought. "I mean, you were runnin' a criminal organization and all."

Lucille laughed, "Well, now you've got a set of balls on you, don't ya? Maybe that's why Carla likes ya. Likes to feel them big ol' testicles slappin' up against her coochie when you mount her from behind. Noble, are you layin' it to my granddaughter? Are you givin' it to her good?" Noble could feel the blood rush from his toes straight to his head. It was all he could do not to bolt for the door and probably would have if Sanderson had not been standing next to him. Lucille slapped her leg and laughed so hard she began to cough. When she regained control, she grinned up at the two men, "You should see your faces. Talk about priceless. And for your information, Mr. Know-It-All Noble, it won't be long until weed is legal in this state."

"Well, until it is," Noble, regaining some of his composure, countered, "it's still a criminal activity."

Lucille waved her hand as if to indicate he was not worth arguing with before saying, "Since you're here and since the Good Lord seems to think there's a reason I should talk to you, what is it exactly that you want to know?"

Noble took a second to collect his thoughts and was about to speak when Dan said, "Well, ma'am, according to the story you told Noble and he told me, we think all the animals are dead except the Shadow. Unless of course, the Shadow was Judge Hall."

Noble turned to Sanderson, who had turned to look at him. What if the Judge was the Shadow? What if they had all the characters in the story wrong?

"I've been thinkin' on that story a bit myself," Lucille crossed her arms over her chest as she spoke, "and I think Frank Nelson was the Woodpecker, Sam Wilson was the Snake, that doctor who got killed in Ardmore was the Crow, and Jason Hall was the Wolf. Of course, there's no doubt that Billie Hilton was the Dog."

"So, who do you think the Shadow is?" Sanderson asked her.

"Beats the hell out of me," she answered. "Could be just about any white man who lived in Love County when it happened."

"Why do you say white man?" Noble asked.

"Because she hated white people," Lucille answered. "Hated them with a passion. When she wasn't tellin' the story about the Indian maiden, she talked constantly about how white people had sucked the souls from her people."

"Did she ever mention Judge Winchester?" Sanderson asked.

Lucille sat silent for several seconds as if in thought before answering, "Not that I recall."

Noble looked from her to Sanderson. Sanderson shrugged as if to say, "I'm out of questions."

Noble turned back to Lucille, and after a moment's thought, said, "I think we're out of questions. Thank you for your time."

As he and Sanderson turned to leave, Lucille said, "Hey, I've got a question for you, Noble."

Noble turned back and asked, "And what might that be?"

"How long are you gonna make Carla wait before you bend her over and…"

Noble did not wait for her to finish the sentence. He gave Sanderson a shove to get him moving and stepped out into the hall.

As they made their way toward the common area, Sanderson, between bouts of laughter managed to say, "She is something else, isn't she?"

"Yes, she is," Noble agreed as he made the corner at the end of the hall and stepped into the common area. From across the room, the silver-haired wheelchair lady locked eyes with him, jutted her lower jaw out, squinted her eyes down tight, and slowly raised her hand high in the air with her middle finger once again extended.

Sanderson caught sight of her and roared with laughter. He was still laughing when Noble opened the front door of the nursing home.

CHAPTER 31

Lincoln carefully removed the bandages from his shoulder. Two days of rest in Lawton had helped his mental state, but the shoulder was stiff and sore. It would be several more days before the stitches could be removed, and Lincoln knew he could not wait several days to kill the Shadow. It needed to be done soon so he could put Love County behind him once again.

He thought of the places he might go. South America was a possibility. He had always wanted to visit Chile. There had been times in the last two days when he had considered leaving without killing the Shadow. Deep inside, he knew he could not. Grandmother would haunt his mind until the Shadow had been eliminated.

What was it she had said? How had she explained it?

"*Impa Shilup* is the worst of the bad men," Grandmother had told him. "He does not kill their bodies; he is the Shadow that steals their souls."

At the time, Lincoln was thirteen. To better understand his Choctaw heritage, he had checked out books from the library and studied them.

"But Grandmother, *Impa Shilup* is a giant spirit, not a man," he had told her.

Even now, he shuddered remembering her response, "Oh, so now Coahoma thinks he is Choctaw. Thinks he knows more than his *pokni*. He thinks a giant spirit cannot become a man. But Coahoma is also Lincoln, the poor little white boy whose mother left him. Lincoln thinks he is Choctaw because Grandfather gave him a Choctaw name. Lincoln is Coahoma. Coahoma is Lincoln, and Lincoln is a white boy. Lincoln is nothing. Without *Chahta Pokni* to teach him purpose, Lincoln has no reason to live, but no, now, Lincoln knows more than *pokni*."

A full week had passed before Grandmother had spoken to him again. When he got up in the morning, his breakfast was on the table, and Grandmother was on the front porch in her chair. On the third day, Lincoln had taken his plate to the porch. When he sat down on the front steps with it, Grandmother stood up and went inside.

The seventh day after his mistake, for that was how he thought of it, he arrived home to find Grandmother cooking in the kitchen. Setting his books down on the kitchen table, he waited for her to turn around and said, "Grandmother, I am sorry. I was wrong to doubt you. I was wrong to think I knew more about Choctaw things than you. Please, forgive me."

Grandmother had turned back to her cooking, but when she was finished, she turned around again and said, "*Impa Shilup* is the worst of the bad men. He does not kill their bodies. He is the Shadow that steals their souls. And he is not the only Shadow; there are many Shadows. Not everyone can see them for what they are. Even your grandfather could not, but I can."

Lincoln had never questioned her again. Over four years between then and his high school graduation, Grandmother had explained in more detail how the Shadows feed on the innocent, especially the Choctaw. She told him how they entered minds and removed important things like culture and heritage. Of all the Shadows in the world, she was convinced that the one that had ruined his mother's life was the vilest of them all.

Lincoln forced the memory from his head. It was time. Slowly, he began to work the soreness from his shoulder.

Noble found Granny Harris sitting in her rocking chair on the front porch. She had her jelly jar half-filled with whiskey in her right hand and her Bible laid open in her lap. The trip to the nursing home seemed to have been a waste of time, and he told her so as he eased into the rocking chair beside hers.

She had looked up from the Bible when Noble stepped on the porch, now her eyes returned to the Good Book. Noble rocked gently and waited. When she was done reading, Granny closed the Bible and turned it sideways in her lap with the spine pointed away from her body. Noble did not need to look at her to know this was so, he had seen it too many times both at home and at church.

"I was reading in Mark this evening," Granny took a sip from her glass before continuing. "The fifth chapter, where he tells the story about the man filled with unclean spirits who lived in the tombs, and people were afraid of him. Do you remember the story?"

"I think so," Noble answered. "That's the story where Jesus asks the unclean spirit its name, and it said something like Legion or Legions because we are so many."

"Yes, that's the one," Granny shook her head and took another sip of whiskey.

The sun had moved far enough to the west so that the porch was shaded and comfortable. The view, the sound of the chairs rocking, and the occasional bird call brought a momentary peace that Noble badly needed. He had just begun to enjoy it when Granny spoke, "I've been wonderin' if maybe Lincoln is filled with unclean spirits."

Noble mulled it over in his mind for the next couple of minutes before responding, "Maybe he is, and maybe he isn't, but unless Jesus himself comes down and convinces me otherwise, I'm gonna kill him."

For several seconds, neither Noble nor Granny spoke. Then Granny asked, "Because of the men he killed, or because of what he did to Jacqueline?"

Noble shrugged. "A bit of both, I suppose, but mainly because of what he did to Jacqueline."

"Seems a little beyond an eye for eye," Granny offered.

"And I don't think killin' Lincoln is gonna bring Jacqueline around any faster."

Noble nodded his agreement. "Yeah, I know. Actually, I'm not sure anything is gonna bring her back."

"Are you prepared for that?" Granny asked.

Noble shrugged again but did not verbalize his answer. He thought he was ready if it happened. He had even tried to mentally prepare himself for it the last few days, but still, he was not sure.

"Did Lincoln say anything to Jacqueline during the time he had her?" Granny asked.

Noble stopped rocking. Why had he not thought to ask? Because he was more worried about her physical health than debriefing her, he answered his own question. And now, she did not want to be contacted by him.

"I don't know," Noble answered Granny's question.

"Think you should find out?"

"She doesn't want to talk to me," Noble's mind was racing, "But maybe she would talk to Davenport. I'll give him a call."

He pushed himself out of the rocking chair and dug his cellphone from his pocket. As he dialed the number, Sanderson's voice echoed in his mind, "Bits and pieces, bits and pieces."

Death headed east on Highway 7 out of Lawton. He had not bothered to check out with the front desk. Since he was paid through tomorrow and checkout time was not until eleven o'clock, he saw no sense in it. He considered swapping the truck for another vehicle but then decided to wait until after the Shadow was dead.

He had rolled both truck windows down before leaving the motel. Now, as he gained speed, he was glad. The feel of the cool night air as it blew through the cab felt refreshing. He tried resting his arm on the windowsill but quickly figured out that the vibration caused by the road did little for his wounded shoulder.

In his mind, he worked on a scenario in which he killed Noble and his little Harley-riding friend before leaving the country. It was something he had done for the last couple of days to kill time in the motel room. Now, as he tried to drag his mind away from it and back to planning for the Shadow, he was finding it harder than he would have thought. He was Death, he reminded himself. Lincoln had become Coahoma. Coahoma had become Death. And after the Shadow was gone, he would be Lincoln once more. Lincoln and only Lincoln. And Lincoln had to leave the country.

But not if Death decided to kill Noble. He shook his head, trying to clear the thought away.

"How's it going?" Davenport asked as soon as he answered the phone.

"About as well as can be expected," Noble answered. "How's desk duty?"

"It sucks big brown donkey dicks," Davenport replied, and in Noble's mind, he could see Davenport glaring at Tom Jack's office door.

"Why does the donkey have to be brown?" Noble asked.

"Because it does," came Davenport's response, "but I'm guessing you didn't call me to discuss equine genitalia."

Noble shook his head. "No, I did not. I need a couple of favors."

"Just a couple?" Davenport grunted. "Let me check my schedule…yeah, I'm good…looks like a couple more months of desk duty will fit nicely right here after I'm free from the last favor I did you."

"Man, I said I was sorry," Noble apologized. "But you know you should look at the bright side, after all, you did get to shoot someone."

Davenport gave a snort. "Yeah right, and look at how that worked out. So, what are these two favors you need?"

"I need you to debrief Jacqueline," Noble answered and waited.

After a long pause, Davenport asked, "Why don't you do it?"

"She's doesn't want to see or hear from me right now," Noble answered as he fought back the heaviness in his chest.

"Man, I'm sorry," Davenport said. "Should I call her or just drop by?"

"Your call," Noble replied.

"Alright, I'll think on it. Now what's the second favor?" Davenport asked.

"I need the photographs from the motel room wall down in Denton," Noble told him. "I have some on my phone, J.T. sent some additional ones he took. I never got a chance to take a look at those. They're on my computer. You know the password. Can you send them to my phone? I want to look them over tonight."

"Can do," Davenport responded. "I'm on it."

"Thanks, partner," Noble said as he hit the end button on his cell.

In his mind, the conversation with Lucille mixed with that of Granny's and caused a weird kaleidoscope of images and questions to form. Somewhere in the spinning mess was an answer, he knew it. Now he needed to take the bits and pieces and sort them out as if he were doing a puzzle. He checked the time on his cellphone and wondered how much more time he had before Lincoln made a try for the Shadow, whoever that might be.

CHAPTER 32

Davenport's text read, "On my way over to Jacqueline's. I called her, and she said she'd rather do it at her apartment than the office, and the sooner, the better. Also, images are on the way."

Noble texted back, "Okay and thanks." Then waited while the images downloaded.

He thought about making a quick trip to Walmart in Ardmore to print all the images so he could lay them out, but decided to wait until he had scanned through them first. He could hear Granny tinkering around in the kitchen and thought that while he waited, he would see if she needed help.

He made the trip up the hall and stepped into the kitchen as she was putting the last of the dishes she had washed in the cabinet. When she turned and saw Noble, she asked, "Wanna nightcap?"

"I might have to run to Ardmore, so I guess I better not," he told her.

"Well, I'm in for the night," she smiled, "so there's nothin' stoppin' me."

Noble chuckled, "Guess not. How 'bout I sit with ya while you drink it?"

Noble's cellphone dinged, indicating a text, as Granny began to pour three fingers of Gentleman Jack into a jelly glass. "What's that about?" she asked as Noble tapped the phone's screen.

"Text from Davenport," Noble answered.

"What's it say?" Granny wanted to know.

Noble shook his head, "Give me a second to read it."

The text read, "Did the images come through? And did you want me to call you tonight after I talk to Jacqueline?"

Noble texted back, "Coming through now. And, yes, please."

A thumbs up emoji appeared instantly beside Noble's text.

He laid the phone on the table and seated himself before saying, "He's on his way to talk to Jacqueline. He's gonna call when he finishes interviewing her, and he wanted to know if I got the images he sent me."

"What images?"

"The ones from the Lincolns' motel room in Denton," Noble answered.

"You still think the Shadow is someone besides Judge Winchester?" Granny asked between sips.

Noble shrugged. He was beginning to wonder if he even knew what he thought anymore. "I'm not sure. I'm hoping the photographs, along with the two conversations I've had with Lucille Muncy and the one Davenport is having with Jacqueline, will shed some light on something—anything, really."

Granny swirled the last bit of her whiskey around in the bottom of her glass before tossing it back. "Looks like my nightcap is done, and looks like you have work to do. If you have to go out, try to be quiet about it. This old woman needs her beauty sleep."

"Yes ma'am," Noble grinned up at her as he spoke.

As she put her glass upside down in the sink, he opened the images on his phone. He had flipped through the first several when he heard the door to her bedroom close. He wondered how the interview with Jacqueline was going and thought to himself, "Looks like another late night."

Death made a left turn at the intersection Highway 81 and Highway 32 in Ryan, Oklahoma. He had filled the gas tank in Comanche, and now it was almost a straight shot east to Marietta. One last appearance, and Death would disappear forever this time. He had made the decision somewhere between Duncan and Comanche.

Tomorrow he would kill the Shadow. By this time next week, he would be on a beach somewhere in Chile. It was a good plan.

Noble laid his phone on the table and stared across the kitchen. He had viewed all the pictures Davenport had sent. Deep down, he knew there was something in them, but he could not put his finger on it. He recalled a game show he had watched with his Granny somewhere in the past. On it, contestants answered questions, and if they got a question right, a puzzle piece would be removed to reveal a portion of an image. As the image was uncovered, the contestants would guess what or who the completed picture would be.

Noble felt a bit like a contestant now. The only difference was he had to make up and answer his own questions, and there was no one to tell him if his answers were correct. He picked up the phone intending to look through the pictures again when it rang. It was Davenport.

"How'd it go?" Noble asked as soon as he pressed the accept icon.

"Better than I thought it would," Davenport answered. "Anything jump out at you from the pictures?"

"Not yet," Noble replied. "Did Jacqueline say anything helpful?"

"I'm not sure. She told me Lincoln took her from her work right after she opened up. When I asked her why no one reported her missing, she said she had showings scheduled all day, and it was not unusual for her to drop by, open the office, and leave the front door open, especially if she knew someone was coming in right behind her."

"Why didn't anyone notice her car?" Noble asked.

"Funny you should ask," Davenport said. "Seems she has a girlfriend who works at a car dealership, and she was test-driving a new car for the day to see if she wanted it. It was like the perfect storm. Lincoln might just be the luckiest asshole on the planet. He could not have planned it any better. Anyway, that's why no one missed her the day she went missing."

"Alright," Noble muttered. "How'd he get her to go with him?"

"Force," Davenport answered. "He knocked her out when she went for the gun in her purse. She woke up zip-tied in the back of his van. At one point, during the trip to the cemetery, she said he went off about his grandmother giving him purpose. Something about him not being Choctaw, or only part, and because of that he was nothing. When she was talking about it, she almost sounded like she felt sorry for him."

"Stockholm syndrome?" Noble interjected.

"I don't think so," Davenport continued. "He didn't have her long enough, and she seemed pretty pissed at him for cutting her and leaving her in the woods."

"Any chance my name came up?" Noble asked.

"Briefly," Davenport sighed, and Noble got the idea his friend was struggling with whether he wanted to say anything more on the subject.

"And?"

"And she mentioned that you showed up and untied her. Then she skipped forward to going by ambulance to the hospital. That was the only time your name came up. Sorry, partner."

Noble exhaled the breath he had not realized he was holding. "Okay, well, thanks for talkin' to her."

"Just a heads-up," Davenport said, "Jacqueline was not happy when I told her my visit was unofficial and that someone else from the agency might be by to talk to her later."

"How unhappy? Noble asked.

"Some cussing," Davenport answered, "and while she didn't exactly kick me out, I'm pretty sure I'm not welcome back."

"I'm sorry, man," Noble apologized. "I owe you."

"Just get this asshole, and we'll call it even," Davenport said and the line went dead.

Noble laid his phone back on the table and tried to meld the latest information into the bits and pieces running through his head. He was more convinced than before that Judge Winchester was not the Shadow. He was even more convinced that if he did not figure something out soon, whoever the Shadow turned out to be would not be alive long.

"The Wolf is dead," Death spoke in a whispered tone.

Seated at the foot of Grandmother Mosley's grave, he felt a deep sadness. He was not a genius; he knew this, but he was intelligent. Intelligent enough to know that some part of him would slowly wither away and someday cease to exist once he left this place. Grandmother had been an anchor of sorts, the lifeline that held him to a specific spot on the world map. She had given him a mission, a purpose. That purpose had charted the course of his life. That purpose ended when the Shadow died. With no anchor and no purpose, how would he live? He knew where he planned to go, but knowing where he was going and having a plan for life were two very different things.

"In the morning, I will kill the Shadow," he whispered, "and then I will leave. I will not return. I will not visit. I will have done what you wanted. Once the Shadow is gone, we are through, and I do not want to hear you anymore."

Silence followed. He waited, half-expecting the whistle of a train or the cry of some nightbird. Nothing, no train, no sound, and still he waited. Was Grandmother's response the silence itself? Death decided it must be. Slowly, he stood, satisfied that after he killed the Shadow, Grandmother would no longer haunt his mind.

Exhausted, he walked to his truck. He would find a quiet spot hidden from view to park and sleep until morning—then he would find the Shadow.

CHAPTER 33

Noble sat in one of the rocking chairs on the front porch, waiting for sunrise. He had slept very little throughout the night, and what little sleep he had gotten was riddled with dreams. Dew hanging on the grass sparkled in the light coming from the living room window. Somewhere, a cricket chirped.

Slowly, Noble began to rock. The rhythmic motion helped him think, and he closed his eyes. In his mind, he recreated the wall from Lincoln's motel room in Denton. He had scanned through the images on his phone so many times that he had memorized them. Now, with care, he placed each piece where it had been until he could see the whole of Lincoln's insane collage.

Near the top of the wall were articles about the Muncy twins' accident that led to the discovery of the sheriff's badge. The word *"ofi"* was scribbled on the bottom of one of the newspaper clippings—the Choctaw word for dog. Halfway down the wall, centered between those two articles, was a picture taken from what Noble figured was Marietta's local newspaper. In the photograph Frank Nelson was handing an award of some kind to another man. The word *"biskinik"* was handwritten beneath it. Frank Nelson the 'news bird,' the woodpecker.

The maps were tacked out on the edges with no reasonable explanation Noble could find. Large red Xs marked the places where Frank Nelson and Sam Wilson had been killed. Noble studied the blue circles. The hospital was the largest of the blue circles. To the right of the circle was a large blue question mark. A house several blocks south of Sam Wilson's residence was circled. Two businesses on Main Street had blue smudges near them. It was possible those meant nothing, but Noble's mind would not let him rule them out.

The front door opening as Granny stepped out of the house caused Noble to open his eyes, and the picture slowly disappeared. As the last remnant of it faded, the clipping of Frank Nelson handing the award to the man, flashed in Noble's mind.

"Up early, I see," Granny said, her voice still heavy with sleep.

"Couldn't sleep," Noble told her as he pulled his phone from his pocket.

"Expectin' a call?" Granny asked.

"No," Noble answered. "Just need to look at somethin'."

He typed in his passcode, tapped the camera icon, and scanned quickly through the pictures until he found the one he was looking for. Using his fingers he enlarged the picture until only a portion of the newspaper clipping with Frank Nelson in it was visible. The caption underneath was blurred badly where the word "*biskinik*" had been scribbled over it in red. No matter how hard he tried, Noble could not make out the words.

"What is it?" Granny asked as she seated herself in the rocking chair beside him.

Noble handed the phone to her. "This is a picture taken of part of the wall in Lincoln's motel room. It's a newspaper clipping, I think from Frank Nelson's paper. The quality of the photo isn't great, but I knew because of the word written below it that this man was Frank." He leaned over and pointed at Frank, then at the other man in the photo. "I recognize the other man, but I can't put a name to his face, and until now, I didn't think it important. I was trying to read the caption, but as you can see, it's pretty much covered by the red ink."

"That's Brother Ken Thomas," Granny told him without looking up from the phone. "He pastors the First Baptist Church and has for years. I remember this photo. I can't tell you exactly what it read, but the gist of it was that he was gonna retire, and Frank was givin' him a plaque for his years of service."

"How long has been the pastor?" Noble asked.

"Oh, my," Granny shrugged, as she handed the phone back to Noble, "I'm not sure. A long time, I know that."

"Any chance he would have been pastor there when Lincoln's mom was raped?" Noble asked.

Granny's brow narrowed and Noble knew she mulling his question over in her mind. After several seconds, she nodded, "It's quite possible. It would have been within a year or two one way or the other. Why? What are you thinkin'?"

Noble rocked forward in his chair allowing the motion to help him stand. "Do you know where Frank Nelson attended church?"

"Yes," Granny answered, "He attended First Baptist. Now what's this all about?"

"What if Frank asked Brother Ken to help him defuse the situation when nothin' was done about the rape?" Noble asked.

"I don't know," Granny shook her head. "That's a stretch."

"Maybe, but I'm gonna make a call and check it out," Noble said.

Granny pushed herself up from her rocking chair and motioned for Noble to follow her inside. "Might as well have some breakfast and coffee. Ain't nobody out of bed yet, so your call is gonna have to wait a bit."

The sound of a semi-truck roaring to life brought Death out of a deep sleep. He sat up in his truck and looked around. The eastern horizon showed the slightest hue of orange, announcing that dawn would soon arrive. He must have turned wrong in his sleep because his shoulder was aching more than usual.

Once the semi had pulled away, he stepped out of the truck and stretched. Walking to the back of the truck, he checked to make sure he was out of view of the truck stop and relieved himself.

Looking out across the field behind the graveled parking area, he thought about the coming day. Unless the stolen truck had been reported and he was stopped, getting to the Shadow should not be a problem. If all went well, there would be no one at the church but the Shadow. He found himself hoping that the Shadow was alone. He did not wish to kill an innocent.

Whether or not to drive away in the stolen truck was a question he had been trying to answer. He had considered taking the Shadow's vehicle once he was dead, after all, he would have no need for it anymore. He figured as soon as the body was found, the police would put an all-points bulletin out on the Shadow's car, so he decided that was not the best idea. Stealing another car in broad daylight did not seem like a better idea, though.

Still undecided but leaning toward just leaving in the stolen truck, he walked around to the driver's door and stepped back inside. Pulling his duffel from the passenger-side floorboard, he took out a gun and a knife.

At eight o'clock, Noble could wait no longer. The phone rang three times before an answering machine picked up. A lady's voice gave the hours for the weekly services and then said that the office hours were tentatively nine o'clock a.m. to three o'clock p.m., with lunch from eleven thirty to one.

Noble hung up without leaving a message, then decided leaving one might not hurt. The phone rang twice, and then a male voice said, "First Baptist Church of Marietta, Dean speaking. How can we help you?"

Noble, who had been preparing the message he would leave in his mind, stammered, "I'm.. I'm lookin' for Brother Ken Thomas. Is he there?"

"Brother Ken usually arrives just about nine o'clock," Dean told him. "Can I give him a message?"

Noble thought about it and decided it would be best not to

wait. "Sir, my name is Noble Harris, I'm an agent with the OSBI. Could you give me the pastor's personal number, please?"

"Well, we usually don't give out personal numbers," Dean answered. "Who did you say you were with again?"

"The Oklahoma State Bureau of Investigation," Noble told him. "And what is it you do at the church, sir?"

"Mainly cleaning," Dean answered.

"I see," Noble said. "It's really important that I talk to the pastor as soon as possible."

After a long silence, Dean finally spoke. "I guess if it's important."

With help from Noble, Dean managed to text the pastor's information. Noble hung up, retrieved the text, and called Brother Ken.

"Hello, who's calling?" a male's voice answered on the fourth ring.

"Noble Harris. I'm with the Oklahoma State Bureau of Investigation," he answered. "Is this Ken Thomas?"

"It is," Ken replied. "What is this about?"

"Brother Thomas, I hate to bother you at home, but I need to know if you ever had any dealings with Nita Mosley?"

"Goodness, I haven't heard that name in quite some time," Brother Thomas said. "But to answer your question, yes, I tried to help her when she was going through a tough time many years ago."

"I think we should talk," Noble said.

"I was just heading out the door," Brother Thomas told him. "Can you meet me at the church?"

"I can," Noble answered. "See you there in a few."

CHAPTER 34

From half a block away, Death watched as a man came out of the back door of the church, pushing a large plastic trashcan piled high with bags. The man was not the Shadow, and Death hoped he would leave soon.

The man and the trashcan vanished from Death's view around the corner of the building north of the main church structure. After several minutes, he returned, pulling the now-empty trashcan behind him. He did not seem to be in any hurry as he sauntered along. Death was not sure why, but for some reason, he found the man's lackadaisical attitude bothersome. As the man opened the door and pulled the trashcan inside, Death wondered if he was subconsciously finding fault with the man in case he had to kill him to get to the Shadow.

He looked down at the knife lying beside him on the truck seat. It was almost over, he told himself. Just a little while longer. He could feel the darkness spreading through his body and mind. It came anytime he began to anticipate a kill. The first time he felt it was the night he slit the Dog's throat.

Picking up the knife, he leaned forward and slid it into the sheath behind his back. He considered the gun lying in the passenger seat. It did not have a silencer on it, and firing it would draw attention. He thought about leaving it but decided it would not hurt to take it along.

As he started to open the truck door, a light brown Nissan sedan turned into the church parking lot. Death removed his hand from the door handle and waited.

The driver of the Nissan parked in the space closest to the

church's back door. Death inhaled through his nose, then slowly exhaled. Seconds ticked by, the darkness built inside him.

Finally, the door of the Nissan opened, and the Shadow stepped out. It was time.

"Sorry, Trashcan man," Death whispered, "It's not personal."

Noble made a left onto North Fourth Street and another left into the church parking lot. A brown Nissan was the only vehicle in the lot, and a man was stepping out of it as Noble turned in. The man was Brother Ken.

Noble pulled to a stop in the space next to Brother Ken's car and stepped out. As he did, the church door opened, and a man dressed in a pair of lightweight blue coveralls stepped out. Brother Ken looked from Noble to the man in the doorway and then back to Noble. "Noble Harris?" he asked.

"Yes, sir," Noble answered and offered the pastor his hand.

"Nice to meet you," Brother Ken said as the two shook.

"And you as well," Noble returned as he watched the man in the coveralls approach.

"How's Brother Dean this mornin'?" the pastor asked as he turned his attention from Noble.

"Doin' good, pastor, doin' good," Dean responded. "Just wanted to let you know, I need to run out to the house and grab some tools. The sink in the ladies' bathroom ain't drainin' like it should. Thought I'd check the P-trap to see if it's clogged. Should be back shortly."

"Sounds good, Dean," the pastor smiled, then as Dean looked at Noble, he said, "Oh, I'm sorry, gentlemen. Noble, this is Dean Jones. Dean, this is Noble Harris, he's with the OSBI."

"Spoke to ya on the phone earlier," Dean stuck his hand out as he spoke.

"Yes," Noble said as he shook the man's hand.

"Shall we talk inside?" Brother Ken asked as he motioned toward the church.

Noble nodded, said, "Nice to meet you" to Dean, and started for the door. Behind him, he heard Dean say, "Oh, yeah, I almost forgot, someone left the projector on in the sanctuary. You know I don't mess with anything technical like that."

"I'll take care of it," Brother Ken told him.

Death stared in disbelief as Noble shook hands first with the Shadow and then Trashcan Man. The darkness surrounded him, enraged him. Jaws clenched, eyes wide open, he watched as Trashcan Man walked around the corner of the building and got into an old blue Toyota truck while Noble opened the door to the church and held it for the Shadow to enter. Death wanted to scream. His chest pounding, he could hear every beat of his heart in his ears. Stepping out of his truck, he started for the church.

"Not today, Noble, not today," he hissed as he shoved his gun into the waistband of his pants.

Noble followed the pastor down a hallway, through a door, and into the sanctuary. Brother Ken pointed to the center pew as the two made their way along the front row, "Have a seat. I'll just be a minute and then we can talk."

Noble did as he was instructed. Turning sideways in the pew, he watched as Brother Ken walked up the slight incline to the back of the sanctuary. Once there, he stepped behind a barrier, and seconds later the projected images on each side of the stage disappeared.

Death opened the door and stepped inside the church. No one was in sight. Knife in his right hand, gun in his left hand, he slowly made his way from door to door, looking for Noble and the Shadow. On the short walk from his truck to the door, he had forced himself to breathe and calm down. It did not work as well as it had in the past. His pulse still sounded loudly in his ears. He clenched his teeth, then relaxed them, trying to get it to stop.

Door after door, he checked rooms. He looked back often, knowing that churches were often built circularly. Noble stepping into the hallway behind him would not be good. In frustration, he reached the end of the hallway. It turned sharply to the right, and after a few feet ended at a door that was ajar.

As Death flattened out against the wall and reached for the door, he heard the Shadow say, "So, Noble, what was it you wanted to know about Nita Mosley?"

Death froze.

A long silence followed. The sound of footsteps, then something rustled before he heard Noble respond, "On the phone, you said you tried to help her when she was going through a tough time."

"Yes," the Shadow responded.

"By tough time, did you mean the rape of her granddaughter?"

Again, there was a long silence, then, "Yes."

"Was she a member of your congregation?" Noble asked.

Death nearly laughed.

"No," the Shadow answered, "but her granddaughter had attended several services."

"Rita Burns attended services here?" Noble sounded shocked.

"Well, she actually went by Rita Mosley," the Shadow answered, "but, yes, she attended a few services before the incident. She never returned after it."

"So, how did the grandmother, Nita Mosley, end up here?" Noble asked.

"Frank Nelson brought her," the Shadow answered. "He worked hard to try to get justice for that young woman, but there really was not much that could be done. You see, it was a she-said-he-said kind of situation, and the 'he' was sheriff of the county. Plus, there was no physical evidence."

"Actually, there was evidence," Noble interjected. "The doctor did a rape kit."

"I heard about that," the Shadow said, then continued, "as I said, Frank was really agitated about the whole situation, but there came a time when it was obvious that nothing could be done, so he brought the grandmother to see me. I think he hoped that being counseled by a man of God would help her understand that…well, I'm not sure what he thought it would do, but I don't think anything I said helped."

"Why is that?" Noble asked.

"I'm not sure I can put it into words," the Shadow said. "She listened, but after I told her there was nothing I could legally do about what happened to her granddaughter, it was like she tuned me out. She did not leave, but her demeanor changed. Have you ever seen someone meditating with their eyes open? It was like that. She was sitting there, but her mind was a million miles away."

"So, afterwards, you never felt threatened?" Noble asked.

"Oh, heavens, no," the Shadow responded. "It was a strange experience, and to this day I regret I couldn't do more for her and her granddaughter, but there were no hard feelings. As a matter of fact, as she was leaving, she said something to me in her language. Even though I didn't understand it, I think it was a blessing of sorts."

"Do you remember what she said?" Noble asked.

"I probably won't get the pronunciation right," the Shadow said, "but it was something along the lines of *Impa Shilup*."

Noble shook his head. "Sir, that was not a blessing."

"No?" Brother Ken gave him a confused look. "Then what was it? What does it mean?"

"In the Choctaw language, it's the name of a soul-devouring spirit," Noble told him. "And it means that you are the final name on Lincoln Burn's list."

"Lincoln Burns?" Brother Ken looked stunned.

"Yes, Lincoln Burns," Noble said. "Nita Mosley's grandson. The same man who killed Frank Nelson and…"

"Sam Wilson and Judge Hall." The blood had drained from Brother Ken's face.

Death smiled at the fear in the Shadow's voice. He considered throwing the door open and shooting both him and Noble, but the thought faded as quickly as it surfaced. That would not be the right way. The Shadow must feel the knife.

"So, what now?" the Shadow asked.

"Now, we get you into protective custody until we catch him," Noble answered.

"Okay, but I'll need to get some things from my office first," the Shadow told him.

Death stepped across the hallway and flattened himself against the wall behind the door.

Noble stood and started across the sanctuary. Brother Ken followed behind him. Bits and pieces went through Noble's mind as they reached the door. Sanderson, he needed to call Sanderson, and soon.

"I need to make a couple of calls while you get your things together," Noble said as he stepped through the door into the hall.

He heard Brother Ken's gasp as he reached the corner and instinctively pulled his service revolver as he turned. Lincoln Burns smiled from behind the pastor. He held a knife to his throat and had a gun pointed at his head.

As Noble's gun came up, Lincoln pulled the knife across the pastor's throat. Instantly, blood sprayed from the opened arteries and life faded from Brother Ken's eyes. Noble's gaze moved from Brother Ken's face to Lincoln's, and as their eyes met the barrel of Lincoln's gun moved away from the pastor's temple and toward Noble. Noble pulled the trigger and fired at the only part of Lincoln he could see, his face.

One shot. A hole appeared in the cheek below and to the right of Lincoln's right eye. Noble pulled the trigger again as something hit him hard in the shoulder. Second shot. Lincoln's left eye exploded. Noble pulled the trigger once more, or thought he did, as something smashed into his head. There was an explosion of lights, then in a blink, darkness descended. It started at the edge of his vision and quickly closed until he could see nothing but blackness. He felt like he was falling through it with no way to stop. Fear gripped him as pain sent shockwaves of agony through his body, and he heard someone far away scream. He tried to force his mind to concentrate, but the darkness prevailed and…

CHAPTER 35

Light far away down a tunnel filtered in. He tried to move toward it, but could not. Voices shouted, but he could not understand them. Was that a face? He was not sure. He blinked, and everything went dark again.

Pain. His body ached. His throat felt raw. He forced his eyes open. Bright light to his left seared through his eyeballs and into his head. He winced.

"Noble," a female voice to his right spoke.

He turned his eyes but not his head toward the voice.

"Noble, I'm Sabrina. I'm your nurse. You're in the hospital. Please don't try to talk, you're intubated. Do you understand?"

He blinked and thought he nodded, then faded back into darkness.

"Noble, it's me," Granny's voice floated through the darkness and found him.

He opened his eyes and tried to speak. His throat refused to work, and he choked.

"Don't try to talk," another voice, this one masculine, instructed. "Ms. Harris, I'll go see if the doctor is still on the floor."

His head felt like something had exploded in it, and when he tried to move, pure agony shot through his entire right side. He willed himself to remain, even though the darkness pulled at him.

"It's going to be okay, grandson," Granny's face appeared above him. "Just relax."

The sound of footsteps drawing closer caught his attention. A memory flashed across his brain. Lincoln Burns's gun exploded five feet in front of him. He blinked it away.

"Mr. Harris," a tall man in a white overcoat leaned over him as he spoke, "It's good to have you back, sir. You gave us quite a scare. I'm Doctor Siva."

Noble watched as he pulled the sheet away from his body. The feel of cold air against his skin caused him to shiver. The shiver caused pain, and the last thing he heard was, "I believe it will be okay to remove the…"

Noble opened his eyes and stared at the ceiling. His throat felt dry but not swollen like before. He mumbled, "Water."

Granny Harris's face appeared. "You're awake."

"Water, please," he repeated.

Granny took what looked like a paint sponge from a cup and pressed it to his lips. His look of confusion must have tickled Granny because she chuckled before instructing him to suck.

He did, and the cool liquid felt good as it filled his mouth and cascaded down his throat. After several more sponges, Noble managed to whisper, "Enough."

Granny put the sponge back into the cup and stood smiling down at him. Behind the worry, Noble could see the relief in her eyes.

"How long?" he forced the question past the soreness in his throat.

"It's been eight days," Granny answered.

"Why?"

"You were shot. You took two bullets. One shattered your shoulder, the other fractured your skull," Granny explained. "You've had two surgeries—one to repair your shoulder and the other to relieve the pressure on your brain."

"Lincoln?"

"Dead," Granny answered. "You shot him."

Noble sat staring out the window of his hospital room. He was tired and frustrated and wanted to go home, but the doctors seemed to think they needed to monitor his head injury a bit longer. Of course, he disagreed. A rap on the door caused him to put his little pity party on hold.

"Come in."

The door swung open, and Davenport sauntered in, followed by Tom Jack. Noble mentally braced himself for the ass-chewing he was sure was coming.

"Well, I'll be damned," Davenport laughed. "Looky here, boss, Sleeping Beauty is back from the dead."

"I see that," Tom Jack grinned. "And he's got a new haircut and a beard."

Noble attempted a half-hearted smile.

"I don't know if you can rightly call that scruff a beard, boss," Davenport joked.

Tom Jack laughed. "How are you feelin'?"

"Like I want to get out of here," Noble answered.

"Oh, I wouldn't get in too big a hurry," Tom Jack's smile faded. "I'm pretty sympathetic when my guys are all banged up in the hospital, but buddy, as soon as you get out of here and back to the office…well, let's just say your ass is mine."

Noble looked from Tom Jack to Davenport. Davenport shrugged and, with a smile, said, "I've already taken my ass-chewing partner. Don't know what to tell you."

Noble eased into the shirt on Granny had brought him to wear. Daily physical therapy had done little to loosen up the new shoulder, and he nearly gave up on wearing the shirt entirely before he managed to get it on and buttoned.

Six weeks of sick leave with orders to attend physical therapy daily in Ardmore provided him a glimpse of his future. He picked up the baseball cap and stared at it. Blue with the Dallas Cowboys' star embroidered on it, it was a gift from Davenport. Noble hated ball caps, but the bald spot where they had shaved his head to drill into his skull was not something he wanted people staring at, so he put it on.

He checked his phone for the fourth time in ten minutes. Granny should be here any minute. He hoped they would not make him ride in a wheelchair on the way out.

A rap on the door caused him to look up from his phone. "Come in."

The door opened, and Jacqueline stepped in. He tried not to act surprised. When he had asked Granny if Jacqueline had visited while he was out, she had simply shaken her head.

"I'll make this brief," Jacqueline said. "I've moved everything of yours from my apartment back to yours and taken everything of mine from yours. I thought I was okay with dating a cop, but it turns out I'm not. I won't apologize for that, and I don't want an apology from you. I just want to move on with my life, and I need to do that without you." She moved across the room and laid a house key on the end of the bed. "That's the key you gave me to your house. When you can, please mail my house key to me." And without another word, she turned and left.

Two days after his release from the hospital, there was a knock on the front door. Granny had run to town for supplies, so Noble pushed himself out of the recliner he had been napping in and answered it.

"Well, look at you," Carla was all smiles.

Not sure how to respond, Noble said, "Not much to look at, huh?"

"Oh, I don't know," Carla reached out and ruffled his beard. "The scruff is kind of sexy, but I think I prefer you clean-shaven."

Noble laughed, "Is that so?"

"It is," Carla replied. "Oh, and MawMaw sends her regards, and she said I should have you tell me about y'all's discussion on genitalia."

"Oh, did she now?" Noble chuckled.

"She did indeed," Carla answered. "What does a girl have to do to get invited inside around here?"

"Not talk about genitalia, for one," Noble answered as he stepped back to allow her entry.

"No promises," she giggled as she stepped past him.

"What brings you out?" Noble asked as he motioned her toward the couch.

"Oh, I don't know," Carla replied as she seated herself. "Maybe, I just wanted to see what a hero looks like…or maybe I heard there was a new bachelor in town, and I wanted to throw my hat in the ring."

Noble smiled, and for the first time in many weeks, the smile reached his eyes.

Two weeks of therapy had started to loosen Noble's shoulder up, but his gun still felt strange in his hand. He had considered trying to learn to shoot left-handed but decided to wait until after he was released from physical therapy to make that decision. His hope was that time would help.

As he sat in one of the rocking chairs on Granny's front porch, sipping bourbon from a jelly jar and lamenting life, he heard a vehicle coming up the drive. Standing up, he walked to the edge of the porch in time to see Sanderson step out of his personal truck.

"How's the therapy goin'?" he asked as he made his way along the porch to the steps.

"It's goin'," Noble shook his head, "I'd say it's gettin' better, but sometimes I'm not so sure. I think I'm just aggravated because all I do is sit around all day. I'm ready to get back to work."

"Funny you should mention that," Sanderson grinned.

Noble gave him a sidelong look, "What do ya mean by that?"

"Well, partner, there's a young girl missin' from up in Carter County," Sanderson answered. "And you'll never guess who the primary suspect is."

"Who?" Noble asked.

"The son of one of Sheriff Hughes's cousins, and it looks like drugs may be involved," Sanderson eased into one of the rocking chairs and looked up at Noble. "Wanna hear more?"

DEAR READER,

First and foremost, I want to say *Thank You* to **You**. Without you, the reader, books are simply marks on paper. It takes You to complete the cycle. Now, thanks to you, the letters on the pages of this novel are no longer just random words; they are the shared story they were meant to be.

It is my hope that you enjoyed getting acquainted with Noble Harris. This novel is the first in a series I plan to write. I cannot vouch for all writers, but I know more than a few who weave bits of reality into their fiction. With that in mind, I must confess that after the first chapter of this book, I found myself in a quandary as to how to start the next chapter twenty-two years later. In the end, a visit to the dentist rectified the problem. Although the names were changed and the bulk of the narrative seriously dramatized, a bee tree limb story similar to the one at the beginning of chapter two was shared by my dentist. I would therefore be remiss if I did not let him know how much I appreciate his sharing the tale, so Thank You, Travis Storts.

As with any story, movement from an idea to the reality of a book, took a number of special people. With that in mind, I would like to thank my dad, from whom I inherited my love of a good mystery, and my mom, who is the major driving force behind my writing. A huge *Thank You*, to my cultural reader, Damon Robinson, my copy editor, Makela Robinson, and my proof editors, Kayla Arnold, Tammara Cook, and Wade Couch. And without my formatter, Judi Fennell, there is no telling what the pages within these covers would look like, so Thank You, Miz Judi.

Until next time,

Charles Lemar Brown

OTHER WORKS BY
CHARLES LEMAR BROWN

Novels
The Road To Nowhere
The Neon Church Journal
The Seventh Date

Short Stories
Raised Redneck, Vol. 1
Raised Redneck, Vol. 2

Poetry
heart breaks and cannon fodder
tattoos on my soul

Also Included In the Following Anthologies
Wild In Deadwood—Wild Deadwood Reads Anthology, Vol. 1
Wild In Deadwood—Wild Deadwood Reads Anthology, Vol. 2

ABOUT THE AUTHOR

Charles Lemar Brown is an author, a cover model, and a photographer who spends much of his time writing and traveling. In addition to this work, he has also published three novels, two collections of short stories, and two books of poetry. His photographs have been sold around the world. He lives in rural Love County, Oklahoma, where he enjoys spending time with his seven children and twenty-two grandchildren. Left alone too long, he is likely to be found making TikToks, working out in his home gym, or, during the season, kicked back watching whatever football game he can find on the television. His favorite quote is—what doesn't kill you makes you stronger, and I ain't dead yet.